D0801834

# No Laughing Matter

BETTY ROWLANDS

# No Laughing Matter

Hodder & Stoughton

Copyright © 2003 by Betty Rowlands

First published in Great Britain in 2003 by Hodder and Stoughton
A division of Hodder Headline

The right of Betty Rowlands to be identified as the Author
of the Work has been asserted by her in accordance with the
Copyright, Designs and Patents Act 1988.

1 3 5 7 9 10 8 6 4 2

A CIP catalogue record for this title is available from the British Library

ISBN 0 340 82679 7

Typeset in Plantin Light by Phoenix Typesetting, Burley-in-Wharfedale, West
Yorkshire

Printed and bound in Great Britain by
Clays Ltd, St Ives PLC

Hodder and Stoughton
A division of Hodder Headline
338 Euston Road
London NW1 3BH

To the memory of my brothers Geoffrey and
Donald Howard, with love.

# I

A pale-faced, grey-haired woman who introduced herself as Mrs Sinclair, deputy manager, greeted Melissa Craig on her arrival at Framleigh House Retirement Home. 'I'm afraid Mrs Wardle is a little behind schedule with her appointments,' she apologised. 'She regrets the inconvenience and asks me to say that she hopes not to keep you waiting for too long. In the meantime, she has suggested that I show you round.'

'Thank you, that's quite all right.' Melissa would in any event have asked to see the house and its amenities before deciding whether it was the kind of place where her mother would be happy, but Mrs Sinclair evidently felt the need for further explanation.

'A new resident has just arrived and the formalities are taking a little longer than expected. A member of her family has brought her here and . . .'

The unfinished sentence was accompanied by a vague gesture and a compression of the speaker's colourless lips, which suggested to Melissa, a shrewd judge of intonation and body language, that the said relative was proving diffi-cult. By way of relieving the hint of awkwardness that hung in the air, she repeated that she was perfectly happy with the proposal and went on to admire the design of the badge pinned to her guide's light green uniform, which bore a representation of a bird bearing a strong resemblance to a

Picasso dove, surmounted by the monogrammed letters PHF.

Mrs Sinclair received the compliment with evident pleasure. 'It represents the Framleigh philosophy of peace, harmony and freedom,' she said proudly. 'It sums up the atmosphere we try to maintain for the benefit of all our residents.' She conducted Melissa along a maze of carpeted corridors, from time to time opening a door with a flourish to announce, 'This is the residents' lounge. They like to foregather here for a drink before their meals,' or 'This is the dining room. It has a lovely view of the garden, don't you agree?' In the TV lounge the curtains were drawn against the afternoon sun; a few greying heads turned briefly and eyes peered in the dim light towards the source of the interruption before switching their attention back to the screen. Finally, Mrs Sinclair showed Melissa a small, barely furnished room smelling of stale tobacco, which she described as the 'smoke hole'.

'Not many people use it, I'm pleased to say,' she commented, wrinkling her nose in distaste. 'We don't encourage smoking; in fact it's forbidden in the bedrooms because of the risk of fire. If they must indulge their habit we prefer them to go outside, but of course we are obliged to provide somewhere indoors where they can go in inclement weather.' She made the addiction sound like a cardinal sin. 'Does your mother smoke?'

'No.' The question conjured up for Melissa a sudden terrifying mental vision of her late father's wrath had either she or her mother been caught with a cigarette. 'Neither do I,' she added, and received a nod of approval.

'And this,' continued Mrs Sinclair as they reached a door labelled Activity Centre, 'is our very latest amenity. We are confident that it will bring considerable benefit as well as enjoyment to many of our residents.' She opened it to reveal a small swimming pool from which an elderly woman in a bathing suit had just emerged and was being helped into a towelling robe by a white-coated attendant whom she introduced to Melissa as 'Mrs Pettifer, our physiotherapist. Everyone using this department does so under her supervision. And this,' she continued, opening yet another door, 'is our gymnasium. There's no one here at the moment, of course. They're mostly having a rest before changing for supper.'

More out of politeness than interest, Melissa popped her head inside to look at the assortment of exercise machines. 'I'm not sure my mother would spend much time in here,' she commented, 'but I know she'd love the pool. She and I often used to go swimming together when I was a little girl.' Happy memories. Keep them alive. Try to blot out the pain. Aloud, she added, 'I understand from your brochure that Framleigh is not a nursing home.'

'That is correct. Our residents are still able to care for their personal needs and most of them enjoy a considerable amount of independence. We provide these facilities to help them keep fit and mobile for as long as possible. Naturally, we care for them if they fall ill with some minor ailment – Mrs Wardle and I both hold nursing qualifications – but should they become in any way permanently disabled then obviously they or their families have to make other arrangements.' The woman hesitated for a moment before saying, 'I understand your mother has recently had major surgery.'

'Yes. She's convalescing in a nursing home near Reading, but she's made excellent progress and her consultant has given full approval to her coming here. She tells me you have a very good reputation.'

'I'm delighted to hear it!'

Melissa felt that she had delivered a personal compliment, so evident was the pleasure that greeted her words. She was touched by this show of enthusiasm for the work of the home. It strengthened her hopes that her mother, who had been through so much, would here find peace and be fully restored to health. She found herself offering a silent prayer: Please, God, after all these years of estrangement, grant us some quality time together. Memories of the past few traumatic weeks crowded in and for a second or two she found herself battling against a wave of emotion.

'Mrs Craig, are you all right?'

The words seemed to come from a long way off. Melissa took a deep breath and swallowed hard. 'Yes, I'm all right. It's just that . . . well, Mother has been so ill and for a while . . .' To her embarrassment, her voice faltered and her eyes began to sting. 'It's been a very anxious time.'

'Of course it has.' The voice that had up to now been brisk and businesslike took on a warm, sympathetic note, and a comforting hand was laid on Melissa's arm. After a moment, Mrs Sinclair said gently, 'I think Mrs Wardle should be free now. I don't want to rush you . . .'

Melissa fished in her pocket for a handkerchief and blew her nose. 'Thank you, I'm all right now. I've seen all I need to for the time being and I expect you have plenty to do.'

'If you're sure.'

'Quite sure, truly.'

'It's just that it's nearly suppertime and one of the girls is off sick so I've promised to lend a hand. Sheila on reception will direct you to Mrs Wardle's office.'

'No problem. Thank you for showing me round.'

'It's been a pleasure.'

Once again, the warmth in the speaker's voice made it clear that this was not just a polite formality. Mrs Sinclair might have her prejudices, but there was no doubting her dedication. Melissa felt encouraged.

'Mrs Craig, I'm delighted to meet you.' A slim, middle-aged woman in a plain but well-cut navy blue dress walked round from behind a heavy oak desk and held out a hand. 'I'm Geraldine Wardle, the manager of Framleigh House. I'm so sorry to have kept you waiting.'

'There's no need to apologise,' Melissa assured her. 'I've enjoyed having a look round. The house is lovely and the rooms look very comfortable.'

'I'm glad you think so. Do take a seat.' Mrs Wardle indicated a group of three easy chairs in the far corner of the room, one of which was already occupied. 'May I introduce our new resident who joins us today? Mrs Cherston, Mrs Craig.'

'Delighted!' A well-preserved but rather heavily made-up woman of about seventy extended a carefully manicured and generously bejewelled hand, accompanied by a waft of expensive perfume. She wore a clover-pink jacket and skirt with an ivory silk blouse, with 'designer' written all over them, a gold chain round her neck, diamond earrings and a diamond brooch on her lapel. 'You planning to move in here too?' she enquired. A pair of surprisingly bright blue eyes scrutinised Melissa as she sat down beside her. 'Bit early for you to think of retiring, innit?' A hint of nasality in the voice located her in the Home Counties.

'Oh no, I'm not retiring. I'm here on behalf of my mother,' Melissa explained. 'She's recuperating after an operation. She's coming to live with us in a few months' time, but we're having the house extended so I've been looking for somewhere nearby where she can stay until it's ready.'

'That's nice. She's lucky to have a daughter to look out for her. I've got two sons by my ex, but they don't wanna know me. Snobs like their old man. My stepson and his wife think I'm a pain in the fanny, so I've ended up here for the time being. The feeling's mutual,' Mrs Cherston added, almost casually. 'The last thing I want is to shack up with that pair of tossers.' She turned back to Mrs Wardle. 'Sorry Des gave you such a hard time, Geraldine. He's got this fixation about getting value for money so he wants to be sure I'm not being ripped off. Not that he cares about me personally,' she added with a flash of bitterness. 'He's just looking after number one. He's hoping to get his claws on his dad's fortune one day.'

'I'm sure he has your welfare at heart, Mrs Cherston,' said Mrs Wardle, a little stiffly.

'Oh, please, call me Lily.'

Mrs Wardle cleared her throat and her smile took on a slightly glacial quality. 'Thank you, Mrs Cherston, but I prefer to accord our residents the dignity of being addressed by their correct titles.'

Melissa detected a hint of disdain, although she was uncertain whether it was a reaction to the sentiments, style of speech or general appearance and demeanour of the speaker. She concluded that it was probably a little of each.

Lily Cherston shrugged. 'Whatever you say. I prefer a bit of informality meself. Anyway, I thought this was supposed to be a home from home, not a hotel.'

'We do pride ourselves on offering every possible home comfort, combined with special care for those in need of it on account of their age. At the same time, we try to offer the amenities of a first-class private hotel.' The words had a familiar ring and Melissa realised that the manager was quoting from the brochure. 'You wouldn't expect hotel staff to address you by your first name, would you?' Her manner became almost coaxing, as if she were speaking to a child.

Lily Cherston shrugged again. 'Suppose not. Does that mean I have to call them Miss or Mrs?' A gleam in the carefully made-up eyes told Melissa that the new resident was being deliberately provocative.

This impression, however, was evidently lost on Mrs Wardle, who gave a slightly condescending smile and said, 'Of course not,' in the same indulgent tone.

'And what about the other residents? Do they expect Mr or Mrs or whatever?'

'That is for them to decide.'

'That's all right, then.' The gleam became almost prurient.

Melissa found herself taking an instant liking to the woman. She liked her candour, the directness of her gaze, the warmth of her smile and the hint of devilment that lay behind it. She could, however, think of no obvious contribution to the present conversation, so she smiled and remained silent. She had not so far met any of the other residents but, reading between the lines while being escorted round the building, she had sensed that Mrs Sinclair's casual references to membership of golf, bridge and theatre clubs and a convenient taxi service for shopping or cultural trips to Oxford, Cheltenham or Bath were intended to convey the impression that the ambience at Framleigh House was unashamedly middle-class. In contrast, there was undoubtedly a rich seam of earthiness, even vulgarity, lurking beneath Lily Cherston's colourful exterior, which made a sharp contrast to the formal courtesy of the manager and her deputy. It would be interesting to see how she fitted into her new environment.

Mrs Wardle broke in on her thoughts. 'Well, Mrs Craig,

I understand that you're unable to stay for supper, but perhaps you have time to join us for a drink in the residents' lounge before we have our little chat?'

'Thank you, that would be very pleasant,' said Melissa politely, concealing a smile at the euphemism for the more straightforward 'business discussion'.

'Did I hear the magic word "drink"?' said Mrs Cherston roguishly. She stood up and smoothed her skirt, which failed by several inches to reach her still shapely knees. 'Lead me to it!'

As they made their way to the lounge, Mrs Wardle was briefly detained by another member of the staff. Lily Cherston took the opportunity of whispering an aside in Melissa's ear. 'Did you see the look she gave me when I asked her to call me Lily? Talk about po-faced!'

Melissa giggled. 'Yes, and did you see her expression when you called her Geraldine earlier on?' she whispered back. 'As if she'd bitten on a sour lemon.'

'No, I missed that. What a pity. Never mind, there'll be other chances to wind her up.' The prospect amused Lily so much that she let out an uninhibited shriek of laughter, causing heads to turn. 'Ah well, time to meet some of the other inmates. Let's hope they'll be a bit less stuffy.'

It occurred to Melissa that the term 'inmates' would also incur managerial displeasure, but forbore to mention it for fear of provoking another explosion. 'It will be very interesting to find out,' she agreed demurely, unaware that 'interesting' would turn out to be a less than adequate description of the situation that was about to develop.

# 2

Light from the setting sun cast a golden patina over the residents' lounge. Glass-topped occasional tables sparkled. The Turkish carpet glowed fiery red. The air held a subtle blend of leather and lavender. No smell of tobacco, thank goodness. Smoking was allowed only in a separate room set aside for the purpose – and, as it happened, seldom used.

Laurence Dainton settled in his favourite armchair by the French window, his customary glass of whisky and soda in one hand. The chair had a high back where he could rest his neck and shoulders, and was so positioned that merely by turning his head he could choose between admiring the view and observing the comings and goings of the other residents. It was mostly comings at this hour because the kitchen staff would soon be serving what the cook was pleased to call supper.

Even after living at Framleigh House Retirement Home for nearly five years, Laurence still found himself feeling slightly put out by the custom of referring to the midday meal as dinner and the evening meal as supper. He had to be careful, when glancing at his watch after a morning round of golf, not to comment that it was 'getting on for dinner-time'. Eyebrows would have been raised. Everyone he knew socially outside the home came from a background similar to his own, where one ate lunch at midday and dinner in the evening.

He had mentioned this to the manager, Mrs Wardle, on the Friday of his first week. As was her custom with new residents, she had invited him to take a glass of sherry in her sitting-room 'before supper'.

'Yes,' she had agreed, 'it is a little . . . well, *unusual* I suppose.' Not a word he would have chosen, which would probably have been 'proletarian' or 'working-class', but she had gone on to inform him that it was already an established tradition when she was appointed. She continued at considerable length – peppering her speech with vocal italics – explaining that in its early days Framleigh House had not been perhaps quite such an *exclusive* kind of establishment as now, *if you know what I mean*, the residents not *quite* of the same, well, *background* was one way to describe it. One had to be so careful nowadays not to offend people, what with all this *politically correct nonsense*. She had inherited the best of the original staff, including our *absolutely superb* cook, who was a perfect *gem* but did tend to use some slightly *non-U vocabulary*. One couldn't afford to upset good staff; they were like *gold dust* nowadays. Cook in particular had been there *for ever* and if Cook – who had risen from quite a *humble* background and trained in one of the *very best* cookery schools – maintained that the meal she served at half past twelve (one o'clock on Saturdays and Sundays) was dinner, then dinner it was. 'I can't be sure, but I think she probably feels it keeps her in touch with her *roots*,' the manager concluded with a flourish of her empty sherry glass (her second). And since Cook's so-called suppers (at least she didn't call them high tea) were substantial three-course affairs with coffee and mints to follow, Laurence had to accept that to quibble was pointless. He certainly didn't want to be the one to cause Cook to hand in her notice, as had been darkly hinted.

Besides, he reflected with satisfaction as he settled his long legs a little more comfortably and took another pull from his whisky and soda, no one could find fault with the food itself. It was never less than acceptable; most of the time it was very good and occasionally, particularly if it was someone's birthday, it was almost memorable. He surveyed the room with approval. It compared favourably with a lounge in many a country house hotel: furniture of excellent quality and design; décor in impeccable taste; wall-paper chosen to complement curtains which had been draped just so by a professional hand. There were good quality reproductions on the walls and the whole place shone with cleanliness.

Even more important, the bar was kept well stocked with all the best brands. Gary, the handyman who doubled as barman, had been there from the time the home changed hands and the new owners moved it up-market. Gary knew all the residents' tastes, always greeting them by name with a smile of welcome before taking their orders. He was sensi-tive to their moods as well; his casual remarks as he poured the drinks and made a note of their room numbers were designed to give the cheerful a chance to crack a joke and the depressed or out of sorts to share their problems.

Yes, Laurence mused, it was on the whole not a bad place to see out one's days. He finished his drink and glanced at his watch. Over half an hour to go before the gong. Plenty of time for a refill. He didn't usually start his evening tipple this early and his normal limit was one Scotch followed by a glass or two of claret with his meal, but today he was cele-brating. He had been on the golf course that afternoon for the first time since his hip operation and although he had played only nine holes he felt pleased with the way it had gone. He had a lot of ground to recover after the enforced rest, but he had none the less managed a couple of birdies and finished only three strokes above par. What was more important, apart from a slight stiffness in the shoulder muscles, there were no residual aches and pains. Yes, another Scotch was definitely in order. Just this once. Mustn't make a habit of it. He got up and wandered over to the bar, *en route* exchanging polite nods of greeting with Seb Riley and Chas Morris, who glanced up from their study of the City pages of the *Daily Telegraph* as he passed.

As he returned to his seat in the corner, more of the other residents began to appear. At the head of a little procession was Mrs Flavia Selwyn-Tuck, leaning heavily on her silver-topped stick but still setting a cracking pace. Her pedigree black poodle, Gaston, waddled panting at her heels. She bore down on Gary, ignored his greeting and demanded, 'Me usual, please,' in the fruity, penetrating voice with a faint drawl which Laurence had encountered so often during his cub reporter days and instinctively associated with women who had married 'above their station' and gone to great lengths to ape the accents, attitudes and *mores* of their new social environment. Flavia loved to give the impression that she moved among the landed classes and was fond of dropping references to 'Sir Donald Thingummy' or 'the Honourable Mrs So-and-so of such-and-such a stately home'. Laurence had once wryly remarked to Seb and Chas that all her acquaintances seemed to live in remote corners of a distant county, thus minimising the risk of her coming face to face with someone who actually knew them. If, indeed, they actually existed; although she showed an insatiable curiosity about the past lives of her fellow residents she was inclined to be evasive concerning her own.

Behind Flavia came one of the only two married couples at Framleigh House, Sidney and Sybil Wooderson. Within a week of their arrival they had chummed up with the Hammonds, Peter and Dulcie, and they played bridge together every evening. Following their usual routine, Sidney installed Sybil at a corner table before going to the bar for their drinks. As they sipped their sweet sherries they chatted in a polite, desultory fashion with two elderly women already ensconced at an adjacent table when Laurence arrived. As soon as the Hammonds turned up, the four card players began an animated discussion of a recent bridge problem in *The Times* and ignored everyone else for the rest of the evening.

A couple of paces behind the Hammonds was a recent arrival to whom Laurence had not yet been formally introduced, although he had learned that her name was Angela Fuller. She was slight and petite, and she clutched a small purse to her chest with both hands as if terrified of having it snatched from her grasp. Scared of her own shadow, that one, Laurence reflected with a blend of pity and amusement as he settled back in his corner with his second drink. He enjoyed observing people and for some reason he found 'the little Fuller', as he privately thought of her, of particular interest. The previous evening he had observed with a hint of admiration how she quietly turned aside Flavia Selwyn-Tuck's blatant attempts at cross-examination, leaving that lady in a state of ill-concealed frustration. He had enjoyed a quiet chuckle over that.

Laurence occasionally amused himself by weaving background lives for the other residents, based initially on what they chose to reveal of themselves but often, where such revelations were thin on the ground, enlivened with embellishments from his own fertile imagination and his experience as a journalist. Now and again he toyed with the idea of writing a novel; certainly, there was no shortage of potential characters at Framleigh House to people it. He had cast the little Fuller as the genteel paid companion, or possibly poor relation, of some person of wealth, rather like a character from a 1930s detective novel set in a grand country house full of weekend guests and obsequious servants, all of whom had dark secrets. Perhaps the sole heir to the property had turned out to be a ne'er-do-well who had been disinherited for leading a life of debauchery, after which the head of the family had settled a substantial sum on the innocent nursery governess who had been cruelly wronged by the dissolute son. She would, of course, have needed a pretty comfortable inheritance to afford to live at Framleigh. He put her age at about sixty, on the young side to be living in a retirement home. She had an interesting face that might once have been beautiful. Laurence decided it might be diverting to get to know her.

She had ordered a small dry sherry (he noted with approval the brand she had chosen) and was glancing round the room as if uncertain where to go. Her eyes met his for a moment, then slid away in obvious confusion. He got to his feet, gave a little bow and said, 'Good evening, Miss Fuller. Would you care to join me?'

Her reaction was surprising. She gave a slight start, hesitated, and then without a word almost ran towards the chair that he indicated. He wondered if perhaps she recognised him, which would have been rather flattering. Or it could have been relief at not having to make herself conspicuous by sitting at a table on her own. Whatever the cause, he noticed as she set her glass on the table and sat down that her hand was trembling and that there were tears in her eyes. Out of consideration he looked out of the window and said quietly, 'This is a good spot to enjoy the sunset, isn't it?'

'Yes, it's beautiful,' she agreed. Her voice was not quite steady and she was evidently making a desperate effort to compose herself.

Laurence sensed that she needed someone to confide in, but was afraid to do so. There could be several reasons. Scared of breaking down and making an exhibition of herself in public, perhaps? Or uncertain whether he was the right person? She had certainly shown no inclination to shy away from him when he invited her to his table; on the contrary. He waited, still feigning an interest in the sunset while covertly observing how she took a handkerchief from her little purse and dabbed discreetly at her eyes. She had rather nice eyes, he thought: blue-green with long brown lashes innocent of mascara so the tears produced no unsightly smudges. The thought of mascara brought a brief, unwelcome flash of memory of other eyes, heart-wrenchingly beautiful despite their heavy make-up, that had once stirred him more than he had ever believed possible.

He glanced back at his new companion. She had pulled herself together, put away the handkerchief and picked up her glass. With a brief half-smile, she raised it in his direction and he acknowledged it with his own.

'How do you know my name?' she asked shyly. 'Mrs Wardle has introduced me to a few people, but I don't believe I . . .'

'Laurence Dainton.' He leaned forward and offered his hand. She took it briefly; hers was cool and pleasant to his touch. 'I overheard someone greeting you this morning. It's a pleasure to know you, Miss Fuller.'

'Likewise, Mr Dainton.' He was relieved that she did not invite him to call her Angela. In his youth he had enjoyed a reputation as a fast worker, but these days he preferred to 'play it cool', as his grandchildren would have put it. Many an unattached woman of a certain age would find a seventy-five-year-old bachelor with a comfortable income a target worth pursuing.

Angela Fuller took a couple of sips of sherry and appeared to relax a little. 'It's been a lovely day, hasn't it?' she said.

He gravely agreed that the day had been perfectly splendid. 'Quite a fresh breeze out on the links, though,' he added.

'You play golf?'

'I enjoy the occasional round. How about you?'

She shook her head. 'I'm afraid not. I used to play tennis, years ago.'

The wistful note in her voice made him fearful that she was about to become emotional again and he hastily changed the subject by asking, 'Not been here long, have you? How are you settling in?'

It was not, he realised immediately, the most tactful of questions. Her face clouded again. 'It will take a while to get used to it. Everyone's very kind, of course, but . . .' She bit her lip and fiddled with her glass.

'Not what you've been used to?'

'Something like that.'

As a journalist of many years' experience, Laurence considered himself to be as hard-bitten as they come, yet there was a vulnerable quality about this softly spoken woman that aroused his sympathy. 'The years bring their changes. It happens to all of us one way or the other,' he pointed out gently. 'Life doesn't stand still, not for anyone.'

'I know.' She was close to tears again. Laurence looked

out of the window. During the past few minutes the sky had faded from flaming orange to a delicate shade of apricot, warm gold flushed with rose pink. Before long, the dusky indigo of evening would start to creep in. A person's life could change colour as quickly as that.

He became aware of a movement on the other side of the room. Two women were about to enter, escorted by the manager. A member of staff approached and drew her to one side; they conversed in low voices while the others waited in the doorway. They were both strangers to him. One was good-looking and fresh-faced, with rich chestnut brown hair and an air of vitality. He had a feeling he might have seen her before. She was too young to be considering entering Framleigh House as a resident, more likely here to suss the place out on behalf of an elderly relative. The other he judged to be about his own age, possibly the new resident Mrs Wardle had mentioned at breakfast. He eyed her, sizing her up. Expensively but not quite appropriately dressed for her age: fluffy blond hair, over-bright clothes and too much make-up. Carried herself well though; good legs. There was something familiar about this one too. Disturbingly so. Couldn't immediately place her either. It was frustrating; the old memory wasn't what it used to be in the days when he had instant recall, especially of women he'd previously met and dallied with. One thing was for sure: she was not a member of the golf club.

She was whispering to her companion, who smiled and whispered something back. The blonde newcomer evidently found the exchange amusing, for she gave a sudden burst of loud, unmusical laughter. Heads turned. Laurence felt as if he had been doused in cold water. He had never thought – or wished – to hear that laugh again.

It was not until some hours later, when he'd had time to

recover from the initial shock of meeting the woman from whom he had been so acrimoniously divorced some forty years ago, that he remembered where he had seen the other. It was quite recently, when she was signing her latest novel in a Cheltenham bookshop. She was the bestselling writer, Mel Craig.

# 3

Some twenty minutes later, Melissa found herself reluctantly accepting a second glass of sherry from a half-empty bottle produced from a locked cupboard in the manager's office. She was on the point of refusing; she was not particularly fond of sherry, although she had to admit that Gary, the jovial barman of the shining pate and gold earring, stocked an exceptionally good selection. Then she caught Mrs Wardle looking at her with an almost pleading expression, as if she badly needed another herself and would not have felt comfortable drinking alone.

'It's my little weakness,' she explained as she poured. 'After a busy day, you understand, it helps me to relax. I don't care for spirits or wine, but a good sherry takes a lot of beating.' She gave the bottle an affectionate pat before returning it to the cupboard.

Her manner was almost defensive, which struck Melissa as being a little out of character. There had been no hint of it earlier; on the contrary, in the exchanges with Lily Cherston her attitude had verged on the authoritarian. Melissa wondered if the change had anything to do with the fact that Lily Cherston and Laurence Dainton, the distinguished-looking man sitting by the window in the residents' lounge, appeared to know one another. There had certainly been an undercurrent of tension during the formal introductions: the startled recognition on his face, quickly suppressed and replaced by a somewhat frigid composure; his momentary hesitation before briefly and, it seemed to Melissa, almost reluctantly clasping the clover-tipped fingers held out to him; the mockery in Lily's voice and the mischievous twitch of her carefully lipsticked mouth as she returned his polite greeting. Perhaps Geraldine Wardle had sensed a potential threat to the harmony lying at the heart of the Framleigh House philosophy as outlined by Mrs Sinclair, and was uneasy at the prospect.

She sat down behind her desk, politely waved her visitor to a chair facing her and took a generous mouthful from her own glass before setting it down on one of the two silver coasters she produced from a drawer. As if she had been reading Melissa's thoughts, she remarked, 'I have the impression that Mrs Cherston and Mr Dainton already know one another.'

'I thought so too.'

'If that is the case,' Mrs Wardle went on in her precise, well-bred voice, 'I find it somewhat surprising. I would not have expected them to move in the same circles.'

'You mentioned that Mr Dainton was a journalist,' Melissa pointed out. 'He must meet all kinds of people in the course of his work.'

'Yes, that must be it.' Mrs Wardle appeared to draw comfort from this explanation. 'Now, I know you're a little pressed for time, but there are one or two things . . .' She drank some more sherry before opening a folder that lay on the desk and drawing out a single sheet of paper. 'I understand from your letter that you're thinking in terms of a three- or four-month stay for your mother.'

'That's the situation at the moment. As I explained, my fiancé and I are getting married at the end of August. Completion of the extension to Hawthorn Cottage is scheduled for mid-August, so that if everything goes according to plan, it should be finished a fortnight before the wedding.'

This optimistic statement was greeted with a wry smile and the comment, 'Knowing how builders work, that sounds like a big "if".'

'We're prepared to coexist with them for a while, if necessary. You never know when the unexpected may crop up, especially when you're dealing with an old property.'

'Well, I hope for your sake that things go well.'

'Thank you. It will take us a week or two after we get back from our honeymoon to get straight and my mother's room furnished, but we're aiming to have everything ready for her by the end of September.'

'That will suit us very nicely.' Mrs Wardle finished her drink, glanced at Melissa's and betrayed a hint of disappointment at seeing it barely touched. 'It so happens that a gentleman who was expecting to join us at the beginning of next month has had a stroke and will be in hospital for an indefinite period,' she went on in her best professional manner. 'In fact, it is by no means certain that he will ever be fit enough to take up his place.' Her fingers moved restlessly on the stem of her glass, prompting Melissa to take a sip from her own. 'We shall do our best to make your mother happy and comfortable during her stay with us.'

'I'm sure you will. She's looking forward to coming here. It's only a short drive from my house so I'll be able to visit her regularly.'

'Ah, yes.' Mrs Wardle glanced again at the letter. 'I see you live in Upper Benbury. Such a pretty little village, I'm told. Now, if I could just have your signature on this form . . .'

'Yes, of course.'

From somewhere not far away a gong sounded. Mrs

Wardle took the completed form, slipped it into the folder and stood up. 'Ah, that means supper's ready, so I must ask you to excuse me. Please don't hesitate to give me a call if you have any further questions.' She walked to the door and paused before opening it to say in a confidential, almost apologetic tone, 'It's dinner really, of course, but our cook always calls the midday meal dinner and the evening one supper.' She gave a slightly forced laugh. 'Terry's *cuisine* is excellent, but her background is definitely *working class*. Now, may I leave you to find your own way out?'

'Of course.'

'It's been a pleasure to meet you, Mrs Craig. My staff and I look forward to receiving Mrs Ross at the weekend.'

They shook hands and said goodbye. As Melissa walked away, she heard the office door close behind her, but a backward glance showed an empty corridor. Feeling slightly guilty at having left her sherry almost untouched, she hurried back to the front door, encountering on the way several elderly ladies and gentlemen making their way unhurriedly to the dining-room. They were all impeccably turned out and they smiled politely as she passed.

The telephone rang shortly after Melissa arrived home. Joe was calling from London. 'What's the verdict on Framleigh House?' he asked.

'On the whole, very favourable. I'm sure Mum will be comfortable there.'

'Let's hope she takes to it.'

'When I saw her in the convalescent home yesterday she had a very positive attitude, so I know she's prepared to like it. Anyway, it's only for a few months and I'll be close at hand to visit and take her out and about.'

'It sounds fine.' There was a pause before Joe added, 'Just

so long as you don't forget you have a deadline to meet.'

'Have I ever let you down?'

'There's always a first time.'

'Can't you forget for a moment that you're my agent? I'm also your bride-to-be, remember?'

'Of course you are, but we have to get our priorities right.'

It was part of an on-going joke between them and normally Melissa would have made some wisecrack in return, but this time she felt her hackles unexpectedly rising. 'I *hope* you're kidding,' she said, more sharply than she intended.

In an instant, his tone changed. 'You know I am, darling. What's the problem?'

'I'm sorry, I'm a bit tired, that's all. It's been quite a stressful day, although I've met some very interesting characters.' The recollection chased away the momentary ill humour. 'One or two might find their way into a novel one of these days.'

'Tell me.'

'Well, the manager is a very ladylike woman called Geraldine Wardle, a terrible snob with a taste for sherry. Then there's a barman called Gary, who doubles as resident handyman and is built like a prize-fighter. One of the residents is a horsey woman with a fat dog, very pretentious and would like to be taken for a duchess—'

'The dog?'

'No, silly, the woman.' Her mood lightened still further at the nonsense. 'There's also a new resident called Lily Cherston who arrived today,' she went on. 'She was being introduced to everyone at the same time as I was. A bit flashy – in fact, I got the impression Mrs Wardle thought she was rather vulgar but was too diplomatic to say so. I thought she was rather jolly and from the load of rocks she was wearing she's obviously filthy rich. Another of the residents is a rather distinguished-looking gentleman called Laurence Dainton and I have a hunch that he and Lily already know one another, although neither of them referred to it. Mrs Wardle noticed it as well and found it "somewhat surprising".'

'Laurence Dainton? The writer and political commentator?'

'Yes, I suppose he could be. I never thought. Now you mention it, I think I've read some of his stuff. Not exactly New Labour, as I recall.'

'Hardly. More old Genghis Khan, only a bit further to the right.'

'On reflection, he didn't strike me as the kind who'd have much in common with Lily Cherston,' Melissa said thoughtfully. 'He didn't appear exactly overjoyed at the reunion.'

'It sounds an interesting situation. Get to work on it at once.'

'For goodness' sake, Joe Martin, let me finish the current book first!'

'Just kidding.' He gave a low, slightly sensuous chuckle that sent ripples of pleasure chasing one another through her body. 'Take care then, my love,' he said softly. 'See you soon.'

# 4

'It was really clever of you to find Framleigh House, Lissie.' Sylvia Ross put down her empty teacup, brushed a few crumbs of honey cake from her skirt and sat back in her basket chair with a little sigh of contentment.

'So you reckon you're going to be happy here?' said Melissa.

'I'm sure I am. Everyone's so friendly – I feel quite at home already and I've only been here for three days.'

'I'm so relieved to hear that.'

'You sound as if you had some doubts, dear.'

'No doubts about the place itself.' Melissa finished her own tea and reached for the teapot. She refilled the cups and handed one to her mother. 'It seems ideal to me, but . . .'

'But you were concerned that I might be wondering why you've been so anxious for me to like it, weren't you?'

'Whatever do you mean?'

'I mean that not every woman who's about to get married wants an aged parent invading her and her new husband's domain. It's quite understandable.' The words were spoken lightly, but Melissa detected a hint of unease in the way her mother, who did not take sugar, concentrated on stirring her tea. 'Isn't this pretty china?' she added inconsequentially.

'Never mind the china. I want to know what prompted this. I've told you umpteen times that both Joe and I are looking forward to having you living with us.'

'Yes, you keep saying so, but I can't help thinking perhaps you might be hoping I'll settle down here so well that I decide to stay permanently.' Sylvia's voice wavered on the final word.

'Oh, Mum, that never entered my head, honestly.' Melissa reached for the hand that continued to fiddle with the teaspoon and gave it a squeeze. 'If I sounded doubtful, it's because I've been afraid you might find it frustrating to have to spend more time being cosseted and waited on when I know you're dying to get back some of your independence.'

'That had crossed my mind,' Sylvia admitted, 'but I feel better about it now I'm here. Doctor Freeman all but had me packed in cotton wool for the journey.' Visibly relaxing now, she gave a little gurgle of laughter at the recollection, in which Melissa joined, remembering fun days spent together long ago, just the two of them.

'You'll have all the support you need while you're here and you'll be back on your feet by the time the work on the house is finished,' she said. 'I'm sure you'll enjoy living in Hawthorn Cottage. It's very quiet, but it's only a short walk into the village and there's a good local taxi service if you want to go off somewhere on your own.'

'Thank you, dear, that's very comforting and I promise not to be any trouble or interrupt you when you're busy with your writing.' Sylvia settled more comfortably in her chair and sipped her second cup of tea. She glanced round the spacious conservatory. The only other occupant was an elderly woman sitting in the far corner, apparently absorbed in a book. 'Isn't this pleasant?' she went on. 'I'm surprised more people don't have their tea out here, but most of them seem to prefer to sit in the lounge and gossip. I'd be happy to spend all day just enjoying the view.'

'You'll do no such thing!' Melissa wagged a finger in mock reproof. 'You know Doctor Freeman said you need regular, gentle exercise; and you have to keep your mind occupied as well.'

'Yes, dear, I know, but you must admit the garden is really pretty. And those lovely pink shrubs – do you know what they're called?'

Melissa studied the plants in question. They made a spectacular show, tall heads of blossom erupting from wooden tubs on the patio outside the conservatory. 'I'm not sure,' she said after a moment's thought. 'They look rather exotic. Iris would know what they are.'

'Who's Iris?'

'She's one of my dearest friends. She's an artist; she owns the cottage next door to mine, but she and her husband run an arts centre in the south of France and they spend a lot of their time there. She's a keen gardener and she knows a lot about plants.'

'She sounds nice,' Sylvia remarked. 'I'd like to meet her.'

'I'm sure you will before long. She pops over to England quite often for exhibitions and things.' Melissa gave an involuntary sigh. She missed Iris, missed her unquestioning friendship, her dry humour and down-to-earth approach to life. There were times when she felt a spasm of resentment against Jack Hammond for marrying her and taking her off to Provence for most of the year. Not that she begrudged Iris her happiness, or Jack either – far from it.

Her mother, sensing the hint of nostalgia in her daughter's voice, reached over and patted her arm. 'Never mind, dear, you'll soon have your Joe to take care of you.'

'Yes, of course.' The reminder gave Melissa an immediate lift. 'I've had a letter from Doctor Freeman, by the way,' she went on. 'She recommends regular physio and hydrotherapy sessions, and plenty of contact with other people. They offer those treatments here and several more, and from what I've seen of the other residents I'm sure you'll find some congenial folk to chat to.'

Sylvia chuckled. 'Oh yes, chat is the word. I've already been "engaged in conversation" by a very distinguished-looking gentleman called Laurence Dainton. He's very charming. He tells me he's a writer and he's very interested in you. He says he knows of your books.'

'I wonder if he's actually read any of them?'

'He didn't say, but I'm sure he'd like to meet you.'

'We've already met. He's one of the residents I was introduced to when I was being shown round, but he didn't appear to recognise me. As a matter of fact, it was a bit embarrassing.'

'Embarrassing?' Sylvia raised her eyebrows, furrowing a forehead that was remarkably unlined for a woman of seventy. 'In what way?'

'There was a new resident being shown round at the same time, a Mrs Cherston.'

'Ah yes, Lily Cherston.' Sylvia's face lit up. 'She's a real live wire.'

'That was my impression when I met her. She struck me as maybe a little *outré* for some tastes, but very likeable.'

'That's Lily. She can be quite outspoken.'

'Yes, I noticed. She had Mrs Wardle looking down her nose once or twice.' Melissa smiled at the recollection.

'Is that what you meant when you said it was embarrassing?'

'No, that was later when Mrs Wardle introduced her to Mr Dainton. It was obvious they had met before, although neither of them actually said so. Lily seemed to find the situation amusing, but it was pretty clear he wasn't terribly pleased to see her.'

'You're absolutely right, Lissie.' Sylvia glanced across at the elderly woman; her book had slid from her lap and she had evidently nodded off. None the less, Sylvia leaned sideways, put her mouth a couple of inches from Melissa's ear and dropped her voice to a whisper. 'Lily told me in confidence that they used to be married, she and Laurence that is, but they got divorced about forty years ago. Lily says he's terribly clever; he started out as a reporter on some provincial paper and ended up a very distinguished journalist.'

'That's right. Joe and I were saying—'

'He's written books as well,' Sylvia went on, brushing aside the interruption. 'Not your kind of books, though, very clever ones about economics and stuff like that. Biographies too, although I forget who of.' In her enthusiasm, she forgot to keep her voice down. The slumberer gave a slight start and emitted a strangled sound between a cough and a snore before her head sank once more on to her chest.

Melissa feigned indignation. 'So my books aren't so clever as Mr Genius Dainton's then?'

Sylvia gave a self-conscious titter. 'Don't be a goose, Lissie, you know what I mean. Lily says he should have gone into politics, or been a lawyer,' she went on, once more lowering her voice. 'She says he could always twist everything she said and use it against her. I find him interesting, though. I enjoy hearing him talk about all the important people he's met.'

'I'm sure he enjoys it as well,' Melissa remarked drily.

The gentle irony was lost on her mother. 'Oh, he's too much of a gentleman to say so, but to someone like him Lily must seem a little, well, vulgar. She is a bit, I suppose, and she's got rather a loud laugh that makes people turn round. It makes you wonder how they came to be married, doesn't it? Anyway, she found herself a rich husband soon after their divorce, but she's been a widow for several years and living quite comfortably on her own.'

'So why is she here?'

'She's had some problems with her health and she found looking after a big house with a lot of garden too much for her. She doesn't seem to get on very well with her children, which is a pity.'

'I got the impression from what she said in Mrs Wardle's office that there'd been some friction.'

'Yes, I think you're right. Anyway, she's very jolly in spite of it and she wears some lovely clothes.' Sylvia glanced down at her own plain dress with a slightly wistful expression.

'If you want to buy some new things, we can go shopping in Cheltenham or Bath,' Melissa promised.

'That would be lovely.' Sylvia finished her tea, put down her cup and saucer, sat back and closed her eyes for a moment. Then she thought of something else. 'There are two gentlemen called Charles and Sebastian who can't seem to take their eyes off Lily,' she confided. 'I have quite a chuckle to myself, watching them.'

'I'm delighted to hear it. It's time you had a bit of fun in your life, and Joe and I are going to make sure you have plenty in the future.'

'Dear Lissie, you and your Joe are so good to me. I'm sure you're going to be very happy. You certainly deserve it.'

'I think we all deserve a bit of real happiness,' Melissa replied with a touch of bitterness. She reflected for a moment on the pain they had both suffered as a result of Frank Ross's inflexible puritanism and then resolutely pushed the negative thoughts aside. 'Things are going to be wonderful for us from now on,' she declared. She finished her own tea and put her cup, saucer and plate on the tray beside her mother's. 'That honey cake was absolutely delicious.'

'I expect it was home-made. The food here is very good. Lunch today was excellent, especially the dessert. Terry – she's the cook – says "dinner" and "afters", which Laurence thinks is terribly non-U!' Sylvia added gleefully.

'It's good to see you so relaxed, Mum. A few weeks here will put you on your feet again and once you're settled in Hawthorn Cottage we can make some plans. There are loads of things we can do together, to—' Melissa broke off in confusion; she had been about to add 'make up for all the years of separation', but checked the words just in time, knowing how much they would hurt.

'I don't want to be any trouble, you know,' Sylvia repeated earnestly. 'Once I'm quite fit again, I'll be able to do most things for myself.'

'Of course you will, and I promise not to treat you like an invalid. So long as you're happy to stay here until the house is ready?'

'Haven't I just said so? There are lots of interesting things to do and everyone is so helpful. All sorts of different people, you know. You might find some of them useful in your books.' Sylvia went once more into conspiratorial mode. 'There's a dreadful creature called Flavia Selwyn-Tuck, for example,' she whispered. 'She's got a fat dog called Gaston – she's always boasting about the prizes he's supposed to have won.'

'I'm surprised dogs are allowed.'

'That's the only one that I know of. I think it's all right as long as the owner looks after it and doesn't let it bite anyone. Mrs Selwyn-Tuck had only been here five minutes, Laurence says, before she began poking her nose into everyone's business. She doesn't give away much about herself, though. She tried to quiz me, but I told her I wasn't in the habit of telling my life story to perfect strangers. She was quite miffed, but Laurence thought it was very funny.'

'That's the third or fourth time you've mentioned Laurence in the past few minutes,' Melissa teased. 'I do believe you've taken a fancy to him!'

'Lissie, it's very naughty of you to say that. I assure you I—'

'Sshh, better drop it for now, here he comes.' Through the glass door that connected the conservatory to the main building, Melissa had caught sight of a tall, upright figure approaching them. 'Would you like me to leave you two alone?'

'Don't be absurd, dear.'

Despite the protestation, Melissa detected a faint flush in her mother's pale cheeks. 'He doesn't look very happy,' she whispered slyly. 'Perhaps he's had a run-in with Lily.'

The glass door slid open and Laurence Dainton stepped into the conservatory. He made a beeline for mother and daughter, with barely a glance at the third, still somnolent occupant in the corner. 'Good afternoon, ladies,' he said with a stiff little bow. 'May I join you?'

'Of course. Do sit down.' Sylvia indicated a vacant chair and he drew it towards them. 'I believe you've met my daughter, Mrs Craig.'

'Yes, indeed.' He sat down, frowning, with a brief nod in Melissa's direction. His mind seemed to be elsewhere.

'You're looking a little put out, Mr Dainton,' Sylvia remarked. 'Haven't you had your tea?'

'Had it and nearly threw it up again,' he remarked with none of the old-fashioned courtesy that Melissa had noticed at their earlier meeting and privately written off as affectation. 'That infernal dog of Flavia's started puking and shi—' He hastily broke off and started again. 'Making a disgusting mess on the carpet, just as I was enjoying one of Terry's delicious cakes. Quite revolting.'

'Oh dear!' Sylvia's pale features registered concern. 'I wonder what's upset the poor little thing.'

'Overeaten itself, probably. That silly woman is always stuffing it with titbits. I've said all along that they should never have allowed it here in the first place, but not enough people objected so Geraldine Wardle fell for some sob story that it's old and hasn't got long to live anyway. Should have been put out of its misery long ago, that's what I say.' Laurence waved a dismissive, immaculately manicured hand. 'Let's not talk about it any more. Just the thought of it turns my stomach.'

Not much sympathy there for the poor old dog, or its owner, thought Melissa. Totally self-absorbed. It doesn't surprise me.

Her reflections were interrupted by the sound of a woman's hysterical screams coming from inside the house. They looked round, startled. The sleeper jerked awake and Laurence stood up. 'I'll see what's going on,' he said. The incoherent screams rose in intensity and then subsided into heart-rending sobs. Several minutes passed before Laurence returned. 'The dog's keeled over,' he informed them. 'Someone's volunteered to take it to the vet, but from the look of the beast there won't be much he can do.'

'Oh, poor Gaston,' said Sylvia. 'Flavia will be heart-broken.'

'I wonder if he picked up something noxious while they were out for a walk,' Melissa suggested.

'That's the obvious explanation,' Laurence agreed, 'but Flavia will have none of it. She's insisting that her precious pooch has been deliberately poisoned.'

# 5

That evening, after taking a leisurely shower, Lily Cherston spent a good ten minutes massaging her body with one of the most expensive body lotions on the market. The procedure, as always, gave her considerable satisfaction. For a woman only a few months short of her seventieth birthday, her skin was in exceptionally fine condition, her limbs smooth and rounded, not a trace of cellulite anywhere.

She puffed a little, feeling her pulse rate quicken slightly as she went through the contortions necessary to reach the area between her shoulder blades. This involved manipulating a special pad on a stick designed and made for her by the husband of her beautician. It worked a treat (Kim said Nick was thinking of patenting it) once you got it directed at the right spot. This was one of the occasions when Lily missed her late husband George, fondly remembered as Pudgie on account of his portly figure. He had always been only too ready to rub the creamy, fragrant lotion on her back – and on other parts of her body too – until the dreadful day when he complained of feeling unwell and keeled over from a heart attack that came out of the blue and left her a sorrowing widow within twenty-four hours. A very comfortably provided for widow, none the less. Things would have been a great deal worse, she reflected, had Laurence popped his clogs during their marriage. He'd only just begun to carve a career for himself and money was scarce in those days. He must have made a pile since, to be able to afford to live at Framleigh House.

Having finished the anointing process, Lily put on a silk kimono, sat down at the dressing table and began to dry her hair. That too was in good condition, thick, lustrous and, as always, expertly cut. Not many traces of grey either, just the occasional gleam of silver lurking in the (almost) natural blond. Pity about the neck, she thought with a frown. Definite signs of ageing there, although not yet enough to make her experiment with the filmy scarves sported with a kind of desperate panache by some of her contemporaries, or to discourage her from flaunting any of the costly neck-laces dear Pudgie had lavished on her. She laughed aloud when she recalled the envy in the eyes of Martha, her stepson's wife, whenever Pudgie insisted that she show off the latest addition to her collection. There had been anger, too, as she discovered later when she overheard Martha saying, 'Doesn't your father realise he's spending your inheritance on that bloody gold-digger? And if you were going to say it'll come to us when she dies, I wouldn't put it past her to leave it all to that tarty cousin of hers.'

It hadn't up till then occurred to Lily to leave anything at all to Cousin Sophie, whom she saw only once in a blue moon and didn't really get on with anyway, but the descrip-tion of herself as 'a bloody gold-digger' and one of her relations as 'tarty' riled her so much that she went to a solici-tor the very next day and instructed him to add a codicil to her will, leaving all her jewellery to Sophie. It was true she wouldn't have married Pudgie if he'd been poor, but she was genuinely fond of him if not wildly in love. They'd had some good times together and the tears she shed at his funeral were genuine.

She switched off the hair dryer, slid the kimono from her shoulders and began riffling through her clothes, trying to decide what to wear for dinner. Or supper, as they called it here. 'I'll bet that gets up Lol's nose!' she said aloud with a smirk. After a moment's thought she pulled out the plain black number with a high neckline and lace inserts that she'd worn the previous evening. It was unheard of in Lily's book to wear the same dress two nights running and this one was pretty boring anyway, although the inserts did show a nice bit of cleavage. Not that there was anyone here that she fancied. A couple of gays, some boring old farts with equally boring wives . . . and of course, there was Laurence. She had to admit that he cut a pretty dashing figure for his age.

She gave a little sigh, twirling the dress on its hanger, wondering why of all the dresses she had at home she'd bothered to bring this one. There was room for only a fraction of her wardrobe in this shoebox of a cupboard. She'd been feeling so tired and stressed while packing for the move that she'd grabbed a pile of stuff at random. She sighed again, put on the dress, chose some jewellery, did her make-up, sprayed perfume, gave her hair a final pat and left the room. *En route* for the lounge, she tapped on Sylvia Ross's door.

'Who is it?' Sylvia called. She sounded startled.

'It's me, Lily. You ready for a snifter, Sylv?'

'Oh!' This time Sylvia's voice registered surprise and there was a moment's hesitation before she said, 'Well, I don't see why not. I'm almost ready. Do you mind waiting just a minute or would you rather go on down?'

'No problem. I'll wait by the lift.'

There was a short interval before Sylvia appeared. Lily noticed that she too was wearing the same dress as the previous evening, dull red with long sleeves and a cameo brooch at the neck. There was a note of wistful admiration in her voice as she said, 'You look lovely, Lily. Black really suits you.'

'Thanks.' It did not occur to Lily to return the compliment. 'It's nothing special – there's no point in wearing anything sensational here. The other residents would either be shocked or have their snouts so deep in the trough they wouldn't even notice.'

'I'm sure some of them would – notice, I mean. I saw those two gentlemen called Sebastian and Charles looking at you with great admiration last night.'

Lily threw back her head and gave a huge laugh. They were just entering the lounge and several heads turned. She flashed a smile round the room and said, 'Evening all,' as she led Sylvia to the bar. 'What're you going to have, Sylv?'

'Oh, just an orange juice, I think.'

'Sure you don't want anything with a bit more kick?' Lily scrutinised her face with concern. 'You feeling all right? You look a bit pale.'

'I . . . it's just that I'm still feeling a bit upset about poor Gaston.'

'That smelly dog that Flavia drools over? What about him?'

'Haven't you heard? He died. Flavia thinks he was poisoned. She's asked the vet to do a post-mortem.'

'Stupid old bat. He probably died of overeating.'

'I'm surprised you hadn't heard.'

'I was feeling tired so I spent the afternoon kipping. Well, if you're feeling upset by the tragedy you need a stiffener. How about a spritzer?'

'What's that?'

'White wine topped up with soda or tonic.'

'That sounds nice. Yes, I'll try a – what did you call it?'

'Spritzer. Make that two, will you, Gary? Mine's dry with soda, ice and lemon. Same for you, Sylv?'

'Oh . . . yes, please.'

Gary put two glasses on the counter and uncorked a bottle of wine. 'Just a sec, let me have a look at that,' said Lily. She took the bottle and inspected the label. 'Australian Chardonnay,' she commented. 'That'll do. Wouldn't serve this one at table, mind, but it's okay for spritzers. Can't have them serving us cheap supermarket plonk, can we?' she added in an aside to Sylvia, who gave a shy smile, bemused by this display of expertise.

Lily picked up the drinks and cast an eye round the room. 'Let's sit over there.' She led the way to a table in a corner opposite the French window. Laurence Dainton was already in his usual place, whisky tumbler in hand, staring out at the garden. Lily paid him no attention. As soon as they were seated she raised her glass, said 'Cheers!' and took a generous mouthful. A little cautiously, Sylvia followed suit. 'How's the drink, then?'

Sylvia took a second sip, swallowed and nodded. 'It's very nice,' she said. She fingered her glass for a few seconds, then looked at Lily and asked, 'Why did you laugh just now?'

Lily thought for a moment and then gave another, more subdued, cackle. 'You mean when you said about Seb and Chas giving me the eye? D'you reckon they fancy me?'

Sylvia turned pink. 'Well, you did . . . you do look very glamorous, especially in that dress, and I just wondered . . .'

'Old Sylv, you are an innocent.' Lily's eyes danced with mischief. 'You haven't noticed?'

'Noticed what?'

'They're gay, silly.'

Sylvia looked blank. 'What does that mean?'

Lily shook her head in disbelief at such naïvety. 'I mean, they're an item. They aren't interested in women.'

'Oh, I see.' Sylvia took a little time to digest the information, then said, 'My late husband called men like that something different.'

'I can imagine, but gay sounds nicer, don't you think? You met many?'

'None, so far as I know. Frank was very much against that sort of thing.'

'Bit of a stuffed shirt, was he?'

Sylvia bit her lower lip and stared down at her glass. 'If you don't mind, I'd rather not talk about him just now.'

'Sorry, love.' Lily took another swig from her drink, jerked her head in Laurence's direction and said, 'I've no objection to talking about mine – my ex, that is, him over there. Snooty old bugger.'

'You still feel bitter towards him, don't you?' Normally, Sylvia would not have dreamed of making such a personal comment, but she was unused to any form of alcohol and the spritzer was already beginning to have an effect.

Lily shrugged. 'S'pose I do,' she admitted. 'It's the kids more than him. Two boys. He turned them against me. They're married now and got kids of their own, but I don't see much of them either. They're ashamed of me, the boys I mean. Think I'm common.'

'That's dreadful! You're a very kind person and I'm sure you were a lovely mother.'

'Ta.'

Sylvia took another mouthful of her drink. 'You know something,' she went on, 'I've never seen my grandson at all and he's nearly thirty.' She brushed the back of her free hand across her eyes and began fumbling in her handbag for a tissue.

Lily gave a puzzled frown. 'Why's that? I thought you and your daughter was good mates.'

'We are now, but it's a long story.'

'You don't have to tell me if it upsets you.' Lily's eye fell on Sylvia's glass, which she had just emptied. 'How about another spritz?'

'Oh no, thank you. One's quite enough. I mean, it was very nice, but . . .' Sylvia's voice shook a little, then steadied as she went on, 'Lissie's promised to arrange for me to meet Simon soon. He lives in New York so she doesn't see all that much of him herself.' She compressed her lips and closed her eyes for a moment before continuing. 'Her father was very upset when she told us; she had this boyfriend—'

'Who ditched her when he found out she was in the club?' Lily's normally warm, if slightly nasal, voice became acidic. 'Not unusual.'

'It wasn't quite like that. I believe he was a very nice boy, although I never actually met him. He was killed in a car crash, you see. He never knew about the baby, and when Lissie's father found out . . . it was terrible, he was a very stern man but I'd never have thought he could be so hard on her. He thought the world of her.' Her voice faltered; her face was the colour of chalk.

Lily reached across the table and gave her arm a squeeze. 'Sorry, didn't mean to pry. Don't say any more if it upsets you.'

'I don't mind you knowing. You're so sympathetic.'

Lily's mascara-laden eyes twinkled. 'Mother confessor Lil, that's me. And I promise it won't go any further. Oh, look!' Her gaze slid past Sylvia and focused with interest on a little scene being played out opposite. 'Lol's being all gallant to Angela Fuller, standing up and holding her chair. That's how he was with me fifty years ago, the creep – and

I fell for it.' More acid spiked the final words. 'It didn't take long for things to go sour and I used to wonder why the hell he married me if he thought me so far beneath him. Took me a while to twig it was because I wouldn't let him get into me knickers any other way.'

Sylvia looked momentarily startled and turned pink, then clapped a hand over her mouth and gave a stifled giggle.

Lily nodded approvingly. 'That's better. Laugh it off, that's my motto. It wasn't so easy at the time, though; until Pudgie came along, bless his heart. He's been gone ten years now, but I still miss him.' The corners of her mouth drooped for a moment, then lifted at the sound of the supper gong. The residents rose to their feet *en masse* as if summoned by royalty. 'Come on; let's get at the nosh. I'm starving.'

Joe said, 'I'm in the club lounge at Heathrow, waiting for the flight to be called.'

'Will it be leaving on time?'

'No one's said anything about delay so far.'

There was no need to ask what time his plane was due to take off; she had every detail of his itinerary pinned to the notice-board in her office. Just the same, she needed to say something to keep the conversation going. 'You said your ETA in New York is 20.00 hours?'

'That's right.'

'Let's hope it keeps to schedule.'

'Let's hope *you* do. I'm expecting that new book on my desk when I get back, remember.'

'Slave driver!' The hint of awkwardness, the reaching for something meaningful to say, evaporated as they both chuckled. It was so silly, Melissa thought, suddenly to start having these drawn-out, phatic exchanges just because Joe was off on a business trip. He'd been doing it for years; it went with the job. Until now she had hardly spared him a thought during his absences, being too busy with her own life, which – apart from their professional relationship – was no concern of his any more than his was of hers.

Now, it was different. Joe *was* her life. Now she was unable to relax until he'd called to say he'd arrived safely and checked into his hotel without incident. Now, however brief the trip, she received a call each day until his return. Loving someone made an incredible difference, even when it was someone you'd known for ages without realising you loved him.

Joe broke into the reverie she had drifted into. 'Mel, are you still there?'

'Yes, of course. I was just thinking . . .'

'What?'

'Never mind. I can't explain now. Listen, Joe, guess what. You remember I mentioned a ghastly woman at Framleigh House with a dog called Gaston?'

'What about it?'

'Gaston had a violent and rather revolting stomach upset this afternoon while I was having tea with Mum.'

'That must have put you off your tea and buns.'

'We didn't actually witness it, although we had an un-necessarily graphic account from one of the other residents. The dog died not long after and the owner had hysterics and claimed he had been deliberately poisoned.'

'Surely not. Whoever would do a thing like that?'

'I don't believe anyone did, but believe it or not there's to be a post-mortem, and if it turns out it was poison she – the owner – is talking about a police investigation.'

'She must be a complete nutcase.'

'Eccentric, certainly. She puts on airs and graces, and drops names as if she's intimately acquainted with half the aristocracy. No one believes the stories she tells.'

'She sounds a real pain.'

'I suppose she is, but I can't help feeling sorry for the poor old thing. That dog was probably all she had in the world to love.'

'Mel, you're getting soft in your old age.'

'What do you mean, old age?' She feigned indignation. 'Fifty is today's thirty.' In the background, she could hear a voice requesting passengers to proceed to the departure gate. 'Is that your flight being called?'

'Yep, got to go. See you in a week's time. Oh, by the way . . .'

'What?'

'If the police won't take on the case of the poisoned pooch, make sure you don't let the old bat know you're a crime writer. She'll have you on the case before you can say Sherlock Holmes!'

# 6

Over tea in the conservatory the next day, Melissa explained to her mother about the deadline and was reassured by her response.

'Now don't you worry about me, dear,' Sylvia insisted, bright eyes gazing earnestly into the ones that were so like her own. 'I know how busy you are and I'm very comfortable here, so you get on with finishing your book and just pop in and see me when you can spare the time.'

'I'll telephone you every day.'

'There's really no need to fuss. I had enough of that from Doctor Freeman and I'm not a baby, you know.' Sylvia shook Melissa's arm in playful reproof. 'They take really good care of us here. Mrs Wardle came to my room this morning to ask if I was settling in all right. She says if there are any problems I must let her know at once. Laurence says she speaks to all the residents at least once a week. He says they should bring back managers like her to all the hospitals.'

Laurence again. Well, what of it? Melissa told herself to stop being so negative; she should be glad her mother had found a congenial companion. Aloud, she said, 'Remember the old-fashioned matrons? They used to rule hospitals with a rod of iron, didn't they? I remember when I had my appendix out, the nurses hopped around like scared rabbits getting everything ship-shape for her daily visit. All the patients had to sit to attention in bed with their hands folded while an old gorgon in a starched cap went around saying, "Good morning. How are you?" to each one in turn. If anyone tried to say anything except, "Very well, thank you, Matron," they got told off afterwards by Sister.'

'Yes, I remember. When I was a trainee nurse, I don't know who was more scared of Matron – us or the patients.'

'Whereas nowadays people will moan about almost anything,' Melissa observed.

'It's not like that here,' her mother assured her. 'Most people seem very happy, but there are one or two who always make a point of finding something to complain about, Laurence says.'

'I believe there's also the odd difficult relative,' Melissa commented, thinking of Lily Cherston's apologetic reference to the attitude of her stepson.

'Yes, I expect so. They say Mrs Wardle's very good about listening patiently and making soothing noises, though. And if there are any health worries, she calls the doctor right away. As a matter of fact he's been twice to see Flavia Selwyn-Tuck. She got so overwrought when her dog died and she has problems with her digestion and high blood pressure, so I'm told.'

'Poor old thing.' There was a short pause while they enjoyed their tea and home-made jam tarts. Then Melissa said, 'By the way, how are things between Lily and her ex these days? Are they on speaking terms yet?'

'Sshh!' Sylvia hissed reproachfully. She glanced round and lowered her voice, even though they had the conservatory to themselves. 'I promised not to tell anyone about . . . you know.'

'You told me.'

'You're my daughter, that's different. Poor Lily has some hard things to say about Laurence and I sympathise up to a point, but I'm sure he wasn't entirely to blame. I mean, it's easy to see why the marriage failed, isn't it? He's so refined and gentlemanly, and she—' Sylvia broke off, evidently not wanting to make any kind of derogatory remark about her new friend. 'I really like Lily,' she hurried on, 'she's very kind and jolly and I think it's a shame the way her children neglect her.' Still speaking in a whisper, she gave a slightly bowdlerised account of Lily's confidences of the previous evening. 'At least she was happy with her second husband, although he was much older. He died about ten years ago, leaving her very well off, but her health isn't too good these days.'

'She looks as fit as a flea to me.'

'She says she experienced what she calls "a shot across the bows" – something to do with her heart, I understand – so she has to take life very quietly from now on. She's staying here while her house is being converted into sheltered flats and then she'll move into one of them. I have a feeling it can't be too soon for Laurence, although he never says anything against her, never mentions her in fact. He's too much of a gentleman. What's so funny, dear?' she added, aware that Melissa's eyes were sparkling with amusement.

'You are. You have the makings of a diplomat, Mum, the way you manage to keep on good terms with two sworn enemies.'

'Enemies? Oh no, I'm sure they don't wish one another any harm. In fact' – at this point Sylvia grew slightly reflective – 'it would be nice if they were to bury the hatchet and at least be friends again. At their time of life it's silly to bear grudges. The Church preaches forgiveness, doesn't it? Perhaps I could—'

'Mum, you're here to recuperate, not act as a marriage guidance counsellor.'

'I only meant . . . when I was doing my nursing training, you'd be surprised how many patients confided in me when they were feeling low. They said it helped them to talk about their troubles with someone completely detached.'

'I'm sure it did, but in this particular situation, putting in your two penn'orth of advice might not be appreciated.'

'Lissie, do give me credit for a little common sense.'

'I'm sorry, Mum. It's just that I'm concerned you might get caught in the crossfire. Emotional upset isn't good for you. Don't you think it would be better to leave them alone to sort it out for themselves – if they want to, that is? From what you've already told me, they don't have much in common.'

'That's true,' Sylvia admitted with a sigh. 'They seem to go out of their way to avoid one another.'

'There you are, then.'

'I suppose you're right, but it would have been nice.'

Melissa stood up and said, 'I'm going home now, but I promise to come again as soon as I've got this book off my back. And you'll be sure to call me in the meantime if there's anything you need, or that you're worried about?'

'All right, dear, but there's no need to fuss. I'm absolutely fine here, really I am.'

'She seems almost pathetically anxious not to be a nuisance,' Melissa observed to Joe when he called that evening from one of the hotels on his North American itinerary. 'It's almost as if she feels guilty at all the trouble she's caused by being so ill.'

'I doubt if it's just by being ill,' said Joe.

'How do you mean?'

'What about all the years you had to cope on your own without her love and support? They must weigh pretty heavily on her conscience.'

'We've been over that umpteen times and she knows I don't blame her.'

'But has she forgiven herself?'

'Possibly not, although she's never actually said so.'

'Maybe she's keeping it bottled up instead of talking about it.'

'You could be right.' She thought for a moment, then said, 'Joe, do you think she needs counselling?'

'I hardly think that will be necessary.' Joe's voice betrayed a hint of exasperation, recalling the cynical reference he had once made to the present-day obsession with what he dubbed the 'counselling and compensation' syndrome. 'There's been a huge upheaval in her life and it will take time for her to adjust. I'm sure she'll be fine once she's settled with us at Hawthorn Cottage.' His tone became gentler again. 'Don't worry about her, darling.'

'I'll try not to.'

'Good girl. How are things with you?'

'Fine. I've almost finished the final draft of the book and the builder's confirmed that work will start next Monday.'

'Great. All being well, I'll be back on Saturday and with you on Sunday. Can't wait to see you again.'

'Me too.'

The following morning the ebullient Gloria Parkin, devoted wife of Stanley and proud mother of Darren, Wayne and Charlene, came to do her weekly stint of cleaning while bringing Melissa up to date with the latest news and gossip from the twin villages of Upper and Lower Benbury. Today she arrived in a state of high excitement mixed with a tinge of doom-laden apprehension as she held forth about the week's prime sensation.

'Terrible thing about that poor dog being poisoned, weren't it?' she exclaimed. She hung up her jacket and donned an overall patterned with overblown red roses that had the effect of enhancing her already generous proportions. 'I hears they're having one of they *past-mortiums* like what they does when someone gets topped in one of your books. I expect you knows all about it, with your mum being at Framleigh House. Fancy it just throwing up and dying like that!'

'However did you hear about it?' Melissa asked curiously, although with little surprise. Gloria's sources of information were astonishingly wide-ranging.

'My Charlene's friend Lottie's Auntie Maddie works there,' Gloria explained. 'She told me all about it. Said the old woman what owns the dog threw a fit when it happened and they had to call the doctor. Were your mum very upset?'

'She was sorry about it, of course. I expect everyone was.'

'Not everyone. Lottie's Auntie Maddie says it were fat and smelly and several people was glad to see the back of it, didn't think it should've bin allowed there in the first place. They all reckons it picked up something nasty when it were out walkies, but the owner's going round saying someone done it on purpose.'

'Yes, I heard that too, but I find it hard to believe.' Melissa was rapidly losing interest in the drama of the dead dog. 'I really must get on with some work,' she added pointedly.

Gloria took the hint. 'Mustn't stand here gossiping, must I?' She put on her rubber gloves and went to the cupboard where she kept her cleaning equipment, but it was clear from the sparkle of relish in her toffee-brown eyes that she still found the subject fascinating. She continued with her commentary as, speaking over her shoulder, she reached for her basket of polishes and dusters with one hand while manoeuvring the vacuum cleaner from its place with the other, almost jamming her ample posterior in the narrow doorway during the process. 'Maddie says she wouldn't be surprised if someone did bump that dog off,' she announced, as she finally emerged, puffing from her exertions. 'She says she wouldn't be surprised if they did for old Mother Something-Tuck next. Here!' Gloria's eyes expanded till they threatened to start out of her fluffy blond head. 'What if the poison were meant for her? Maybe it were in her cake! Maddie says she were always accusing Terry, she's the cook, of hating her silly dog 'cos she wouldn't let the girls pat it or give it titbits when they came round with the cakes at teatime.'

'That was probably for reasons of hygiene. Dogs carry all sorts of germs in their mouths.'

'Might've bin, I s'pose, but Maddie reckons the old bag had it in for Terry. She moans about the food too, but Maddie says it's real fancy. Maybe Terry got so fed up she decided to have her own back by poisoning her cake, only she gave it to her dog!' The black humour in this outrageous hypothesis suddenly sent Gloria rocking on her heels in a spasm of gurgling laughter. 'D'you s'pose that's the way it happened?' she wheezed when her power of speech returned.

'I don't think so for one moment and I don't think you should let any of this get back to Maddie,' said Melissa severely. 'It could cause all sorts of trouble for Terry if Mrs Selwyn-Tuck heard about it.'

Gloria took a few moments to reflect on this proposition before saying, with a hint of regret, 'I s'pose you're right. Well, I'd better get on. See you at coffee time.' Evidently feeling that she had milked the episode dry, Gloria set to work and Melissa retreated thankfully to her study.

Absorbed in the task of completing her new novel, which both she and Joe were confident was going to be her best so far, Melissa lost all track of time until, while drinking her early morning cup of tea and listening to the six o'clock news, she realised that it was Friday and she had not spoken to her mother since her previous visit. A polite note in the Framleigh House brochure requested relatives not to telephone before ten o'clock except in cases of urgency. Reminding herself that Sylvia had assured her there was no need for a daily phone call, and that in any case had anything been seriously amiss she would have been notified immediately, she found herself waiting impatiently for the time to pass.

The secretary/receptionist at Framleigh House, after an interval during which Melissa was treated to a version of 'Your Sheep May Safely Graze' played on a musical box, returned with the news that Mrs Ross was 'absolutely fine', was at the moment out for a stroll in the garden with Mr Dainton and did she wish her to be summoned to the telephone?

'No, that's all right,' Melissa said. The grounds were extensive and it could have meant a wait of several minutes. In any case, she had no wish to cause her mother unnecessary anxiety. 'If you'd kindly get someone to tell her I phoned, and say that if she's not planning to go out I'll pop round this afternoon.'

'I'm sure she'll be delighted to see you.'

Feeling relieved, Melissa returned to her task. By midday, the completed final draft of the novel lay on her desk and she sat back in her chair with her eyes closed, flexing the muscles in her arms and back and wishing Joe was there to massage her neck and shoulders. She fell into a pleasant daydream; on Sunday he'd be home and they'd have a few precious hours together before life became disrupted by the imminent building work.

After a few minutes, she got up, opened the window and leaned her elbows on the sill, breathing deeply of the fresh country air. There had been rain the previous evening and the overnight temperature had been low for June, but the sun had steadily gained in strength throughout the morning and now shone warmly on her upturned face. A constant stream of swifts, swallows and house martins rushed across her vision as they swept the skies for food, recurring patterns of curving black shapes against a background of china-blue decorated with cloud-white. Aware that she had been almost chained to her desk all the week, with little or no exercise, she decided to go for a walk before lunch. She had just changed her shoes and put on a light jacket against the gentle breeze when the telephone rang. She was tempted to leave the answering service to do its work, but something made her pick up the receiver. It was her mother.

'Lissie, I got your message. I'm so glad you're coming this afternoon.'

'I'm sorry I haven't been in touch before—'

'It's all right; you don't need to apologise. I just wanted to make sure you haven't had to change the arrangement.' Sylvia's voice dropped to a whisper as she added, 'I want to talk to you about the death of that poor little dog.'

Melissa's heart sank. Was she never to hear the last of this canine saga? 'What about it?' she said, a little wearily.

'It's just that the more I think about it, the more I think

maybe Flavia had a point when she said someone had poisoned him.'

'And do you have a suspect?'

'Well, as a matter of fact,' Sylvia gave a slightly embarrassed giggle, 'that's what I want to talk to you about.'

# 7

'Now, Mother, what's all this about a suspect?'
Sylvia fidgeted and looked embarrassed. 'I'm afraid you're going to think I'm being rather silly.'

'Silly about what?' asked Melissa, as her mother seemed reluctant to go on.

'It came to me all of a sudden, you see, after I'd spoken to the gardener about my flower arrangements.' Sylvia glanced around as if to make certain they were alone before saying in a low voice, 'I don't want anyone else to hear this, in case I've got it all wrong.'

'Mum, you can see for yourself that there isn't a soul about.'

They were sitting in a small gazebo overlooking the feature described in the Framleigh House brochure as 'our own private lake', although it was little more than a large fishpond where golden carp twisted and darted to and fro in the clear shallow water. It was none the less a very pleasant spot, well maintained and reached by paths of lush green turf, partially shaded by trees and far enough from the road to be undisturbed by traffic. It was a haven for wildlife as well: several rabbits had hopped into the bushes at their approach, dragonflies skimmed the water in bright flashes of blue and green and bees hummed and feasted among the wild flowers that patterned the grass. Almost as many species of birds as Melissa regularly counted in her own secluded Cotswold garden sang and chirruped, flew to and fro with beaks full of food or rummaged in the undergrowth.

'Just listen to that thrush!' whispered Sylvia in delight at the sparkling song pouring from an invisible perch above their heads.

'It's lovely,' Melissa agreed, this time unable to conceal a touch of impatience, 'but I don't think you brought me here to listen to birdsong. What have you been up to?'

'I haven't been up to anything, as you put it, just thinking. I haven't said anything to anyone else yet, not even Laurence.'

'Never mind Laurence. Just take your time and tell me.'

'Well, as I said, it started with the flower arrangements.'

'What flower arrangements?'

'Didn't I tell you? I offered to do some with real flowers, not the artificial ones they put in the lounges. It seemed a pity not to have fresh ones, and I thought it would give me something to do. I know they put one or two real carnations in little vases on the tables in the dining room and of course they do wonderful things with plastic nowadays—'

'Mum, will you please stick to the point!'

'I'll try, dear. I'm sorry; I sometimes find it difficult to get my thoughts in order since my operation. I am getting better, though, aren't I?' Sylvia's expression as she turned to her daughter was full of anxious pleading.

'You're doing brilliantly, truly you are. I'm sorry if I was pressuring you. Just take your time and tell me exactly what happened.'

'It's only what I think might have happened.' There was another pause, during which Sylvia sat staring at the water, apparently deep in thought. Resisting the temptation to prompt her a second time, Melissa waited in silence for her to continue. 'I hate to think anyone would deliberately harm a little dog,' she began, 'but it does seem strange, him dying so suddenly after being horribly sick.'

'Are you saying you agree with Flavia that Gaston was poisoned?'

'She claims to have proof that he was. She's talking about hiring a private detective to find out who did it, but Laurence says Mrs Wardle won't allow anyone to go round asking a lot of questions and upsetting people.'

'I'm sure he's right – but you say you think you know who did it?'

'I thought so, but ever since I spoke to you, I've been wondering how such a nice man could do anything so wicked. I may be doing him a terrible injustice.'

'You surely don't mean Laurence?'

'Oh my goodness, no!' Sylvia looked shocked at the suggestion. She dropped her voice again and whispered, 'The gardener.'

Melissa drew a deep breath, mentally counted to five and said, 'Why on earth would the gardener want to poison Gaston?'

'As I was saying, I had a word with Mrs Wardle about the arrangements and she had no objection, in fact she was quite pleased so long as I paid for the flowers and didn't expect the staff to look after them. I told Laurence about it and he thought it was a lovely idea and offered to take me to a nursery to get flowers and oasis and so on. Wasn't that kind of him?'

'Yes, very kind. When are you going?'

'Oh, we went this morning. It was such a nice nursery and we had coffee and cakes in the coffee shop. I think Laurence quite enjoyed the trip – he seemed really interested and helped me to choose the flowers.'

'That was nice. So where does the gardener come in?' she

asked as Sylvia paused to reflect with obvious pleasure on the outing.

'Oh yes, sorry. I wanted to start work on my arrangements right away and I asked Terry if I could do them in her kitchen, but she said no because of hygiene regulations and in any case I'd be in the way while she was preparing lunch, I mean dinner, so I asked the gardener to let me use a corner of his potting shed. He said yes and cleared a space for me straight away. It was so kind of him. That's what I was saying, I hate to think that such a nice man . . . anyway,' Sylvia hurried on, evidently reading the hint of exasperation that Melissa found increasingly difficult to conceal, 'we got chatting, and I happened to mention Gaston, and he said he was quite glad to "see the back of the little beast", as he put it, which I thought was a bit shocking.'

'Not all gardeners like having dogs around. Perhaps Flavia let Gaston run on the flowerbeds and damage his plants.'

'It was more because he was always lifting his leg on some of the shrubs and things. He said he'd complained to Flavia about it, but all she said was, "You can't stop doggies doing that, it's their nature".'

'But Mum, you surely aren't suggesting that the gardener poisoned the dog because he'd peed on a few plants?'

'He did seem awfully cross about it, especially the damage to his oleanders. He said the lower leaves have started to go brown because of it.'

'Which are the oleanders?'

'The ones in the tubs on the patio – we were admiring them the other day. I was planning to ask if I could have a few stems for my arrangements, but he seemed so protective of them I decided not to mention it.'

'So that's what they are! Mum, if I were you I wouldn't

think of bringing them into the house, or even touching them.'

'Why ever not, dear?'

'You might get pollen on your hands and it's very poisonous. In fact, every part of the plant is. At least one crime writer has used oleander leaves to murder someone. In one of her books the killer chopped them up and put them in a pâté and gave it to the victim.'

'How horrid.' Sylvia pulled a face. She thought for a moment, then clutched Melissa's arm. 'Lissie, d'you suppose that's how it was done?'

'How what was done?'

'Gaston being poisoned. It wouldn't take very much to kill a little dog, would it?'

'Probably not.' Melissa's thoughts had shot off at a tangent. She recalled reading in a book about poisons that the toxic ingredient of oleander worked very fast. 'Does anyone know what the dog had to eat that day? Presumably Flavia is right when she insists he didn't pick up anything he wasn't supposed to have.'

'That's the point. She was always feeding him titbits from her own plate, Laurence says, as well as his proper meals. And Gaston keeled over while we were having our tea.'

'Mum, you're not suggesting—?'

'Anyone would know that Flavia would give her cake to Gaston.'

'Only part of it.'

'You just agreed it wouldn't take much.'

'Yes, but if someone offered Flavia a poisoned cake, they'd expect her to feed some of it to the dog, but not all of it. She'd surely eat some of it herself.'

Sylvia's eyes stretched in horror. 'Lissie! Are you saying someone tried to murder Flavia?'

Melissa burst out laughing. 'No, of course I'm not. I was only trying to point out that your poisoned cake theory is a little weak. From what you tell me, Flavia does get a lot of people's backs up, but I hardly think anyone would want to murder her.'

'Well, that's a relief. So what do you think about the gardener?'

'I think he gave us the clue when he complained about Gaston peeing on the oleanders. The dog probably had a good sniff round them first, got some of the poisonous pollen on his nose and then licked it off. As you say, it wouldn't take much to kill a dog, and he was pretty old anyway and probably not very fit if Flavia was always feeding him scraps.'

'Oh, Lissie, I'm so thankful to hear you say that.' Sylvia's face lit up and she straightened her drooping shoulders. 'I didn't want to believe it was the gardener.'

'I think we can eliminate him from our enquiries,' Melissa said with a smile. 'Even if he felt strongly enough to want to do away with Gaston, it would have been difficult to feed poison to him without Flavia noticing.'

'Of course it would. She never let him out of her sight.'

'Of course, we shan't know for certain that it was oleander that killed him until Flavia gets the result of the post-mortem, but it does seem the most likely explanation. If it was, you can explain to her that we've worked out how it could have been an accident. That should put paid to all the private detective nonsense.'

'You're the one who worked it out.' Sylvia beamed with pride at her daughter's cleverness. 'I'm not sure I'd have the courage to tell her, though. She's rather an overbearing sort of person.'

'Well, get Laurence to do it. I think he'd quite enjoy it.'

'That's a good idea.' Sylvia glanced at her wristwatch. 'Lissie, I don't want to rush you, but I think I ought to go back now and do some more work on my arrangements. I'd like to finish a couple before supper.'

'Fine.'

They set off back to the house. As they emerged from the shade of the trees and began to cross the wide, sloping expanse of lawn, they saw a man and a woman emerge from the main door and begin a slow promenade along a gravelled path that ran the length of a colourful herbaceous border. The plants, however, appeared to hold little interest for them. The path was wide enough for two people to walk side by side, yet Melissa noticed that Lily Cherston seemed to make a point of keeping a couple of paces ahead of Laurence Dainton – or possibly it was he who deliberately kept behind her. For most of the time they looked straight ahead, although now and again, and without varying her pace, Lily glanced back at Laurence. It was not possible at that distance to judge whether she had spoken or was merely making certain that he was still following.

'Well, well, well!' said Melissa softly. 'They're on speaking terms now, are they?'

Sylvia gave a little cry of excitement and clapped her hands. 'Oh, wouldn't it be wonderful if they could be friends again!' she exclaimed.

'I thought you had your eye on him for yourself, and here you are trying to pair him off with his ex,' said Melissa mischievously.

'Oh, don't be so silly. I'm not trying to do anything of the kind, but it would be lovely if they could make it up so that Lily could see her children and grandchildren more often.'

'It doesn't look to me as if they're in making-up mode.'

'Well, it's obvious they're going to have a serious talk about something. It could be about their relationship, couldn't it? They must have been in love once,' Sylvia added wistfully.

'From what you've told me about Lily, there doesn't seem to be much love lost now.'

'There might be a little spark left. You never know.'

'Mum, I had no idea you were so romantic.'

'There are a lot of things you don't know about me.'

'That's hardly surprising, is it?' The words were out before Melissa could stop them. Sylvia flinched as if she had been stung and she turned her head away without replying. Melissa slid an arm round her shoulders and gave her a squeeze. 'Sorry, Mum, that was a bit cruel.'

'It was no more than I deserve. I don't blame you for feeling bitter. I'm bitter about it myself.'

'We must try not to dwell on the past. We've got time to get to know one another now.'

Laurence stood at the water's edge and stared down at the goldfish. 'I really don't understand why you're telling me all this,' he said.

'I thought you'd pounce on it,' said Lily. 'It'd make a great story.'

'For whom?'

'Oh, for goodness' sake! You're a journalist, you know the score. Any of the tabloids'd pay big money for it. You read about it all the time.'

'And what makes you think I've descended to writing for the gutter press?'

'You can't afford to be too choosy these days. I heard you at dinner yesterday, complaining to Seb and Chas about how the value of investments has gone down. You've got a chance here to earn some serious money. I'll bet lots of editors would offer megabucks for this.'

'It might have escaped your notice that I have a reputation for high-class journalism and that I was once voted Journalist of the Year. One doesn't receive that kind of award for muck-raking.'

Lily threw back her head and shrieked with laughter. A blackbird that had been exploring a nearby patch of grass for worms took flight and departed with squawks of alarm. Laurence winced.

'I do remember that award,' Lily chortled. 'About twenty years ago, wasn't it? Ancient history. And,' she went on, undeterred by her ex-husband's frosty expression, 'you could always do it under a *nomm dee ploome*. Then you wouldn't have to worry about your precious reputation.' She took his arm and gave it a little shake. 'I'm only trying to help, Lol,' she said coaxingly. 'Besides, don't you think that kind of behaviour deserves to be exposed, even after all these years? Think about it.' He stiffened under her touch, but allowed her arm to remain through his.

Encouraged, Lily went on, 'Don't let's be bad friends, Lol. Fate has thrown us together again and we're both getting on.'

This time, he detached himself from her grasp and brushed away an imaginary insect with a flap of his hand. 'The flies are getting troublesome,' he said. 'I'm going indoors.'

# 8

'Just a minute!'

Laurence stopped, but did not turn round. 'I don't think there's any more to be said.' His voice was cold and distant.

'Oh yes there bloody well is!' A furious Lily rushed in front of him and faced him, blocking his path. 'Okay, so you don't think much of my idea. That's your privilege, but it doesn't mean you have to treat me like dirt. I do have feelings, you know, in case you hadn't noticed.'

'You have made your feelings on this point perfectly clear, as I have made mine,' he said coldly. He assumed the resigned 'we've had this conversation before' expression that Lily recognised all too well.

Too bloody right we have, many times, she thought bitterly. What a fool I was to imagine it would be any different, even after forty years. 'Okay, have it your way.' She felt her colour rise, her hands tremble, her heart pound. This wasn't good for her. Doctor Godwin's parting advice at their last consultation echoed in her brain. '*You have to learn to accept the fact that you need to take life more quietly from now on. No more rushing around the world on a whim, or burning the candle at both ends. And try to avoid undue stress or excitement.*' He hadn't actually spoken the words 'stroke' or 'heart attack', but she knew that was what he had in mind. Mentally she brushed the warning aside. People's lives had been damaged, maybe ruined. If something could be done to put the record straight, it would be criminal to ignore it. Laurence had refused to have anything to do with it so it was up to her. She gritted her teeth, ignored her racing pulse and said, 'If you're too holier-than-thou to dirty your hands with this story, I'll go after it myself.'

'If you want to pursue your sordid little game, I suppose there is nothing I can do to prevent you, but I refuse to be associated with it. However,' he continued, for the first time meeting her eyes, 'I strongly advise you to drop the whole idea. You might find you have stirred up a hornet's nest.'

'Okay, so I'll risk getting stung. People shouldn't be allowed to do that sort of damage and get away with it.'

'It's none of your business.'

'I'm going to make it my business. There's such a thing as natural justice. I've heard you banging on about that often enough. Not that you ever let it affect your attitude to me – or the boys.' To her chagrin, she felt a stinging sensation in her eyes and a constriction in her throat as she struggled to keep her voice level. 'You can't begin to imagine what it was like, not being allowed to see Johnny and Harry.'

'I never forbade you to see them.'

'Oh no, you were much too clever for that. You just took them somewhere I could never afford to visit on the miserable allowance you made me.'

He made a weary gesture. 'Do we really have to go over all this again? You only have yourself to blame for that. It wasn't as if you were discreet about your affairs. Or perhaps "one-night stands" would be a more accurate way to describe your behaviour. People were talking and I thought it undesirable for my sons to know that their mother was a loose woman.'

'*Your* sons! They're my sons too.'

'Unfortunately.'

'You sanctimonious bastard!' Frustration and anger rose in a rush of bile to her mouth. The sense of helplessness, the memory of the futile attempts to convey her feelings, the inability to find the right words and the humiliation of being out-gunned and out-reasoned, were as sharp now, forty years on, as on the day when her spirit finally broke and she walked away from a battle she had no hope of winning. 'You froze me out. I was young and made of flesh and blood. What was I supposed to do – live like a nun?'

'You could at least have been discreet about it, if that was what you wanted.' He looked contemptuously down his beautifully chiselled nose, a feature that she had once found so devastatingly attractive. 'You could have shown a little dignity, a little respect for me and your family.'

'Respect!' She almost choked on the word. 'What respect did you ever show me?'

'I did not object to the boys visiting you once they were old enough to understand the situation. You can hardly blame me if they chose to keep contact to a minimum.'

'Oh, can't I? I suppose the fact that you had poisoned their minds against me didn't have anything to do with it.'

'I did nothing of the kind; I merely told them the truth. I see no point in continuing this conversation, but so far as this present hare-brained notion is concerned, I repeat my advice to let well alone. You could be putting yourself in personal danger.'

'A fat lot you'd care about that.'

'You misjudge me. I would not wish any harm to come to you.'

For a brief moment, she glimpsed a hint of softening in his expression and impulsively she held out her hand. 'Lol,' she pleaded, 'don't let's be bad friends.'

He stiffened, and she knew she had made a fatal blunder. 'If you will kindly excuse me,' he said. Ignoring the out-stretched hand, he moved aside to pass her. This time she made no attempt to stop him. She counted up to fifty before she felt calm enough to follow him back to the house.

Melissa and her mother were strolling to the visitors' car park when Laurence appeared from the direction of the lake. He was walking straight towards them, but changed course abruptly in what seemed like a deliberate attempt to avoid them.

'I think that's what's meant by the cliché "a face of thunder",' Melissa commented wryly as Laurence marched through the open front door of the house and disappeared. 'Sorry, Mum, your romantic dream of reconciliation seems to have gone a bit pear-shaped.'

'Oh, what a pity! Of course, it's obvious that he and Lily are from very different backgrounds, but it does seem a shame they can't even be friends. I mean, the way they've been thrown together like this – it's almost like fate, don't you think?'

'If it is, then I'd say fate has played a very dirty trick,' said Melissa thoughtfully, as a few moments later Lily emerged from among the trees. She walked slowly, dragging her feet, her eyes fixed on the ground. She passed within a few yards of them on her way back to the house, but for all the notice she took of them, they might have been invisible. 'It looks to me as if they've had an almighty row, with Lily coming off worst.'

Sylvia made tutting noises. 'I understand that's how their arguments always ended when they were married,' she said with a regretful shake of the head. 'Of course, Lily has a lot of spirit. If Laurence said or did anything she objected to, I don't suppose she took it lying down.'

'Probably not,' said Melissa. She forbore to add, *not like the way you used to cave in when Dad chucked his weight around.*

'Incidentally' – as was her habit when speaking of some topic that she considered delicate, Sylvia glanced round before continuing in a low voice – 'I have noticed him – Laurence, I mean – chatting quite a lot to Angela Fuller. She's very quiet and ladylike, much more his type, I suppose, although I've never thought her very interesting. We've sat at the same table once or twice and she doesn't have much to say for herself.'

'Maybe that's why he finds her attractive: she lets him hog the conversation and appear very clever.'

'You don't like him much, do you?'

'Let's just say I'm more resistant to his charm than you seem to be.'

'Oh, Lissie, I assure you I'm not—' Sylvia broke off as she caught the mischievous twinkle in her daughter's eye. 'All right, you will have your little joke,' she giggled. Then she became serious as a stout figure emerged from the house and strode purposefully towards them. 'Oh dear, it's Mrs Selwyn-Tuck and she's heading this way.'

'Pretend you haven't seen her.'

Melissa took her mother's arm and began propelling her towards the car, but they had taken only a couple of steps when a booming voice called, 'Mrs Craig, a moment of your time, if you please!'

Reluctantly, Melissa stopped and turned round. It was the first time she had come face to face with the unfortunate Gaston's owner, having so far glimpsed her only from a distance. Her general impression had been of a somewhat matronly although well-proportioned figure, a high colour topped by a formidable sculpture of grey hair and a penetrating, aggressively upper-class voice. Closer quarters revealed a pair of strikingly blue eyes, a fine bone structure half buried beneath an over-abundance of flesh and a disarming smile.

'Flavia Selwyn-Tuck,' boomed the new arrival, extending a plump hand, the middle finger of which sported a huge cameo ring.

'How do you do, Mrs Selwyn-Tuck,' said Melissa politely.

'Please, call me Flavia.'

'Nice to meet you, Flavia. I'm Melissa.'

They shook hands. Flavia's was hot and a trifle moist. She took a handkerchief from her pocket and mopped her forehead. 'Bit warmish today, what?'

'Yes, it is.' Melissa hesitated for a moment before saying, 'What can I do for you?', hoping that it might be nothing more than a question about one of her books, but fearing that it was nothing of the kind. The next remarks confirmed her suspicions.

'I'm told you're something of a detective. Know about crime, write about it, that sort of thing.'

'I used to write crime novels, yes, but—'

'But you have also helped the police solve real crimes. Oh yes,' Flavia continued as Melissa opened her mouth to protest. 'I've been making some enquiries and I think you're just the person I'm looking for.'

'To do what?' Melissa asked, resignedly certain that she already knew the answer.

'You can find out who poisoned me dog.'

She pronounced the final word *dawg* and Melissa

suppressed a smile as she replied, 'Really, Flavia, I'm not a private detective.'

'I'm well aware of that. I'd have engaged one, only that fusspot Geraldine Wardle wouldn't have one near the place. That's why I'm asking you to find the wretch who took out their resentment of me on poor defenceless little Gaston.' The booming voice faltered and genuine tears welled up in the clear blue eyes.

'As a matter of fact,' Melissa went on gently, moved by the woman's obvious distress, 'I think it's more likely that Gaston's death was a very unfortunate accident.' In a few words, she outlined her theory. She half expected it to be swept aside, but Flavia's response was surprising.

'You really think so?' Relief spread like a burst of sunshine over the plump countenance. 'You don't reckon anyone did it on purpose?'

'It seems unlikely. It isn't as if Gaston made a nuisance of himself, is it?'

'Of course he didn't. The poor little love was as good as gold, no trouble to anyone.' The tears overflowed and trickled down to mingle with the sweat on Flavia's flushed cheeks.

'It does depend on whether the poison that killed Gaston is contained in oleander,' Melissa pointed out. 'Did you get a full analysis from the laboratory?'

Flavia mopped her eyes and blew her nose with a vigorous trumpeting sound. 'The vet said something about a cardiac stimulator, whatever that means,' she explained. 'He couldn't say where it might have come from without further tests. D'you think I should . . .'

'I've got some reference books about poisons at home. If you like, I could check on oleander and see if it—'

'Would you *reeahly*? It would be most *awfully* kind of you,

*Ai'd* appreciate it *no end.*' Emotion made the 'county' accent even more pronounced and – to Melissa's ears – more artificial. 'If it's not going to be *too* much trouble.'

'No trouble at all. I'll give you a call and let you know if I find out anything helpful.'

'Thanks most *awfully*! You must think me an old silly to make all this fuss, but Gaston was a real pal to me.' Flavia's normally pompous, self-assured manner had momentarily given way to an uncharacteristic humility.

'Not at all,' Melissa assured her. 'I'm so glad I've been able to put your mind at rest.'

'I suppose I'd better go and tell Mrs Wardle the mystery's been solved,' Flavia said, with apparent reluctance. 'She wasn't very helpful – seemed more concerned with the reputation of Framleigh House than with justice for poor little Gaston.'

'That was interesting,' said Melissa thoughtfully as the bereaved dog-owner made her stately way back to the house.

'What was, dear?' asked Sylvia.

'Didn't you notice how she pounced on the suggestion that Gaston might have picked up the poison by accident? And that reference to someone having a feeling of resentment towards her? I wonder what she meant by that?'

'It was a strange thing to say, wasn't it? I do hope she wasn't thinking of anyone here.'

After her abortive conversation with Laurence, Lily returned to her room, took one of her tablets, lay down on her bed and waited for her pulse rate to return to normal. She realised that in telling her ex-husband about what she considered to be an exciting discovery – well, not exactly a discovery, more a sudden flash of memory – she had somehow thought, or at least hoped, that it would in some way establish a bond between them. She had thought about it so much since that moment of startled recognition and recall. The search for proof of her suspicions might have given her and Lol – no, she mustn't make the mistake of using that nickname again, he'd always hated it – given her and *Laurence* an opportunity to put their heads together to work out a plan of campaign and research. Even if in the end he decided not to go ahead with trying to sell the story, at least they would have found some common ground. The word 'common' that came into her head at this point was like a stab from a needle in her brain. That was how he thought of her, wasn't it? That was the reason that lay at the bottom of his refusal to work with her on what she was convinced was a worthwhile project as well as something they might do together. The reference to possible danger was just an excuse. Lily clenched her hands and fought back the tears. Then, as the drug began to take effect, she relaxed and drifted off to sleep.

She was roused by a tap on the door. 'Who is it?' she asked drowsily.

'It's Sylvia. Aren't you coming down for supper?'

'Oh, Lord!' Lily sat up and swung her legs over the side of the bed. Her head swam; she had moved too quickly. 'What's the time?'

'It's nearly half past seven.'

'I don't think I want anything to eat. I don't feel too good.'

'I'm so sorry. Is there anything I can do?'

'No thanks, love, I'll be all right. I'm tired, all I want to do is sleep.'

'If you're sure . . .'

'Quite sure.'

'You should try to eat a little. I could ask Terry to send you up something light.'

Lily thought for a moment. She really didn't fancy anything at all, but if Sylvia was going to fuss, it might be a good idea to agree. 'Well, maybe just a sandwich.'

'What sort of sandwich?'

'Oh, anything.' Lily tried not to sound impatient.

'All right, I'll have a word with her. I hope you feel better tomorrow.'

'Thanks.'

She had dozed off again when there was another tap at the door. Tracy, one of the helpers, entered with a plate of sandwiches and a glass of milk on a tray, which she put down on the table. 'Egg and cress,' she announced in her warm, Gloucestershire accent. 'And I'll turn down your bed now, so's not to disturb you later.'

'That's very kind.'

'I hope you feel better tomorrow.'

'Thank you.'

Lily slowly ate her sandwiches and drank her milk. She was still dog-tired and it was an effort to go through her nightly routine of removing her make-up and applying the various creams and lotions. When at last she was ready to get into bed, she sat on the edge and unwrapped the sweet Tracy had left on the pillow. It was one of the little touches that she liked about this place; it made it seem less like a home for the elderly, more like a hotel.

She fell asleep with the comforting taste of chocolate in her mouth.

# 9

'Lissie, something terrible happened during the night.' It was Sunday morning. Melissa was still only half awake when the phone beside her bed rang, but the shakiness in her mother's voice as much as the actual words had her alert in an instant.

'I'm sorry to call so early.' Sylvia faltered.

'Don't worry about that. I should have been up an hour ago. What's the matter? Are you all right?'

'Yes, I'm all right, except that I'm feeling very upset. It's Flavia . . . Mrs Selwyn-Tuck. She's been taken ill, she's in hospital.'

'Oh dear. What's wrong with her?'

'They say she's been very sick. They're talking about food poisoning, but I'm terribly afraid . . .' Sylvia's voice tailed off to a whisper.

Melissa began to be seriously alarmed. 'You mean you're feeling ill yourself? Have you—'

'No, no, I'm quite all right except that . . . oh, I do hope I'm wrong.'

Over the wire, Melissa heard a series of short, sharp breaths as her mother struggled to steady herself. 'Mum, just take it easy and tell me about it,' she said in the soothing tone she once used when calming her son Simon's childish tantrums. 'You know excitement is bad for you.'

'Yes, I know, but I must talk to someone and you're the only person—'

'What is it you're afraid of?'

'I can't say on the phone in case anyone's listening in.'

'Oh, Mum, you don't seriously imagine there are spies at Framleigh House, do you?'

'You never know, especially if—'

'If what?'

'I'd really rather not say. Lissie, could you possibly come over? It might be—' There was a pause before Sylvia continued in a barely audible whisper, 'It might be a matter of life and death.'

'Whatever do you mean?'

'I can't say any more now. Please, Lissie, I must see you.' She was clearly on the verge of tears.

Melissa's mind flew back to her last conversation with the consultant who carried out the brain tumour operation and she experienced a stab of uneasiness. '*Watch out for signs of paranoia,*' Doctor Freeman had warned. '*Let me know at once if you notice any kind of irrational behaviour.*'

'Mum, please don't upset yourself.' Again, Melissa did her best to sound reassuring and matter of fact. 'I'm sure everything will be all right. I'll come and see you as soon as I'm up and dressed. Have you had your breakfast?'

'I'm not hungry.'

'Why not? Are you sure you aren't feeling ill?'

'I don't feel ill, I just don't fancy anything.'

'I think you should eat something.'

'I couldn't face food. Please, Lissie, come as soon as you can.'

'All right.' Melissa glanced at her bedside clock. 'It's twenty to nine. I'll be with you by half past.'

'Won't Joe mind? You said he was coming home yesterday.'

'Yes, but that won't stop me coming to see you. In any case, he's not here yet; he went straight to his flat in London and he's going to drive down this afternoon, after he's taken care of some paperwork.'

'Suppose he arrives and you're out?'

'Oh, Mum, stop worrying. He's got a key and he can let himself in.'

'Well, if you're sure. You won't say anything about this to anyone, will you? Not till I've seen you?'

'Of course I won't. Just give me time to get dressed and grab a bite to eat.'

'I'll stay in my room till you get here.'

'That's a good idea. Everything will be fine, you'll see.'

'I do hope so.' Sylvia sounded calmer, but by no means convinced.

With a feeling of intense disquiet, Melissa put down the phone. She took a hurried shower, threw on some clothes, downed a hasty breakfast and set off for Framleigh House.

'Now, Mum, just what is all this about?'

Mother and daughter were in Sylvia's pretty little bed-sitting room overlooking the garden. Sylvia, at least partially reassured by Melissa's presence, had been persuaded to drink a cup of milky coffee and nibble, somewhat half-heartedly, at a slice of buttered toast. She took small bites, interspersed with sips of the coffee, as if playing for time. At last, she said hesitantly, 'Lissie, I know you're going to think I'm imagining things, but I really did hear this.'

'Hear what?' prompted Melissa as her mother still seemed reluctant to go on.

'Laurence and Lily – you remember they had that argument on Friday?'

'We don't know for certain that they had an argument.'

'That's true – at least, it was true at the time.'

'You're saying something's happened since then?'

'Yes.' Sylvia bit her lip and fiddled nervously with her coffee cup. 'I suppose I should have come away and not listened, but I really couldn't help hearing. I was out in the garden yesterday after supper; it was such a lovely evening. The garden here is a bit like a maze, with all sorts of little nooks and crannies where people can sit and read or just admire the flowers and listen to the birds undisturbed.' Sylvia's voice suddenly dropped to a conspiratorial whisper. 'I was just about to sit down on a bench,' she went on, 'when I heard . . . voices.'

Resisting the temptation to make a flippant comparison with Joan of Arc, Melissa said, 'Whose voices were they?'

'Lily Cherston and Laurence Dainton. I had my back to a hedge and they must have been behind me on the other side. I really wasn't imagining it, you know,' she added defensively, as if expecting to be challenged.

Melissa drew a deep breath and mentally counted to ten. 'No one's suggesting you were,' she said slowly and deliberately, with pauses between each word, 'so will you please stop beating about the bush and tell me exactly what you heard.'

'That's the problem, I can't remember the exact words, but Laurence seemed to be apologising for something he'd said earlier and Lily said, "All right, no hard feelings." She sounded really pleased. You know' – a sudden change of tone indicated that Sylvia's mind had switched to a different train of thought – 'I do think, in spite of all the unkind things Lily's been saying about Laurence, she might still be quite fond of him. It would be lovely if they made it up, wouldn't it?'

'Yes, Mum, it would, but that isn't what you wanted to talk about, is it?'

'No, dear, I'm sorry. I do find my mind wandering sometimes.' Sylvia turned and peered anxiously into her daughter's face. 'You don't think . . . ?'

'I'm sure it's nothing to worry about,' Melissa said quickly with what she hoped was complete conviction. 'Just take it easy and get on with your story. What did Laurence and Lily say next?'

'He said he'd been thinking about what she'd told him and how he could see her point of view, and it was right for war criminals to be punished years after the event, but this was different because it might hurt other people if she . . . I think "if you go ahead" were the words he used, but I can't be sure. And Lily said, "What about the people who've been hurt already?" and he said, "It's too late to do anything about them".'

'Have you any idea what Lily was planning to do?'

'None at all, I'm afraid. And I couldn't hear any more after that because their voices went very low, but I did get the impression that he was trying to talk her out of something. After a while the voices stopped altogether. I thought they must have gone, but I was afraid to move in case they were still there and heard me. I didn't want them to think I'd been eavesdropping, although I suppose I had in a way, but it wasn't on purpose.'

'And you don't know who they were talking about?'

'They didn't mention any names, if that's what you mean. But just a few hours later, Flavia Selwyn-Tuck was taken ill with suspected food poisoning and I can't help wondering . . . you know, after what happened to her dog, and her thinking someone might have done it to spite her for some reason.'

Melissa stared at her mother in horror. 'Mum! You aren't seriously suggesting that Laurence and Lily conspired to poison Flavia?'

'I knew you'd think I'm being silly.' Sylvia flushed in embarrassment. 'Just the same, it does seem strange that no one else has been affected, doesn't it?'

'There could be several reasons for that. She might have gone out to lunch and eaten something dodgy in a restaurant. Or she might have some gastric problem of her own. We don't know for certain that it's food poisoning; she might be allergic to something that wouldn't upset anyone else. In any case, there's no evidence from what you over-heard that it was Flavia they were talking about.'

'I suppose not,' Sylvia admitted reluctantly. 'It was just because it's Flavia who's been taken ill that I—'

'Put two and two together and made five,' said Melissa. She patted her mother's hand with a smile of encourage-ment. 'It's quite natural, but I'm sure you're worrying unnecessarily – although I agree it would be very interesting to know who Laurence and Lily were talking about. Anyway, it's not your problem. I'll tell you what,' she went on, glancing at her watch, 'now I've finished my book, and you're feeling stronger, why don't you come home with me? We could go to church and then I'll give you some lunch at Hawthorn Cottage.'

Sylvia clapped her hands. 'Oh yes, that would be lovely. I'm longing to see your house.'

'Actually, you've already seen it. We called in on the way to the convalescent home, the day you left the hospital.'

'Did we? I don't remember.'

'That's hardly surprising – you were pretty woozy.

Doctor Freeman had given you something to help you relax during the journey.'

'I'm not woozy now. I'm much better, aren't I?'

The wistful note in her mother's voice and the pleading in her eyes caused Melissa's throat to tighten for a moment. 'Yes, Mum, you're getting stronger every day,' she said, praying that it was true. 'You've let your coffee get cold. If you can be ready in ten minutes there'll be time before the service to make you a fresh cup and a bit more toast when we get home.'

'I'll be ready in five.'

The short drive from Framleigh House to Melissa's home was by a narrow, winding lane that climbed steeply up the Cotswold escarpment and then, after a short distance, dipped again into a shallow valley. Here lay the twin villages of Upper and Lower Benbury, separated geographically and demographically by a shallow brook. Fed by half a dozen springs, the stream meandered through the country-side on its leisurely way to the distant upper reaches of the Thames, creating a haven for wildlife and a source of constant delight to nature lovers. The road was little used other than by local residents, except when a hold-up on a nearby trunk road sent queues of impatient motorists invading the peaceful byway in search of an alternative route to their destinations, causing congestion, ill-temper and a storm of complaints from residents to the police, the county council, their member of parliament and the local press.

This sunny Sunday morning it was almost deserted. Sitting beside Melissa as the Golf made its tortuous way to the top of the hill, Sylvia exclaimed in admiration as each twist and turn revealed a glimpse of grazing sheep or cattle, a swathe of creamy hawthorn blossom, a meadow sprinkled with wild flowers or the spire of a distant church. For the last quarter of a mile they passed through a wood where branches of beech and ash formed a green arch above their heads and rabbits hopped out of their way into invisible holes in the grassy banks on either side of the road.

When at last Melissa drew up outside her cottage with the announcement, 'Here we are, Mum. This is where you'll be living when the extension's finished,' Sylvia was almost speechless with pleasure.

'It's beautiful, like something off a calendar!' she exclaimed.

'It'll look more like a battlefield when the builders move in next week,' said Melissa wryly. She got out of the car and was about to open the passenger door when a second car swung into the gravelled track that served the two adjoining cottages and pulled up behind the Golf. Her jaw dropped as a familiar figure alighted, waved both arms and shouted, 'Surprise!'

'Iris!' Forgetting her mother for the moment, Melissa ran forward and hugged her friend. 'How lovely to see you! Why didn't you let me know you were coming?'

'Didn't know till yesterday. Had a call to say my old prof is in London for a couple of days. Haven't seen him in years. Booked a flight, hired a car. No time to send messages.'

'How long are you staying?'

'A week or two. Thought I'd take in a few exhibitions while I'm here. That your mother?' Iris switched her gaze to Sylvia, still seated in Melissa's car.

'Yes, do come and meet her.'

'Delighted.'

Looking slightly bemused, Sylvia scrambled out and took the thin brown hand extended to her. 'I'm so glad to meet you,' she said shyly. 'Lissie's told me so much about you.'

'We're going indoors for a quick coffee and then to church,' said Melissa. 'Will you come with us?'

Iris shook her head. 'Bit tired after the trip. Think I'll have a bath and a rest.'

'Join us for lunch, then.'

'Veggie?'

'Would I dare offer you anything else?'

'Then I'd love to.'

'Great. About one o'clock?'

'Fine.'

After the service the three of them sat down to pasta in a cheese and tomato sauce with roast vegetables. Melissa had explained Iris's passionate dedication to a vegetarian diet and offered her mother an alternative meat dish, which she declined with the earnest assurance that she didn't want to cause any extra trouble, later praising the food with such enthusiasm that Iris offered to lend her a vegetarian cookery book.

'Unrepentant carnivore, your daughter,' she declared, with a disapproving shake of her bobbed, mouse-brown head in Melissa's direction. 'Can't think why. Cooks perfectly good veggie nosh. You try and convert her.'

Sylvia gave a shy smile, but avoided making any such commitment by turning the subject to the rector's sermon, which kept them going until the dessert. They were just finishing their first helping of gooseberry crumble, made with fruit from Melissa's garden, when the telephone rang.

Melissa put down her spoon and started to her feet. 'That's probably Joe. I'll take it upstairs,' she said. 'I won't be long – help yourselves to seconds.'

'Take your time,' said Iris with a knowing twinkle in her sharp grey eyes. 'Want me to make the coffee?'

'Thanks.'

It was a good twenty minutes later that Melissa came downstairs to find Iris in the kitchen looking out of the window at the garden. 'Your apples are setting nicely,' she commented.

'Yes, aren't they? I was afraid the tree might have to go to make room for the extension, but the architect managed to save it.'

'That's good. Everything okay with Joe?'

'Yes, fine, except that he has to stay in London for a second night, so he'll be driving down tomorrow instead of this afternoon. Have you had coffee?'

'Not yet, waited for you.' Iris indicated the cafetière on the table beside two mugs and a small jug of milk. 'Shall we have ours here? Sylvia doesn't want any. She's in the sitting room, having a nap.'

They sat down and Melissa poured the coffee. 'She's been a bit overwrought today,' she explained. 'One of the other residents was taken ill in the night, and it's upset her.'

'I know. Says she's worried the woman's been poisoned.'

'Oh Lord, is she still on about that? I thought I'd persuaded her—'

'You don't reckon there's anything in it then?'

'I sincerely hope not, for the victim's sake, but I'm concerned about Mum. The consultant warned me to watch out for signs of paranoia.'

'Doesn't seem paranoid to me.'

'I hope you're right.'

'Think she's feeling a bit insecure, though. Afraid you're going to regret inviting her to live with you and Joe.'

'Is that what she said?'

'Not in so many words, just kept on about the expense of the extension, and not wanting to be a nuisance.'

'I know,' said Melissa thoughtfully. 'I've tried to reassure her, but. . . .'

'Bound to take time.' Iris finished her coffee and stood up. 'Must be going – things to do. If you're on your own this evening, come for supper. Lots to tell you.'

'Thanks. It's great to have you here, Iris.'

'Great to be here.'

'It's a shame Jack couldn't come too.'

'Someone has to look after the business.'

'Are you having a good season?'

'Pretty good. Most courses fully booked. Funny thing,' she added reflectively, 'miss the Cotswolds like hell when I'm there, miss the Midi as soon as I leave.'

'Nothing odd about that.'

As they parted at the door, Iris lowered her voice and said, 'By the way, your mum is very concerned about your reputation.'

'Whatever do you mean?'

'She's afraid the village folk will suspect you and Joe of having pre-marital relations,' Iris explained with mock gravity. 'Went on to say of course she's sure everything's perfectly proper, even though he does spend the night here from time to time.'

Melissa clapped a hand to her mouth. 'Oh, Lord!' she exclaimed. 'That never entered my head. We'll have to mind our ps and qs, won't we?' Her eyes met Iris's and the two friends collapsed in suppressed giggles.

When Sylvia awoke from her nap, Melissa suggested a walk, but she seemed restless and insisted on returning to

Framleigh House without delay. 'I want to know how Flavia is,' she said.

'I could ring up and find out.'

'Thank you, but I'd rather go back.'

Half an hour later, they returned to be greeted with the news that Flavia Selwyn-Tuck had slipped into a coma and died.

# 10

'What did I tell you?' There was a gleam in Sylvia's brown eyes that was almost triumphant, despite her obvious shock and consternation at the news. 'I said there was something suspicious going on, didn't I?'

'Mum, I don't think you should jump to conclusions. We don't know yet what Flavia died of.'

'But isn't it obvious? She was poisoned, I'm sure of it. Either Lily or Laurence—'

'Now look here, Mum.' For the first time since Sylvia had broached the possibility of a Lily and Laurence conspiracy Melissa felt her patience on the point of running out. 'You really mustn't let your imagination run away with you like this. You can't go round accusing people of murder without a shred of evidence.'

'But I told you, I heard them—'

'You heard nothing to suggest that's what they were planning. And anyway you've admitted that you didn't know who they were talking about when you overheard that conversation in the garden.'

'I'm sure now that it was Flavia. It all fits.'

'It does nothing of the kind. Her death might well be due to natural causes. You told me yourself she had high blood pressure and they had to call the doctor a few days ago. The shock of losing Gaston, and then the violent stomach upset on top of everything else, might have sent it to danger level. In any case,' Melissa went on as her mother obstinately shook her head in disagreement, 'what they were saying doesn't suggest to me that they were discussing murder – on the contrary.'

'I don't follow you.'

'Didn't Laurence warn Lily about the possibility of other people getting hurt?'

'I told you, I can't remember the exact words' – Sylvia's gaze shifted to a point somewhere beyond Melissa's left shoulder – 'but I'm sure they were planning to punish someone for something they had done in the past.'

'Like war criminals brought to trial years after they committed their crimes,' Melissa reminded her.

'Exactly!' Sylvia exclaimed, as if this proved her point. 'And now Flavia's dead. What does that suggest?'

'It suggests to me that Lily wanted to expose some person's past misdemeanours, not plan some kind of Mafia-style execution.'

'It's possible, I suppose,' Sylvia admitted grudgingly.

'And in any case, you had the impression Laurence was trying to talk her out of it. That hardly points to a conspiracy theory, does it?'

Sylvia pondered this argument for a moment before saying, 'Maybe he wanted her to give up whatever she was planning to do so that he could have the story to himself.'

'Story?'

'He's a journalist, isn't he?'

'Yes, but—'

'Well, they're always poking around after what they call "scoops", aren't they? Murky secrets in people's private lives, that sort of thing.'

'That's the ones who work for the tabloids. Laurence

Dainton is a highly respected writer on political and economic affairs. I can't see him stooping to that kind of muck-raking.'

'He might, if it was something that interested him personally. I wonder—' Sylvia broke off as if another thought had struck her, but whatever it was she kept it to herself.

'Wonder what?' Melissa prompted.

'Oh, nothing.' Sylvia's tone was evasive and once again she appeared to focus on a distant object.

'Mum, look at me.' With apparent reluctance, Sylvia complied. 'I want you to promise that you won't go round talking to other people about your suspicions. If there's nothing in them you could be in serious trouble.'

'What if it turns out that Flavia really was poisoned?'

'There'll be a police enquiry, of course.'

'Then I'll have to tell them what I overheard!' There was something almost childlike about the eager interruption.

'I suppose so, but please, Mum, don't go jumping the gun. You're still convalescent after your op and you need to take life quietly. Remember what Doctor Freeman said. Promise?'

Sylvia pouted. 'If you say so,' she said sulkily.

Melissa glanced at the clock on her mother's bedside table. 'It's nearly six. What time do you have dinner on Sundays?'

'They call it supper here.'

'Supper then,' said Melissa patiently. 'What time do you have it?'

'Seven o'clock.'

'Then I expect you'll want to freshen up. Iris has invited me to eat with her this evening, so if you're sure you'll be all right, I'll go home now.'

'Of course I'll be all right. You run along, dear, and have

a nice evening with your friend. You must have lots to talk about.' The tone was indulgent, coaxing, evoking child-hood memories of being encouraged to do something that met with paternal approval. The suspicion flashed into Melissa's mind: Is she trying to get rid of me? Is she up to something?

Sylvia was already on her feet, rummaging in her wardrobe. 'I'd better not wear anything too bright,' she remarked, almost to herself. 'We have to show a little respect, don't we, even if Flavia wasn't particularly well liked.' Over her shoulder, she added, 'I think I'll have a quick shower. You don't mind if I don't see you out, do you?'

'No, of course not.' Melissa got up and went to the door. 'You'll remember what I said, won't you? You won't go spreading rumours about Flavia's death?'

Sylvia put on a hurt expression. 'You know me, Lissie. I'm not the sort of person who spreads rumours,' she said reproachfully.

Just how well do I know you? I was barely out of my teens when you and Father threw me out thirty years ago. I know what effect that had on me, but what did it do to you? These were some of the questions that ran through Melissa's head as she made her way back to her car. She had an uneasy feeling that her mother had something in mind of which she would disapprove.

'She really has me foxed,' Melissa confided to Iris as they sat down to a meal of nut roast accompanied by an assort-ment of vegetables arranged on a plain white dish like the colours on an artist's palette. 'My childhood recollections of her are of someone completely subservient to my father. All those years of having a mind of her own and having to suppress it must have been hell for her. Then she had to go through all that trauma of being suspected of killing him, followed by brain surgery.'

'Enough to knock anyone sideways,' Iris remarked as she carved the nut roast, put a portion on a plate and handed it to Melissa. 'Help yourself to veg. Organic, but not home-grown, I'm afraid. What would you like to drink? There's elderflower bubbly, mineral water . . .'

'Elderflower, please. I need something with a bit of a kick.'

'This is last year's – should be well matured.' Iris eased the cork from a champagne-style bottle of her renowned home-made brew, producing a satisfying pop and a tide of creamy froth. 'Cheers!'

'Cheers!' They clinked glasses. 'It's great to see you, Iris.'

'Good to be here.' Iris picked up her knife and fork. 'Tuck in. Don't let it get cold.'

They ate in silence for a few minutes. Then Iris said, 'You reckon there might be something in it?'

'In what?'

'Sylvia's theory.'

'About Lily and Laurence being involved in Flavia's death, you mean?' Melissa toyed with the stem of her wine glass, frowning. 'My common sense says "no", but I have to admit that it is a rather strange coincidence. First her dog gets poisoned—'

'So it was poison?'

'The preliminary result seemed to confirm it, but so far as I know the exact substance hasn't been identified. Flavia was talking about paying for further tests, but whatever it was there's nothing to suggest that it was administered deliberately.' Melissa outlined the theory about oleander pollen being the cause. 'Gaston could have picked it up by accident.'

'There'll be a post-mortem, I suppose. On Flavia, I mean.'

'Not necessarily. She was seen by her doctor only a couple of days or so ago, and with her medical history—' Melissa broke off as an alarming thought came into her head. 'Even if her death is put down to natural causes, I've an uncomfortable feeling Mum isn't going to be satisfied. She was practically licking her lips at the possibility of helping the police with their enquiries, but if that doesn't happen she's quite capable of nosing round on her own.'

'Thought you'd made her promise not to.'

'I'm not convinced she actually promised anything – except to bear the doctor's advice in mind. She was quite evasive. You know,' Melissa went on thoughtfully, 'when I was a child, she often used to say, "Better not tell your father" if she let me get away with something he might not have approved of. Looking back, it was always something quite trivial, like staying up past my bedtime to watch the telly when Father was out at one of his meetings, but . . .'

'Shows a rebellious streak,' Iris commented. She reached for the wine bottle and topped up Melissa's glass.

'She kept it pretty well suppressed most of the time.' Once again, Melissa felt the bitter taste of resentment that no amount of elderflower bubbly could wash away. 'It would have been nice if just once in a while she'd stood up to him over the things that really mattered.'

'No point in raking over the past.' Iris knew the story that lay behind the long years of estrangement. 'Think what she went through. All those years of repression. Let her have her fun if she wants to play at sleuthing. Can't do any harm, can it?'

'I wish I could be sure of that. Maybe I should have a nose round myself – without letting her know, of course.'

There was a subdued atmosphere in the residents' lounge of Framleigh House that evening. Geraldine Wardle made a brief announcement to the effect that further suspected cases of food poisoning in the neighbourhood had been reported during the previous twenty-four hours and the authorities were investigating the kitchens of a local restaurant where several of the victims had eaten. Flavia had gone into town in the morning and did not return for her midday meal, so it was possible that she too had eaten there. Since no one else at Framleigh House had been affected, it was safe to assume that it was not the source of the infection and, as everyone knew, its kitchens were a model of cleanliness and good practice. Mrs Wardle then wished everyone '*Bon appétit*' and retired to take supper in her own room.

'I can't say it ever occurred to me that Flavia picked up the fatal bug here,' Sidney Wooderson observed to his wife. 'Terry is a stickler for hygiene. And so is Gary,' he added, holding his glass of sweet sherry up to the light. 'The glasses are always spotless.' He took a mouthful as if to give the popular barman a vote of confidence.

'Oh yes, indeed,' agreed Sybil, sipping daintily from her own glass. 'It is awful though, isn't it? About poor Flavia, I mean.'

'Terrible,' Sidney agreed.

At another table, Sylvia sat alone with an untouched white wine spritzer in front of her. As Lily had remarked a day or two previously, it had become her 'regular tipple' and today was the first time she had ordered it by herself. In an odd way, it gave her a sense of achievement. However, it did nothing to allay her anxiety about Lily, who had not yet appeared for supper and who had not responded when she knocked on her door on the way downstairs. She noticed that Laurence Dainton was not in his usual place either, which was surprising because he was almost invariably one of the first to come down.

Angela Fuller entered the lounge and Sylvia noticed that her eye went straight to Laurence's corner. On seeing that it was empty she went to the bar, ordered a drink and glanced round hesitantly as if uncertain where to sit. Catching Sylvia's eye, she crossed the room and said, 'May I join you?'

'Please do.'

'Thank you.' Angela sat down and took a sip from her glass. Sylvia noticed that instead of the usual small sherry she had ordered a schooner. She took a second sip and then a third before saying, 'Is there any news of Mrs Selwyn-Tuck? I mean, do they know yet what she died of?'

'Mrs Wardle seems to think it might be food poisoning.' Sylvia repeated what the manager had said. She took a mouthful from her own drink before adding, 'She seemed certain it wasn't caused by anything she ate here.'

'I'm sure it wasn't. It's very sad though, isn't it?' Angela's face was pale and she fiddled with the brooch at her throat with her free hand. She was evidently shaken by the tragedy. 'Of course, I hardly knew her. I mean, like you I've only been here a few days, but just the same . . .'

'It's very upsetting for all of us,' Sylvia agreed. She was only partly listening to Angela while keeping an eye on the door and wondering what had become of Lily and Laurence. It was all very well for Lissie to pour cold water on her suspicions, but even she would have to agree that it was odd for them both to be absent.

She would have considered her misgivings more than justified had she been aware of a very different discussion on the subject of Flavia's death that was taking place in the garden.

# 11

'Lily, what have you done?'

'Me?' Lily's eyes and mouth – both innocent of make-up because Laurence's demand for an immediate meeting had come while she was still deciding what to wear for supper – flew open in a mixture of astonishment and indignation. She was trembling and a little out of breath; her knees felt weak and she sank down on a stone bench in the secluded corner of the garden where Laurence had been waiting. 'I was going to ask you the same thing,' she panted, glaring at him as he stood upright, looming over her. 'First her dog and now the old cow herself. What did you give them – vitriol? I seem to remember plenty of that in your political articles.'

'If that's your idea of a joke, I consider it to be in very poor taste,' Laurence said icily. His nostrils quivered and his pale eyes bored into hers.

'Who said I was joking?'

'You are being quite ridiculous.'

'So are you.'

He made an impatient gesture. 'Am I? You came to me with your story, almost beseeching me to expose the woman. I made it clear that I was opposed to taking any action against her, no matter how strongly you felt. And a couple of days later she's dead. You must admit—'

'I don't admit anything. I did a bit of thinking after we'd

had our little chat and you know what? I reckon you wanted me to keep quiet so you could have the story to yourself. Oh, don't give me that crap about not stooping to write for the gutter press,' she went on as he opened his mouth to contradict the accusation. 'If it's a fight between hard cash and your precious principles—'

'Do be reasonable. If I intended to do an exposé, I'd have wanted her alive, not dead, wouldn't I?'

'I suppose so,' Lily admitted grudgingly. She was silent for a moment, biting her lips in frustration and wishing her heart would stop racing. Then another idea struck her. 'You told me you didn't want her shown up because of what it might do to other people, so maybe you thought, if she was out of the way, there'd be no chance of me—'

'Lily, stop it.' He sat down on the bench beside her, one hand raised. She shrank away from him, fearing for a second that he was going to strike her – something he had never done before, even in their worst moments – but he merely pressed the hand to his forehead and said, 'Can't you see how illogical you're being?'

She relaxed as she saw his expression soften. 'No more illogical than you, suspecting me of topping the old bag,' she retorted.

'All right, let's just think this through. It's important for both of us that we get things absolutely clear. Do I have your solemn word that you had nothing to do with Flavia's death?'

'Of course I didn't.' Lily put her hands to her temples, trying to still the throbbing. 'I didn't want her dead, I just wanted her shown up, let everyone know what a fraud she was with all her boasting and name-dropping. When it first dawned on me who she was I asked myself, what right has she to be living here in comfort, swanning around and talking all that crap about knowing half the aristocracy while that poor chap, and the others who lost out . . . she didn't give a toss for any of them, just pulled the rug because someone had the cheek to give her the brush-off.' To her chagrin, Lily felt her voice breaking; tears of rage began welling into her eyes and she brushed them away with the back of one hand. 'And her prat of a husband let her get away with it,' she almost sobbed. 'Why couldn't the stupid sod see what she was up to? Everyone else knew.'

'The poor chap had his pride, I suppose.' Laurence put a hand on hers. 'Lily, please don't cry.' His voice was unexpectedly gentle, which made it even more difficult for her to control her emotion. To her astonishment, he pulled a clean handkerchief from his pocket, unfolded it and gave it to her.

'Thanks.' She wiped her eyes and gave it back to him, making a supreme effort to pull herself together. 'Sorry, I should've remembered how you hated it,' she said with a watery smile. 'Good job I'm not wearing me war paint, innit? There'd be mascara all over me face by now.' She gave a nervous titter, then put a hand over her mouth. 'Sorry, it's no laughing matter, is it? Lol . . . I mean, Laurence, what do we do now?'

'We keep quiet. We show decent regret over Flavia's death, the same as everyone else. So long as no one besides me knows of your earlier connection with her, no questions will be asked. In any event, it may turn out that her death was due to natural causes.'

'But if it wasn't?'

'Then' – Laurence drew a deep breath – 'it means that someone had a reason for wanting her out of the way.' His expression was grim as he added, 'Probably someone here.'

'Then there'll be a murder enquiry, won't there? And if

it comes out that I knew who she really was and how angry I got over what she did all those years ago, I'll be a suspect.' Just in time she checked herself from adding, 'And the stupid thing *I* did all those years ago.' Her pulse, which had begun to quieten down, started racing again. 'Oh, God!' she groaned, covering her face with her hands.

'Now just take it easy,' Laurence said firmly. 'There's no earthly reason why you should be a suspect. She never did anything to harm you personally, did she?'

She lifted her head and glared at him. 'That didn't stop you from suspecting me,' she said resentfully.

'And you suspected me,' he reminded her. 'We were both a little hasty, weren't we?' His tone was almost conciliatory. 'We must hope for the best.' From the house there came the sound of the supper gong and he stood up. 'You'd better go indoors and put that war paint on, or you'll miss your first course. I'll follow you in a couple of minutes.' He gave her a fleeting half smile and despite her agitation she felt strangely cheered.

The seating arrangements in the dining-room were purposely kept informal, the idea being for the residents to vary their table companions and thus encourage variety in conversation and the exchange of interests. In practice, this was only partially successful, since the bridge players invariably sat at the same table for four, while Seb and Chas always occupied the same table for two, as did a pair of elderly spinsters who rarely communicated with anyone but each other. By mutual consent, there was normally a discreet scramble to fill the remaining tables, each with four places, to avoid having to put up with Flavia Selwyn-Tuck monopolising the conversation with her interminable anecdotes about goings-on among the landed gentry. This evening, there was no such urgency. When the gong sounded, people drifted almost reluctantly towards the dining-room.

'May I join you, ladies?' Laurence Dainton put a hand on one of the empty chairs at the table already occupied by Sylvia Ross and Angela Fuller and treated each of them in turn to a polite smile that expressed confidence of a welcome rather than any expectation of a refusal.

'It will be a pleasure, Mr Dainton,' Sylvia assured him. 'We've been wondering where you'd got to, haven't we?' she added, turning to Angela, who nodded shyly and turned faintly pink.

'I was a bit late getting back from a trip into town,' Laurence explained as he unfolded his napkin. 'Ah, thank you,' he said to a member of the kitchen staff who brought a half-full bottle of red wine and a glass and set them in front of him. There was a faint hiss as he removed the rubber stopper and poured out a generous measure. 'Wonderful invention, these vacuum gadgets,' he remarked. 'Keep the wine fresh for two or three days. Your very good health, ladies.' He raised the glass and drank. Sylvia responded with her own, which was still half-full.

Angela, who had swallowed the last of her sherry before leaving the lounge, reached for the water jug. 'Allow me,' said Laurence gallantly as he set up her glass and poured. She murmured her thanks and took a few nervous sips.

There was a slightly awkward silence for a few seconds, broken by Sylvia. 'I wonder what's become of Mrs Cherston,' she remarked.

'I've no idea,' Laurence said in a dismissive tone that unmistakably said, '*and of what interest is that to me?*' He picked up the menu and studied it with a frown.

Angela gave him a sharp glance and appeared about to

say something, but at that moment Tracy appeared with a basket of bread rolls in one hand and her order pad in the other. 'The soup this evening's asparagus,' she informed them brightly as she offered the basket to each of them in turn, 'and the pâté's home-made, of course. Terry's special French recipe.'

While they were deliberating over their choice of starters and main courses, Lily entered the dining room. She glanced round, caught Sylvia's eye and took a couple of steps in her direction before appearing to change her mind. She spoke in an uncharacteristically low voice to a couple sitting on their own at a table for four; they looked up and nodded and she pulled out a chair and sat down. Sylvia concluded with regret that she had no desire for her ex-husband's company.

Normally there was a constant buzz of voices during the evening meal as the residents exchanged news and comments about the weather, current affairs and their own activities during the day. This evening, everyone seemed unnaturally subdued, as if by mutual consent no one referred to the topic that was on everyone's mind, while any attempt to introduce any other met with little or no response. '*I think we all felt it was indecent to talk about everyday things after the tragedy,*' Sylvia commented later when reporting the events of the evening to Melissa.

When they had finished their meal, Laurence ceremonially re-corked his bottle of wine with the aid of a small pump that he took from his pocket. Then, with a murmured 'Excuse me, ladies', he got up, handed the bottle to a passing member of staff and left the room.

The minute he disappeared Angela leaned across the table and said in a low voice, 'Mrs Ross, I wonder why Mr Dainton made out he didn't know where Mrs Cherston was when I saw them in the garden just before supper.'

'Together, you mean?'

'Well, no, not exactly.' Angela turned pink again. 'I was looking out of the landing window when I saw Mrs Cherston coming back to the house. She seemed in a bit of a hurry, and when she got closer I noticed that she wasn't wearing any make-up, which I thought was unusual. I mean, she does tend to use rather a lot, doesn't she?'

'I suppose she does,' Sylvia admitted, 'but she puts it on very well,' she added, feeling a touch of irritation at the implied criticism of her friend by someone she had come to regard as a little prissy, with her bobbed hair and hygienically scrubbed appearance.

'Oh yes, I don't deny that, but . . .' Once again, Angela adopted a faintly conspiratorial manner. 'I was still at the window when a minute or two later I saw Mr Dainton coming back to the house from the same direction as Mrs Cherston and I couldn't help thinking they must have been together. I mean, it's a big garden, isn't it? If they'd gone for a stroll separately . . . well, you know what I mean. And so near suppertime; anyway, I thought, I wonder what they've been talking about? I mean, they don't seem to have very much in common, do they? And why did he say he had no idea where Mrs Cherston was when he'd been talking to her such a short time ago?' Angela leaned back in her chair with a trace of a pout on her unrouged lips.

'You can't be sure he'd been talking to her if you didn't see them together,' Sylvia pointed out. It was a similar argument to the one Melissa had used earlier and she felt rather pleased at having spotted the flaw in Angela's reasoning. 'And anyway,' she went on, 'if they'd been having a private conversation, he would hardly want to discuss it with us, would he?'

'I suppose not.' It was clear that Angela did not know that the couple under discussion had once been husband and wife and Sylvia had no intention of passing on the information. At the same time, her own curiosity was immediately aroused and her mind went back to her earlier conversation with Melissa. It would be interesting to have her daughter's reaction to this latest piece of intelligence.

There was a short silence before Angela said, 'Just the same, I can't help wondering.'

'Wondering what?'

'What they were talking about.'

It flashed across Sylvia's mind that this was more than a passing interest. She recalled Lily Cherston's sarcastic comments about the attention Laurence Dainton was paying Angela Fuller. Perhaps the shy, quiet little thing had developed a crush on the suave, polished journalist? In an attempt to set her mind on another track, she said casually, 'Maybe it was the death of Mrs Selwyn-Tuck. After all, it's on all our minds at the moment, isn't it?' She felt vaguely surprised at the way she found herself leading the conversation. It was a role she was unused to and she was rather enjoying it.

'Oh.' Angela appeared to be considering this possibility. 'Yes, I expect that was it,' she said after a moment. She folded her napkin, put it on the table in front of her and stood up. 'I think I'll go and read in my room for the rest of the evening,' she said and left without another word, leaving Sylvia to speculate on this small but, she was convinced, significant development.

# 12

Sylvia waited until the couple with whom Lily had been sharing a table got up and left. Lily herself seemed in no hurry; she sat tracing circles on the tablecloth with her empty glass, a preoccupied expression on her face. Sylvia had sent one or two covert glances across the room during the meal and noticed how little she had contributed to the somewhat limited conversation. She got up, crossed the room, sat down in one of the empty chairs and said in a low voice, 'Lily, can I have a word with you?'

Lily looked up, blinked as if she had been aroused from a doze and said, 'Oh, hello, Sylv. Yes, of course. Sorry I didn't sit with you for supper, but I guess you know why.'

'Because you didn't want to sit with Laurence?'

Lily gave a tired smile. 'Got it in one, plus I couldn't stand watching that dowdy little Fuller creature making sheep's eyes at him.'

'Oh, I'm sure—' Sylvia began, but Lily made a dismissive gesture.

'Never mind her. You said you wanted to talk.'

'Yes.'

For a moment, Sylvia's courage almost failed her. She thought of how Melissa would scold her if she knew what she was planning, then told herself that if nothing came of it she would be none the wiser. And if she really was on to something . . . 'It's about Flavia,' she said.

'What about her?'

'I know they think she died from food poisoning, but suppose it wasn't that?'

Lily's eyes narrowed. She was wide awake now. 'What do you mean?' she asked sharply.

There was something in her manner that made Sylvia tingle with suppressed excitement. She knows something, I'm sure of it, she thought. Aloud, she said, 'You remember what a fuss she made when her dog died, saying she thought someone had poisoned him?'

'Well, what of it? We all knew how batty she was about the silly thing.'

'She asked my daughter – you know Lissie has written a lot of crime novels, don't you? – to try and find out who did it. She said Mrs Wardle wouldn't let her hire a private detective.'

'I'm not surprised. It was a daft idea.'

'Yes, well, Lissie thought of a way that the dog might have picked up some poison by accident, and when she suggested it Flavia seemed really relieved. She said something that made us think she'd been afraid someone here might have been trying to settle a grudge against her by killing her dog.'

'It sounds as if she was paranoid as well as trying to kid everyone she was upper crust,' Lily said with a faint sneer.

'Well, of course, I suppose that's possible, but there could be a reason for her believing it.' Sylvia felt herself becoming bolder every minute. 'You see, it occurred to me that if it was true, it might be someone who knew her before she came to live at Framleigh House, possibly a long time ago. Nobody really believes all the stories she tells – used to tell, I mean – about her past life. She . . . well, I know one shouldn't speak ill of the dead, but she wasn't a very nice woman, was she? She might have made enemies.'

'I can't think what put that idea into your head,' Lily said brusquely. 'If you take my advice, you'll leave it to your daughter to concoct the mystery stories.' She was clearly uncomfortable at the turn the conversation was taking. As if to confirm the impression, she reached for her handbag and almost jumped to her feet. 'If you'll excuse me, Sylvia, I'm going to my room. I've got a bit of a headache.'

'I'm sorry to hear that. Is there anything I can do for you?'

'No thanks.' Lily's expression softened and she put a hand on Sylvia's shoulder. 'Sorry, love, didn't mean to sound crabby.'

Sylvia gave the hand a forgiving pat. 'Don't worry about it, dear. We're all a bit upset this evening. I think I'll have an early night as well. I hope you feel better in the morning.'

'Thanks, Sylv. Goodnight.'

Sylvia waited for a few minutes before returning to her own room. She briefly considered taking the stairs to the first floor, then decided that she had expended enough energy for one day and pressed the button for the lift. When the door opened Geraldine Wardle stepped out. She smiled and said, 'Good evening, Mrs Ross,' and was about to walk past when Sylvia put out a hand to detain her.

'Excuse me,' she said. 'Do you have any further news about Mrs Selwyn-Tuck?'

Mrs Wardle shook her head. 'I imagine it will be several days before all the tests have been completed.' She spoke with an air of patient resignation, suggesting that she had been asked the same question, and given the same answer, more than once that evening.

As soon as she was in her room Sylvia picked up the telephone, impatient to tell her daughter about her conversation with Lily. Surely, she reasoned, Lissie would have to admit now that she had been a little hasty in dismissing her suspicions. The number rang several times before there was a click followed by a recorded voice asking her to leave a message. 'Bother!' she exclaimed and put down the receiver without waiting for the tone. Of course, Lissie had said she was having supper with her friend. It was probably just as well; she would not have told her on the phone about Angela's remarks, or her subsequent conversation with Lily, in case someone was listening in. It was much too late to arrange a meeting tonight so it would have been a pointless exercise anyway. She would try again in the morning and ask Lissie to come and see her so that she could tell her privately what she had found out. Then she remembered it was tomorrow that the builders were starting work on Hawthorn Cottage. Perhaps, she reflected, as she undressed and prepared for bed, it would be better not to bother Lissie just yet when she had other things on her mind. Better to wait until she had gone a little further with her investigations and had something definite to report. Yes, that was a much more sensible idea.

She swallowed one of the tablets Doctor Freeman had advised her to take if she got over-tired or unduly excited and settled down for the night.

A couple of hours later and a few doors away along the corridor, Lily Cherston, unable to sleep, went to her bedroom window, drew back the curtains and stared out into the night. The full moon laid a wash of silver patterned with black shadows over the garden; stars like a scattering of sequins sparkled over the limitless dome of the sky. Somewhere in the darkness an owl hooted; moths, attracted by the light from her bedside lamp, thumped against the glass, fluttering their wings and staring in at her with tiny glowing eyes. The effect was eerie; despite the mild night she shivered, closed the curtains and pulled on a robe before filling her little electric kettle with water to make a cup of tea.

It had been a mistake to get so ratty, but Sylvia's questions had taken her completely unawares. Who would have thought such a quiet little thing, a woman who seemed to have lived such a sheltered life, would show so much insight? It was probably that daughter of hers putting ideas into her head. And now she would almost certainly report how Lily Cherston had flown into a paddy the minute it was hinted that Flavia's death might not have been natural. A crime writer would quite possibly have contacts with the police and probably the press as well. If Mel Craig decided to start poking her nose in, who knew what she might turn up?

It occurred to her to tell Laurence about it in the morning and ask his advice, but she cringed mentally at the prospect of facing his scornful reaction and dismissed the idea without further thought. Instead, she tried to think things through logically the way he had done earlier. Even if they can't find a link between the other cases of food poisoning and Flavia's death, she reasoned, it was still true that she had been far from well. They wouldn't necessarily carry out tests for any other kind of poisoning if her symptoms had been the same. So long as nothing happened to arouse suspicion, the doctor would probably sign the death certificate anyway and that would be the end of the matter.

But if for any reason he wouldn't sign, if there should be the slightest hint that it had not been a natural death, enough to justify withholding that crucial certificate, the police would immediately become involved. They would start asking questions at Framleigh House. They would learn

about the death of the dog and Flavia's fear that someone
with a grudge against her had poisoned it. Had that someone then carried the grudge a stage further? They would
probe into Flavia's past in search of a possible motive for
killing her. They would dig and dig, find out that beneath
the padding of fat and cellulite lay the remains of Esther
Arnold, sexpot, gold-digger and destroyer of lives. They
might even get as far back as that fatal evening and track
down the maid who had admitted Lily to the house and
almost certainly overheard her hysterical tirade against
Esther. There was no doubt that in her fury at the woman's
action and its tragic consequences she had made some
pretty unguarded remarks that could easily be interpreted
as threats. Even if they didn't find the maid – after all, it was
nearly thirty years ago – there were plenty of others in whose
hearing she had expressed her outrage and her views on
some appropriate form of retribution.

The insistent bubbling of the kettle brought her back to
reality. She made a cup of herbal tea and sipped it sitting on
her bed while mulling over all the old images that came
crowding back despite her efforts to drive them from her
mind. 'Pull yourself together, Lily Cherston,' she told
herself. 'You're making mountains out of molehills. Just
because all those years ago you had a run-in with that brassy
little tart, no one could possibly blow it up into a motive for
topping her.' She took some deep breaths, trying to calm her
racing pulse. This wasn't doing her any good; the memory
of her doctor's warnings came back to add to her agitation.
She must think of herself; she had plans for the future; she
didn't want to die just yet.

'Take another pill and get some sleep, why don't you?'
she said aloud.

After a few minutes she began to feel herself relaxing. She

switched off the light and settled down under her duvet. She reminded herself that, as Laurence had pointed out, she had not been personally affected, just stung by the injustice of it all into letting her feelings run away with her, 'opened her big mouth once too often', as Pudgie had put it. He'd been pretty cross with her at the time, but she'd talked him round, been forgiven and . . . she felt a glow of pleasure at the memory of their reconciliation, followed by a twinge of sadness at his loss. If only he were here to comfort and advise her now . . .

He would, she decided, have advised some form of what he used to call a damage limitation exercise. Yes, that's what she'd do tomorrow. Just in case.

After a while the combination of the herbal tea, the drug and her own good advice eventually had the desired effect. Lily slept. But although there was no way she could have known, she was not the only one who knew Flavia Selwyn-Tuck's history and had trouble falling asleep that night.

# 13

Just before eleven o'clock on Monday morning, Joe called Melissa from his London office.

'I've got a few things to see to before I leave here,' he said. 'I hope to be with you around four – is that all right?'

'Of course it is. I should warn you, the place is like a battlefield.'

'I take it the builders have moved in?'

'They turned up at about half past seven and by nine o'clock the garage was a heap of rubble.'

'I hope you managed to get the car out before they started.'

'It was touch and go.' Melissa chuckled at the recollection of stumbling out of the shower at the unexpectedly early pounding on her front door and of sticking her head out of her bedroom window to see a fearsome array of machinery and a team of burly workmen outside. 'They just about gave me time to put on some clothes first.'

'What are they demolishing now? I can hear crashing noises.'

'That's the debris being loaded into the skip. If they're as quick at building things up as they are at knocking them down, they should finish way ahead of schedule.'

'From my experience of builders I doubt if that will happen, but you never know. Have you found a safe place to park?'

'In the field opposite. You'll see my car there and I'll open the gate when you arrive. The farmer gave me a key to the padlock on pain of a slow death if ever I fail to close it securely and his sheep get out.'

'Right. See you later then. By the way, how's your mother?'

'Progressing by leaps and bounds. Almost too fast, in fact.'

'I don't follow you.'

'I'll explain when you get here. It's quite a saga. Drive carefully.'

'Will do.'

Melissa put down the phone and went into the kitchen. She was about to fill the kettle for a cup of coffee when she heard what sounded like an altercation going on outside. She opened the window and peered out at the scene of devastation that a few hours ago had been a reasonably well-tended garden. Even though she had been mentally preparing herself for the upheaval, her heart sank at the sight of a digger tearing clods of lush green turf and rich dark soil from the small patch of lawn outside her kitchen window and dumping the spoil on what until yesterday had been her vegetable plot. At least, she thought resignedly, she had managed to find time to harvest her crop of early potatoes before the invasion.

She glanced across to the place where the garage had stood. Above the noise made by broken window glass and chunks of brickwork landing in the skip, a short, portly gentleman with a straggly white beard was lecturing Ron Piper, the foreman, on the iniquity of obstructing access to a public footpath. The foreman, a normally cheerful man whose bald head was as deeply tanned as his muscular arms, was trying to placate him.

'The path isn't blocked. You can still get to the stile,' he pointed out.

'I dare say we can, but I don't think we should be expected to walk past *that*!' The man gestured with a gnarled walking-stick at the chemical toilet sited against the hedge alongside the stile. 'Especially,' he continued in a querulous, high-pitched voice, 'as there are ladies in the party.' He turned and waved the stick in the direction of about a dozen men and women who stood in a small, silent and in several cases slightly embarrassed-looking group behind him. Melissa noticed that a number of them were wearing T-shirts bearing the logo of a rambling club, most carried walking-sticks and all wore rucksacks. One lady grasped the handle of an extending lead, on the end of which a small terrier was excitedly sniffing around under the hedge.

The foreman considered the offending structure for a moment. 'It has to go somewhere,' he said flatly. 'Anywhere else it'd be in *our* way.'

The emphasis on the pronoun was obviously deliberate and it brought an angry flush to the portly gentleman's countenance. It was unfortunate from Ron Piper's point of view that at that moment, as if in a deliberate attempt to undermine his position, the dog reached the cabin and recognised it as a good place to leave a territorial mark. It lifted its leg and sprayed the door just as it opened and one of the workmen stepped out, still in the act of adjusting the zip fastener of his dusty jeans. The dog gave a startled yelp and backed away. Several of the party hid surreptitious grins, but the complainant waved his stick in a gesture of triumph.

'See what I mean!' he exclaimed. 'It's not only an obstruction, it's positively indecent.'

The foreman was beginning to show signs of impatience.

'It's got to go somewhere, and that's the only place where it's not in the way,' he reiterated and turned away to indicate that so far as he was concerned the subject was closed.

His antagonist took a step forward. 'Now just you look here,' he began. Melissa decided it was time to intervene. She hurried to the front door and stepped outside.

'Good morning,' she said. 'Is there a problem?'

The man swung round to face her. 'You the owner?' he demanded.

'That's right. Do I understand you're objecting to the workmen's toilet?'

'I most certainly am,' he declared. 'It couldn't be in a worse place, right in the public eye.'

'I agree it's not ideal and I apologise for the inconvenience,' Melissa said, and then found herself struggling to suppress a grin at the unintentional *double entendre*. 'Perhaps it can be moved so that the door faces away from the footpath?' she suggested, turning to the foreman.

He gave a reluctant nod. 'I'll see what I can do,' he said curtly and marched away.

The portly gentleman was only partly mollified. He cast a disapproving eye around the site. 'I hope you're not going to ruin this beautiful cottage,' he said officiously.

'I'm having a small extension built,' Melissa admitted, feeling slightly guilty under the accusing stare from a pair of watery blue eyes. 'But it's been carefully designed to preserve the original appearance.'

'Glad to hear it. Everywhere you look, people are having lovely old buildings altered,' he complained, looking anything but glad. 'Barns converted, farm cottages turned into weekend homes, green belt land gobbled up for these confounded so-called executive monstrosities with umpteen garages. Why can't people leave things in the countryside as they are?' He was evidently on a familiar hobby-horse; several of his companions were showing signs of restlessness.

'Yes, it is unfortunate,' Melissa agreed, using her most conciliatory tone. 'I can assure you I'd much rather have left the cottage as it is, but I have to accommodate my elderly mother and there simply isn't room for her unless I have these changes made.'

A little wave of sympathy rippled through the group and the lady with the dog took a step forward and said, 'Come on, Patrick, let's get on with our walk. I'd rather go past the thing than stand looking at it all day.' She made for the stile, the others followed and the self-appointed countryside crusader, realising that support had crumbled, gave a final grunt of disapproval before striding after them.

Melissa went indoors, smiling to herself. She looked forward to recounting the episode to Joe – and to her mother as well. It might help to distract the latter's attention from imaginary murderous attacks on the residents of Framleigh House. That of course was what the old dear needed: a diversion. Well, there were plenty of possibilities: the promised shopping expedition to arrange, curtains and fittings for her new quarters to be chosen and ordered, trips to various places of interest . . .

She was, of course, blissfully unaware that Sylvia Ross had already found a diversion of her own, one that was to place more than one life in jeopardy.

'Good morning, Miss Fuller. I wonder if I could have a word with you?'

Angela Fuller, seated in an armchair in a corner of the lounge with a book on her lap, looked up at Sylvia Ross and returned her greeting with a smile. 'Yes, of course, Mrs

Ross,' she said, indicating the chair beside her. 'Please sit down.'

Sylvia glanced round the room. Several of the armchairs were occupied by other residents, all apparently absorbed in the morning papers. Just the same, she thought, when dealing with such a potentially explosive matter one couldn't be too careful. She cleared her throat, lowered her voice and said, 'Not in here. Would you mind coming to my room? It's rather confidential.'

'Oh, I see.' Miss Fuller's expression of mild astonishment seemed almost a contradiction of the words, as if she found it difficult to believe anyone would want to seek her out for a private conversation. She closed the book after carefully marking her place with a leather bookmark, stood up without further comment and followed Sylvia from the room.

'Would you like a cup of coffee?' Sylvia indicated the hospitality tray on her dressing-table. 'I asked for an extra cup and saucer so that Lissie – my daughter, you know – could sometimes have a cup of something in here with me instead of in one of the public rooms. There are times when one likes to be absolutely private, aren't there?'

'Well, yes, I suppose so,' Miss Fuller agreed without conviction. 'Thank you.'

'You have the chair; I'll perch on the bed when I'm ready.' Sylvia bustled about while her guest settled, a little hesitantly, in the armchair by the window.

'You have a lovely view of the garden,' she ventured after a moment. 'My room overlooks the road. It's a very quiet road, of course,' she added, as if anxious not to appear to be complaining.

'Yes, it is nice, isn't it?' During her preparations, Sylvia had been considering possible ways of introducing the subject that was uppermost in her mind. For a moment, her courage began to fail her and she wished she had been a little less impulsive, but finding Angela Fuller sitting so conveniently on her own like that had seemed a heaven-sent opportunity. She was committed now. Above the singing of the kettle, she said, keeping her tone carefully casual, 'I've been thinking about what you said at supper yesterday about seeing Mrs Cherston and Mr Dainton together in the garden; well, not exactly together, I know, but—'

'Oh, please,' her guest interrupted, 'I don't want you to think I imagined there was anything, well, you know, improper. Perhaps I shouldn't have—' She broke off, turning faintly pink.

'Improper? Whatever gave you that idea?' It had not occurred to Sylvia that her remark would provoke such a reaction. It seemed that, as she had suspected, Angela Fuller was a little sensitive on the subject of a possible relationship between Lily Cherston and Laurence Dainton. 'Didn't I say I thought they might have been talking about Mrs Selwyn-Tuck?' She switched off the kettle, spooned instant coffee granules into the cups and added hot water. 'The fact is,' she continued as she went through the process of stirring, placing the cups carefully on the little cabinet beside her bed and offering milk, sugar and biscuits, 'I once overheard, quite inadvertently, I never meant to eavesdrop, a conversation between them about someone – I'm sure it was someone here – that Mrs Cherston seemed very angry about.' Sylvia gave a carefully edited version of the conversation she had overheard in the garden.

'I don't follow you.' Over the rim of her coffee cup, Miss Fuller's eyes held a puzzled expression. 'Why should you think this person they were talking about was Mrs Selwyn-Tuck?'

'It didn't occur to me at the time.' Sylvia was aware that this was not true, but the deception did not seem so important to her as it would once have done. 'It was only afterwards, when we had the news of her illness, and then her death, I remembered how her dog had died and how she believed he had been deliberately poisoned, and I began to wonder . . .'

Miss Fuller put down her cup. Her expression had changed from bewilderment to horror. 'Mrs Ross,' she began.

'Please, call me Sylvia.'

'Thank you, Sylvia. My name's Angela.' She spoke mechanically; evidently she was trying to come to terms with the implications of Sylvia's unfinished sentence. There was a short silence before she said, 'Are you suggesting that Mrs Selwyn-Tuck's death wasn't natural? That someone . . .' Her voice weakened and died; only her pale lips formed the word that she appeared unable to utter aloud.

'Murdered her, yes,' said Sylvia quietly. 'I do believe that's a definite possibility.'

'But that's a terrible thing to say!' Angela exclaimed, aghast. 'I thought the poor lady died of food poisoning. There have been several other cases recently. Mrs Wardle said so.'

'She doesn't know for certain. No one does, not yet.'

'I don't understand,' said Angela agitatedly. Surely you aren't accusing Mrs Cherston or Mr Dainton of . . . ?' Again, she appeared unable to put the possibility into words.

'I'm not accusing anyone, but I'm almost certain that Mrs Cherston knew Flavia a long time ago and as I said, Flavia herself hinted that she might have enemies here.'

'Have you asked Mrs Cherston about it?'

'Yes, in a roundabout way. I mean, I didn't want to let her know I'd overheard a private conversation. I told her what I've told you, that I have my doubts about Flavia's death.'

'What did she say?'

'She got rather agitated and made it quite clear she didn't want to talk about it.'

'And you think that's suspicious?'

'I have to admit I find it difficult to believe that Lily Cherston is capable of killing anyone, but I'm quite sure she knows more about Flavia Selwyn-Tuck than she's prepared to admit and I've begun to wonder whether she might be covering up for someone else.'

'Who do you think that could be?'

'I've no idea. How much do we know about the other people here? Hardly anything, when you come to think about it.'

Angela shook her head. 'I don't understand,' she repeated, frowning. 'Why are you telling me this?'

'Because' – Sylvia lowered her voice, despite the fact that there was no possibility of being overheard – 'I'm thinking of doing a little detective work and I thought you might be willing to help me.'

'Detective work?' Angela's look of dismay deepened. 'What on earth do you mean?'

'I want to know more about Flavia Selwyn-Tuck's background, find out if there's anyone else here who used to know her. My idea is to chat to people – just casually, you know – and see if anyone lets anything drop that might suggest . . .' Sylvia was by this time becoming uncomfortably aware that she was making a hash of this. It had seemed such a clever idea to start with, trying to enlist Angela's help, but the more she pursued it, the more preposterous it seemed. 'You strike me as a very diplomatic person,' she gabbled on. 'I just thought . . .'

'Mrs Ross . . . Sylvia, I'm sorry, I don't mean to be rude, but I do think you've let your imagination run away with you.'

The words increased Sylvia's discomfiture. That's just what Lissie has been saying, she thought unhappily. I wish I'd never started this.

'I can't believe there are any grounds at all for your suspicions,' Angela said. 'I'm sure it will turn out that poor Mrs Selwyn-Tuck died of food poisoning.' She took a deep breath, as if plucking up courage to continue. When she did, her normally gentle voice held a hint of severity that sounded uncomfortably like a rebuke. 'I'm sorry, Sylvia, but I would prefer not to become involved with what you are proposing.'

'That's all right,' Sylvia replied meekly. 'I quite understand. I hope you didn't mind my asking, and I would ask you not to mention this conversation to anyone.'

'Of course I shan't. I shall forget all about it and I strongly advise you to do the same.' Angela stood up and brushed imaginary crumbs from her skirt. 'Thank you for the coffee,' she said politely, and left the room.

'Bother!' Sylvia muttered aloud as she returned the used cups to the tray. 'All I hope is that Lissie doesn't find out how silly I've been. Perhaps Angela's right and I should forget all about it.'

At that moment, there was a light tap on the door and a voice called, 'You there, Sylv?'

'Lily! Do come in.'

'Ta.' Lily entered and sat down on Sylvia's bed without being invited. Her eye fell on the tray and she said, 'Any chance of a coffee? I don't feel like going downstairs and facing the mob.'

'Of course. I'll put the kettle on. I've just had one but it won't take a minute to make another. Is your headache any better?'

'What? Oh, that. Yes, thank you.'

Sylvia bustled about refilling the kettle and rinsing the used cups. She noticed that Lily appeared far from relaxed; her hands moved restlessly in her lap and her forehead was crumpled in a frown.

After a moment, Lily said, 'I'm sorry I was so ratty last night.'

'That's all right. You had a headache.'

'No, I didn't; that was just an excuse.'

'Oh?' Sylvia paused in the act of unscrewing the jar of coffee. 'Were you worried about something?'

'Yes. It's Des – my stepson, you know. He heard about the food poisoning and how Flavia popped her clogs and he's been on the phone to Geraldine Wardle kicking up a hell of a stink, as good as saying it was the food here that caused it. She asked me to go to her office and sort of hinted that if he's going to keep on causing trouble it might be better if I found somewhere else to stay while my house is being altered. It really got to me and I'm afraid I took it out on you. I'm sorry,' she repeated.

'Please, think nothing of it,' said Sylvia reassuringly. She handed Lily a cup of coffee and sat down beside her. 'I can't imagine Mrs Wardle would ask you to leave. I'm sure she understands your stepson's concern for you.'

'Let's hope so. I really like it here.'

'Well, thank you for telling me, but really, there was no need.'

Lily gave Sylvia a pat on the arm and said, 'You're a pal, Sylv.' As soon as she had finished her coffee she got to her feet and said, 'Ta very much. See you at lunch – I mean dinner, okay?'

'Yes, I expect so.'

After she had gone, Sylvia began to ask herself why Lily had found it necessary to change her story. Despite Angela Fuller's discouraging remarks, the doubts it raised in her mind reawakened her resolve to continue with her quest for more information about Flavia Selwyn-Tuck.

# 14

Joe leaned over and tickled the ears of an inquisitive lamb that had trotted away from its mother to investigate the two-legged strangers standing at the entrance to its field. A few yards away a ewe, less venturesome than her offspring, was keeping a close eye on the situation. Melissa rested her forearms on the top rail of the gate, her gaze idly shifting between the spectacle of the little creature wriggling with pleasure under the caressing fingers and the unspoiled view across the secluded valley. It was a view of which she never tired, but her pleasure in it, and her appreciation of the soft breeze that cooled her cheeks and ruffled her hair, were enhanced now by the presence of Joe at her side.

For a while they stood in silence, absorbing the tranquil beauty of the summer evening. The wide expanse of pasture, dotted with grazing ewes and their playful young, sloped down to the brook flowing along the valley bottom and then climbed up the opposite side to a crown of woodland, pierced here and there by shafts of golden light from the sinking sun. Joe took a deep breath and said, 'This is a wonderful spot, Mel. I'm not surprised you can't bear to leave it.'

Melissa chuckled. 'You thought I was crazy when I told you I'd bought a tumbledown shack in the depths of the country, didn't you?'

'I never thought it would last,' he admitted. 'You always struck me as a committed townie.'

'I suppose I was, in a way. I do wonder sometimes whether I'd have stuck it out if I hadn't had Iris for a neighbour.'

'Oh, you'd have stuck it out all right. I don't think you know the meaning of the word "quitter". That's one of the things I admire you for. You never give up.'

She gave him a sidelong glance. 'I'm expecting a lot more than admiration from you,' she said.

'You won't be disappointed.' He put both arms round her, drawing her close. The lamb, suddenly missing the attention it had been enjoying, gave a hesitant bleat and returned to its mother, who ushered it away unnoticed by its human companions. 'Just the same,' Joe went on after an interval, 'I could never make out what made you buy the cottage in the first place.'

'Just an impulse, I guess. The moment I saw the picture in the estate agent's window, something inside me said, "That's for you, go for it".'

It wasn't entirely true. She had known for a long time that she needed a break, not just from London, but also from everything that went with it, including Aubrey. Especially Aubrey. He had become a habit: a kindly, reliable, considerate, worthy but, alas, an increasingly burdensome habit. For a year or more she had accepted his devotion and the sense of security that went with it, knowing in her heart that she could never return his love yet lacking the courage to tell him so frankly and openly. The upturn in her fortunes brought about by a successful TV series based on her books had made the purchase of the cottage a practical possibility, and with the decision came a stiffening of the will that enabled her to send Aubrey away. That was over five years ago, five years that saw her career as a writer go from strength to strength. Emotionally it was a period of turbulence, but always there was Joe in the background: mentor, stimulating companion, unfailingly reliable friend and now, at last, lover.

She leaned against him with a contented sigh and he kissed her gently on the cheek. 'Happy?' he whispered in her ear.

'What do you think?'

He nibbled at her lobe and the rest of her flesh responded with a surge of pleasure. 'I have plans to make you even happier later on,' he murmured. 'And by the way,' he added in the same seductive voice, 'd'you reckon that casserole's ready yet?'

She shook herself free of his embrace and gave him a thump on the arm. 'Men are always thinking of their stomachs,' she declared in mock indignation.

'A man needs nourishment to cope with a passionate woman,' he said and his eyes held hers for a long moment before they turned and went hand in hand indoors.

Over their meal the conversation was mainly about Melissa's new book. It was not until she brought the dessert that Joe said casually, 'So what's Sylvia been up to then?'

Melissa paused with the serving spoon in mid-air and said, 'I was afraid you were going to ask me that.'

'Why afraid?'

'Because I think you're probably going to tell me I'm worrying about nothing. Iris seems to think so, but I can't help feeling uneasy about her.'

'Why? From what little you've told me, she seems to be making very good progress.'

'Too good. She's like a genie let out of a bottle. She's turned into a people watcher and now she fancies herself as an amateur sleuth. Yes, I know that sounds funny,' she went on as Joe burst out laughing, 'but I really am concerned.'

'Suppose you tell me about it while I enjoy some of that fruit crumble – if you're planning to give me any, that is.'

'Oh, sorry.' She hastily served them both and picked up her spoon. 'I'm not sure how up to date you are with the goings-on at Framleigh House,' she said after a few moments. 'You remember I told you about the dog that got poisoned?'

'I remember. You figured out how it happened, didn't you?'

'I thought of a possible explanation that seemed to satisfy the owner, who'd been going round telling everyone the dog had been deliberately poisoned. In fact, it did more than satisfy her, she seemed really relieved, as if she'd been afraid someone had a grudge against her and settled it by killing her dog.'

Joe thought for a moment. 'Is she the one who's been taken ill?'

'That's right. Well, she died.'

'Poor woman. What happened?'

'They think it was food poisoning – there have been several cases locally within the past couple of days. They're trying to identify a common source, but now Mum's convinced herself that there's skulduggery afoot in Flavia Selwyn-Tuck's case on account of a conversation she overheard between two of the other residents.' As accurately as she could, Melissa repeated her mother's account of the episode in the garden involving Lily Cherston and Laurence Dainton. 'I did my best to convince her she was barking up the wrong tree, but I'm not sure I succeeded.'

'So you think that on the strength of what she overheard, plus your success at solving the mystery of the dog's death, she's planning to play Cluedo among the good folk of Framleigh House?'

'If the doctor is satisfied that Flavia's death is due to food poisoning or other natural causes – I understand she had a number of medical problems – I'm afraid that's exactly what she has in mind. I tried to get her to promise to stay out of it, but she was a bit evasive.'

'And you think that's a serious reason for concern?'

'I certainly don't want her to start pestering the other residents with her enquiries, especially as Geraldine Wardle made it clear to Flavia that she wouldn't allow a private detective to investigate the death of her dog. And I'm not at all happy with this fixation about foul play. Doctor Freeman did warn me to be on the lookout for signs of paranoia and I'm wondering if I ought to have a word with her.'

'What do you expect her to do?'

'I don't know. Help me talk Mum out of it, I suppose.'

'Mel, are you sure that's all that's worrying you?'

Melissa was silent for a moment. She sat toying with her dessert spoon, her forehead puckered in a frown. 'Maybe it's because I've written too many crime novels,' she said slowly. 'I've been trying to convince myself that it's just my writer's imagination overriding my common sense, but I keep asking myself, suppose there's something in Mum's suspicions after all, what then?'

'Then surely the doctor will withhold the death certificate and there'll be a police enquiry.'

'But supposing he goes ahead and signs it while in fact she actually was poisoned? Mistakes like that have been known to happen.'

'You mean you share your mother's doubts?'

'I suppose I do, and it makes me afraid for her. If there's no police enquiry, and she starts asking pointed questions, she might stumble on something that someone would prefer to remain hidden. Joe, if that were to happen, she could be in terrible danger.'

'Hmm.' Joe put down his spoon and pushed away his empty plate. 'This needs thinking about. Why don't I make some coffee while you clear the table? What's that?' he asked as there was a sudden rattle at the front door, followed by the sound of something falling on the floor.

'It's probably the local paper. It usually comes earlier, but now and again there's a delay.' Melissa went out into the hall and returned with that evening's edition of the *Gloucestershire Gazette.* She began leafing through it, then stopped in her tracks as her eye caught the words: 'Food Poisoning Outbreak Claims Elderly Victim'. 'Joe, listen to this,' she said, and her voice shook a little as she read the report aloud. ' "The death of an elderly resident of a local retirement home is believed to have been caused by food poisoning. Several other victims are recovering in hospital. The source of the infection has yet to be traced but is possibly chicken served in a local restaurant." '

They stood facing one another across the table, absorbing the significance of the report. Then Joe said, 'Do you know who wrote that?'

Melissa shook her head. 'There's no byline.'

'You could find out, couldn't you? You've still got a contact at the *Gazette.*'

'Bruce Ingram. That's true. I could ask him to check on the accuracy of the story.' She went into the kitchen, picked up the phone and punched out the Ingrams' number. It was Bruce's wife, Penny, who answered.

'I'm afraid he's not home yet,' she said. 'He's having dinner with some of the cast of that film they're shooting at Thornton Manor.'

'*Is* he?' Knowing Penny's pride in her husband's achievements, Melissa made a point of sounding impressed. 'He certainly moves in exalted circles these days.'

'He's been promoted to senior reporter,' Penny went on.

'Well, good for him. I always knew he'd go a long way. I'd never be surprised if he was head-hunted by one of the national dailies.'

'I don't think he'd want that. It might mean moving to London and we're both happy where we are.' In the background Melissa heard the sound of a baby crying. 'Oh, that's Daisy, she's just woken up. I have to go or she'll wake Kirsty. Shall I ask Bruce to call you when he comes in? It might be a bit late.'

'Thanks, I would like a word with him, but tomorrow morning would do.' Melissa put down the phone and turned to Joe. 'He's out,' she said, biting her lip in frustration.

'So I gathered. Look, love, there's nothing more we can do for the moment and I don't think Sylvia's likely to be having a showdown with any murderers this evening.' His tone was flippant, but the remark brought no answering smile from Melissa. He took her by the shoulders and gave her a gentle shake. 'Just don't let this thing blow up out of proportion. Look at it this way: if the report is accurate, and that woman's death is put down as food poisoning, then it's odds-on it's the right verdict. And if Sylvia does refuse to accept it and goes off doing her Miss Marple act, where's the harm? She'll soon give up once she draws a blank. At the worst, she might get a slap on the wrist from Mrs Wardle.'

Melissa sighed. 'You're probably right. Let's have that coffee, shall we?' They made a point of not referring to the matter again that night, but despite Joe's comforting words, the doubts in her mind persisted long after he had dropped off to sleep.

*

On her way up to her room that evening, Sylvia Ross picked up a discarded copy of the *Gloucestershire Gazette*. When she was ready for bed, she sat down and began turning the pages, pausing here and there to read an account of a recent charity event, check the 'What's On?' columns and smile over some of the entries to a photographic competition. When her eye caught the words 'Food Poisoning' she stopped short and read the report carefully before casting the paper aside with a little snort of disdain.

'Food poisoning my foot!' she exclaimed. 'That woman was murdered, I'm sure of it. If those stupid doctors don't spot it, whoever did it will go unpunished. Well, I suppose it's up to me to do something about it. Lissie certainly won't. It's not going to be easy, though,' she went on, still addressing herself aloud. 'I can hardly talk to Lily and Angela Fuller's made it quite clear she wants nothing to do with it. This needs thinking about.'

She got into bed and switched off her bedside lamp. She was just drifting off to sleep when two names came into her head. She smiled happily in the darkness.

'Of course, why didn't I think of them before?' she murmured. 'I do believe they might have something interesting to tell me. First opportunity I get in the morning, I'll have a word with them.'

# 15

There were only a few people in the Lamb and Shearling, a popular watering-hole for the staff of the *Gloucester Gazette*, when Melissa joined Bruce at the bar a little after eleven the following morning.

'What will you have?' he asked.

'Oh, just an orange juice, thanks.'

He ordered her drink and carried it with his own half-finished mug of beer to a corner table. 'So what have you been up to lately?' he asked as they sat down. Before she had time to answer his eye fell on her left hand, his jaw dropped and he exclaimed, 'You're engaged!'

'That's right.' Melissa gave a slightly self-conscious smile.

'Well, congratulations!' Bruce raised his glass in salute. 'Who's the lucky man?' His smile faded a little as he went on, 'Don't tell me you've changed your mind about that copper you used to go out with, the one who became a private eye and then went off to the States? What was his name – Ken Harris?'

'Oh no, not him.' To her intense annoyance, she felt her cheeks growing warm at the mention of Ken's name. Their relationship had been somewhat turbulent, although it had had its moments, which she preferred not to think about now that she was engaged to Joe. It was ridiculous to be blushing like a teenager. Not exactly a fair comparison, she thought; few of today's teenagers were likely to be fazed by the mention of an ex-boyfriend. She took a hasty gulp from her drink and said, 'As a matter of fact, I'm going to marry Joe Martin, my agent.'

'I'm glad to hear it.' Bruce's expression lifted and his clear blue eyes met hers with the frankness of an old friend who would never hesitate to speak his mind.

'Why do you say that?' she asked curiously. 'You've never met Joe.'

'True, but I had quite a bit of contact with Harris at press briefings when he was a DCI.'

'I remember when I told you he was going to the States that you said something about him not being right for me, but you were a bit vague when I asked what you had against him.'

'There was nothing personal, except . . .' Bruce hesitated for a moment and fingered the handle of his beer mug before saying slowly, 'He struck me as being a shade arrogant – a bossy type. A good quality in his job, but two bosses in a marriage could be a problem.' His smile was disarming, but his tone was serious.

Melissa tilted her chin in the air. 'So you reckon I'm bossy, do you?'

'A little.'

'What do you think that makes Joe?'

He helped himself to a nut from a dish on the table, took a swig of beer and considered. 'Hard to say, not having met the gentleman,' he said thoughtfully. 'Not a yes-man, certainly. That wouldn't suit you at all.'

'No? Would you mind telling me, of your great wisdom, just what kind of man would suit me?'

'Oh, undoubtedly he has to be someone of great insight and tact, whose judgement you eventually accept once your emotional feminine reactions have been blown away by his masculine logic.'

'Well, of all the pompous, macho twaddle,' Melissa began indignantly, and then giggled as she caught the mischievous twinkle in his eye. 'You're just winding me up,' she accused him.

'Thought that'd get you,' he said smugly.

'All right, clever clogs, I'll let you have that one. Now tell me about your experience of hobnobbing with the Hollywood greats.'

Bruce chuckled. 'Oh, it was unreal. My assignment was to interview a couple of the stars of a new TV series and I ended up having bangers and mash with half the cast in their mobile canteen.'

'That sounds like fun.'

He grimaced. 'Not really. I was buttonholed by Gawain Hardcastle.'

'Good Lord, is he still around? He must be ninety.'

'At least, but he still gets wheeled out to play cameo roles.'

'Come to think of it, he did just that in an early episode of my first TV series. That must be at least ten years ago. I never actually met him, of course.'

'You were lucky. He could bore for England. I had to spend most of the evening listening to him reminiscing about his long and distinguished career. He got quite dewy-eyed when he came to the debt he owed to an angel called Pudgie who bankrolled the show that gave him his first big break.'

'Pudgie? That's an odd name.'

'I gather it was just a nickname on account of the chap's girth. His real name was something like Chessington, or maybe Chester – no, they're zoos, aren't they?' Bruce wrinkled his brow. 'Can't remember. It's not important.

Anyway, what can I do for you? I read the reports of your father's death, by the way. It must have been ghastly for you. I'm so sorry.'

'Thank you. It was rather. Did you know my mother had a serious operation very soon after?'

'No, I didn't. How is she?'

'She's made an almost miraculous recovery. In a way, it's on her account that I asked you to meet me.' Bruce listened attentively as Melissa sketched in the background to her mother's insistence that the death of Flavia Selwyn-Tuck should be treated as suspicious, ending with the reference in the short piece in the previous evening's *Gazette* to an elderly victim of the outbreak of food poisoning. 'I'd like to know whether the person concerned was Flavia and if so whether it's accurate,' she finished. 'Can you help?'

'Oh, sure, I can find that out easily enough, but I don't quite understand why it should matter to your mother. Surely if the medics are satisfied as to the cause of death—'

'You don't know my mother,' said Melissa with a rueful smile. 'I'm beginning to realise that I hardly know her myself.'

'Are you saying that she's already convinced there's been foul play?'

'Not only that, but unless the police are called in I'm seriously worried she'll start ferreting around on her own.'

'And you're afraid she might be overdoing it, putting her health at risk?'

'Not exactly, although that is a consideration.' Melissa realised with a pang of guilt that the possibility had not entered her head until that moment. She put down her empty glass and looked directly at Bruce. 'The trouble is, my common sense tells me she's mistaken, but I can't entirely rid myself of the notion that she may be right. And in that case . . .'

He nodded gravely. 'Yes, I see what you mean. If there really is a killer out there, and she shows signs of getting close to the truth, she could be a target herself. You said her suspicions are based on a conversation she overheard. Who were the parties involved?'

'Do you need to know that?'

'No, I suppose not, but as a journalist I'm naturally curious as to why you carefully avoided giving their names.'

'It's just that one of them is a very prominent member of your profession.'

Bruce put down his empty mug and planted his elbows on the table. His face wore the alert expression of the dedicated newshound. 'Now I'm really intrigued,' he said. 'Perhaps we can do a deal.'

'What sort of deal?' Melissa asked warily.

'You give me names – in confidence for the time being – and I'll use my contact at the hospital to find out the exact cause of death of that old bird . . . what was her name again?'

'Flavia Selwyn-Tuck.'

He took out his notebook and jotted it down. 'And the two conspirators your mother overheard?'

'Bruce, they weren't actually conspiring; at least, it didn't sound like it, not according to what Mum told me. All she could say was that the woman was bad-mouthing someone who'd apparently caused a lot of grief to a lot of people many years ago and saying that whoever it was shouldn't be allowed to get away with it, while Laurence—' Melissa broke off as she caught the anticipatory gleam in Bruce's eye, hesitated, then shrugged and went on, 'Oh well, okay, it was Laurence Dainton and his ex-wife.'

Bruce gave a soft whistle. 'Dainton, eh?' He was obviously impressed. 'So what line was he taking?'

'Mum said he seemed to be counselling Lily against any sort of action on the grounds that other people might get hurt.'

'I see.' Bruce spent a short while digesting this new piece of information before saying, 'What's he doing in an old folks' home, I wonder? He's still writing; I saw one of his dyed-in-the-wool, right-wing polemics in the *Monitor* only the other day.'

'I'd put his age at about seventy, but he's still very much on the ball. Framleigh House isn't exactly an old folks' home; that is, it calls itself a retirement home but it's more like a private hotel with special facilities. The residents are all getting on, of course, or they wouldn't be there, but most of them are still pretty active. Lily certainly is in spite of some health problems. She's quite a character.'

'Does she still call herself Dainton?'

'Oh no, she remarried years ago. She's Lily Cherston now.'

Bruce made some notes, then stabbed the air with his pen. 'That's it!' he exclaimed. 'Cherston – that was the name of Gawain Hardcastle's angel.'

'Are you sure?'

'Positive.'

'And his nickname was Pudgie?'

'That's what Gawain said.'

Melissa felt a sudden rush of adrenalin. 'D'you know, I remember Mum saying Lily refers to her late husband – her second husband, of course – as Pudgie,' she said excitedly. 'It's got to be the chap Gawain Hardcastle was talking about. Bruce, could you possibly get me an introduction?'

'I dare say I could, but why?'

'Don't you see? He might recall something that could give me a lead – maybe account for Lily's outburst.'

'You mean he might help establish whether it was this Flavia woman she was on about? That's a pretty long shot, isn't it? I mean, have you any reason to connect her or Lily with the theatre?'

'None at all, but there can't be two angels called Pudgie Cherston, surely? In any case, it's the nearest thing I have to a clue so far.'

'What about asking Lily herself?'

Melissa considered this suggestion for a moment or two and then shook her head. 'I think it would be better to try and find out first if there's a link,' she said. 'If I tackle her directly and she has something to hide, she'll simply brush it aside and say it's a coincidence, but at the same time it'll put her on her guard.'

'Yes, I take your point.' Bruce shut his notebook and put it away. He glanced at his watch. 'Mel, I have to leave you now, I've got another appointment. I'll see what I can do about fixing you up with an interview with old Sir Gawain. What shall I tell him – that you're a lifelong fan of his and burning with a desire to worship at his feet?'

'Don't you dare. Tell him it's in connection with research for my next book. You can say how much I enjoyed his performance in my TV episode if you think it will carry any weight.'

'I'm sure it will. He has a monstrous ego that responds well to massage.'


Gawain Hardcastle lowered his immaculately trousered backside on to an oak settle in the lounge of the Mulberry Tree, reputed to be the oldest public house in the county. He let out a long 'aaah!' of satisfaction as he pulled up a chair on which he placed a pair of surprisingly small feet encased in highly polished black leather shoes. He took a cigar from the top pocket of his purple corduroy jacket and after a certain amount of fumbling and grunting produced a silver lighter from another.

'Take that thing away and find me an ashtray, there's a pet,' he said, indicating a small card on the table in front of him bearing the words *Thank you for not smoking*. 'Oh, don't worry about him,' he added with a dismissive wave in the direction of the young barman polishing glasses behind the counter. 'They all know Gawain and his little foibles. That's right, isn't it, O guardian of the sacred brew?' he called in the kind of declamatory tone he might have used in his heyday when launching into the 'Friends, Romans, countrymen' speech from *Julius Caesar*. He applied the lighter to the cigar without removing the band and said between puffs, 'Mine's a Macallan, thank you, my pet.'

Melissa shot an enquiring glance at the barman, who gave a resigned shrug and indicated an alcove on the opposite side of the room where ashtrays on the tables proclaimed that this was the smoking area. It was obvious that he had encountered this situation before and that there was nothing to be gained from arguing. Having complied with Gawain's request, she went to order the drinks.

'Hope your cash-flow situation's okay,' the barman whispered confidentially in her ear as he took the money for Gawain's Scotch and her own glass of fruit juice. 'He's got a serious thirst and he's never been known to pay for a round.'

'Thanks for the tip,' she whispered back. She carried the drinks to the table where the white-haired thespian was peacefully puffing at his cigar with an expression of bliss on features that still bore traces of the classic beauty that had made him a matinée idol in his youth.

'Thank you, my pet.' He took the glass she handed him and swallowed a good half of its contents at one gulp before she had time to sit down. 'What a delightful surprise this is,' he added, making a gracious gesture in her direction before disposing of the remainder. 'I just love meeting authors,' he assured her, staring ruminatively at the bottom of the empty glass. 'They're always so *interesting* and *warm-hearted* – and so *generous*,' he finished with additional emphasis.

'It's nice of you to say so.' Recognising her cue, Melissa held out her hand. 'Can I get you another?'

He handed over the glass with alacrity while rewarding her with one of the devastating smiles that women of a certain age still found irresistible. 'How very kind. Er, perhaps a large one this time – just to save you jumping up and down.'

'Yes, of course.'

'What did I tell you?' said the barman as she returned with the order. 'Take my tip and sit down *before* you hand this one over.'

'This is quite delightful,' said Gawain as she gave him his recharged glass. He took a mouthful of the spirit and rolled it round his tongue before swallowing it. He nursed the glass in his lap and caressed it with delicate, manicured fingers. He cast his eyes upwards at the low wooden beams, blackened with age, and drew deeply on the cigar. 'I do so love a place with *atmosphere*, don't you?' She agreed that atmosphere was very important.

'Now, my pet,' Gawain said after another hearty swallow, 'what was it you wanted to talk to me about? Your young friend said something about research for another of your wonderful books.'

'That's right,' Melissa replied with what she hoped was due modesty while mentally doubting that Bruce had used that particular adjective. She took a quick sip from her own glass and opened her notebook. 'I dare say he mentioned that it has a theatrical setting and one of the characters is a director who is trying to persuade a very rich and important person to provide the finance for a show he wants to put on in London.'

'Ah yes, he's looking for an angel. How that word takes my mind back! How well I recall the uncertainties that haunt many a production. The hopes that soar one day, only to be cruelly dashed the next. Jobs on the line, careers hanging by a thread . . .' Gawain's gaze appeared to focus on an invisible audience; he polished off the rest of his drink and thrust out the glass in an imperious gesture as if commanding another member of the cast to take it from him. Melissa stood up, prised it from his fingers, had it replenished and sat down again.

'So good of you, my pet,' Gawain sighed. 'I've always said, authors are such *lovely* people.'

'Tell me,' Melissa began, 'do you have personal recollections of any particular angels?'

'Oh, *yes*.' The question seemed to bring him back to reality. 'How could I ever forget dear old Pudgie Cherston? It was all due to him that I got my first important role. I know what you're thinking,' he said with a wag of a forefinger, evidently mistaking her sharp intake of breath as a sign of recognition, 'but it wasn't my Hamlet. That came later.'

'What role was it, then?' Melissa prompted cautiously, as he appeared to fall into a mild trance.

'Jack Worthing in *The Importance of Being Earnest*. Surely, you remember – but no, of course, you're much too young.' He treated her to a fond, paternal smile.

'You're quite right, I never saw that production; but of course I've heard all about it since. The definitive interpretation, I believe the critics said.'

'They did indeed. How clever of you to remember.' He gave her a gracious pat on the hand. 'Now, where was I? Oh yes, Pudgie Cherston. I often ask myself what direction my career would have taken if it hadn't been for dear old Pudgie.'

'With talent like yours, I'm sure it would have been brilliant,' said Melissa earnestly, ignoring the inner voice that said, 'Creep!'

'Lovely of you to say so, my pet.'

'Tell me more about Pudgie. He sounds really interesting.'

'Can't remember a great deal now. It was quite a long time ago, you know.'

'I don't suppose you can tell me how I can get in touch with him.'

At this point Gawain, apparently on the point of becoming lachrymose, took solace in his drink. 'Dead this many a year,' he sighed, holding out the empty glass with a hand that trembled slightly. 'I read his obituary in *The Times* with great sorrow. My heart bled for poor Lily.'

'His wife?' Melissa relieved him of the glass and stood holding her breath while awaiting his reply.

'Indeed. His second wife, of course. I often wonder what became of her. I'm afraid that boy of Pudgie's won't have treated her very kindly. He thought of her as a bit of a gold-digger, you know. Natural, I suppose; after all, she was a lot younger than his father, but I always believed her to be devoted to him. Er, were you going to . . .' Gawain's eye fastened on the glass and Melissa hurriedly repaired to the bar for yet another refill.

'I don't suppose,' she said as she sat down once more, 'you know any other angels I could approach? I mean, it's been absolutely wonderful talking to you, but there are quite a lot of things—' She broke off, at a loss to know how to continue without causing offence.

To her relief he grasped the point straight away. 'Of course, my pet, you want to know all the sordid financial details first-hand. That's something I never got to grips with.' He made it sound as if to do so would have soiled his small, exquisite hands. 'Well now, let me think. There was Bernie Arnold – I believe he's still in the land of the living. Hoho!' He gave a chuckle that seemed to come from the depths of his stomach. 'That reminds me of a story; would you like to hear it?'

Recalling Bruce's warning, Melissa experienced a sinking feeling, but she put on a brave smile and said, 'I'd love to.'

'I thought for a moment I was about to witness a real-life murder!' Suddenly animated, Gawain lowered his feet to the ground and sat up straight. For the moment, he appeared to lose sight of the fact that his glass was once more empty. 'It was all the fault of that brassy tart Esther – Bernie's wife. His ex now, I imagine.'

'What had she done?'

'Persuaded Bernie to withdraw his support for a new show. He and Pudgie were in it together, but Pudgie couldn't afford the whole cost so the show folded before it even got to rehearsal. Great pity; several very promising youngsters lost a chance to break into the profession. Young Lily went for Esther bald-headed, so I heard.'

'Lily Cherston?'

'That's right.'

'What made her so angry?'

'Just that: spoiling it for kids who thought they'd got their first big break.'

'Do you know why Esther talked Bernie out of backing the show?'

Gawain gave another deep, rumbling chuckle. 'Rumour has it that it was because the director wasn't interested when she offered to let him take her knickers off.'

'You mean she did it just out of pique?'

'That's one way of putting it.'

'Did any of the actors who lost out get parts in other shows?'

'Eventually, I suppose. Off hand, I can't recall any who made it to the big time, but of course there's no way of knowing whether they would have done even if the show had run.' Melissa was intrigued to realise that he had dropped his theatrical manner and begun speaking like a normal human being. His mood changed; he fell silent for a moment and stared reflectively into the empty glass. 'I did hear rumours of a tragedy,' he went on in a low voice, almost as if he were talking to himself. 'Disappointments – our profession's full of them.'

'Yes, I'm sure it is.' Melissa forbore to mention that writers had their disappointments as well. 'What sort of tragedy?' Gawain appeared not to hear the question, so she tried another. 'Would you like another drink?'

To her surprise, he declined.

# 16

By the time Melissa had escorted a tottering Gawain Hardcastle to her car and delivered him to his hotel, it was after ten o'clock. On the way she had attempted to get him to talk about the Arnolds in the hope that he might give a clue to their present whereabouts, but he had sat beside her with closed eyes and uttered not a word throughout the short journey. She had asked if the name Flavia Selwyn-Tuck meant anything to him, hoping to glean something to suggest a link between her and Esther, but the question was received with the same impenetrable silence. Whether it was distress at the recollection of the tragedy at which he had hinted, or simply the quantity of alcohol he had consumed making him semi-comatose, was impossible to tell.

As she headed for home she began mentally sorting and sifting everything she had learned from their conversation. Assuming the aged thespian's memory could be relied on – and there seemed no reason to believe otherwise – there now seemed little doubt that the Lily Cherston who had 'gone for Esther bald-headed' some years ago was the same Lily Cherston who was now living at Framleigh House. In the light of the conversation between Laurence and Lily that her mother had overhead, it was conceivable that Esther Arnold and Flavia Selwyn-Tuck were one and the same person, and that Flavia was the unnamed person they had been

discussing. Assuming this to be the case, it would be interesting to know how, when and why the change of identity
had taken place.

When she reached the turning to Hawthorn Cottage half
an hour later the exterior lights were already on; as she drew
up outside the front door it opened and Joe hurried out to
greet her, a flashlight in his hand. He unlocked the field gate
and she drove in and parked the Golf beside his Rover. As
she stepped out of the car he directed the light at the ground
and said, 'Mind where you tread. While you were out
boozing your friendly farmer moved his sheep to another
field and brought cattle into this one.'

'Thanks for the warning, but I haven't been boozing,' she
retorted. She picked her way carefully towards the gate and
waited while he relocked it. He took her arm and they
entered the cottage together.

'How did it go?' he asked.

'It was quite an experience,' she said with a chuckle.
'Gawain's capacity for single malt is awesome.'

'Did he come up with anything interesting?'

'Up to a point. Not as much as I'd have liked, but it was
definitely worth the effort.'

'How about a cup of tea while you tell me about it?'

'That would be lovely.'

Melissa kicked off her shoes and slipped into a chair in
the kitchen while Joe made the tea. She watched him put the
kettle on to boil – he had quickly mastered the Aga, something it had taken her several days to achieve – and take
mugs and a tin of biscuits from their respective cupboards.
As she sipped her tea she felt an inner glow that had nothing
to do with the warmth of the drink. To have him there,
looking out for her, welcoming her return and springing
immediately into action with both practical and moral

support, gave her a sense of security and of being cared for that she found immeasurably comforting.

He sat down opposite her and helped himself to a biscuit. 'Right, love, let's hear it,' he said. He listened without interruption while she recounted the gist of the information she had gleaned from Gawain Hardcastle. 'How much of this d'you reckon is kosher?' he asked when she had finished.

'Pretty well all of it, I'd say. His mind seems as sharp as a needle, despite being pickled in alcohol. One thing struck me as odd, though.'

'You mean, when he turned down the offer of another drink?'

'It wasn't just turning down the drink. Presumably even he has a saturation point. No, it was the sudden change in his manner. One minute he was chortling over the spat between Lily and Esther and the way Esther took the huff because the director gave her the brush-off, and the next he went all serious and reflective.'

'That was after he hinted at some tragedy as a result of the show being called off?'

'That's right. He looked at his watch, said something gallant about what a delightful experience meeting me had been and asked me to take him back to his hotel.'

'Hmm.' Joe pondered for a moment while absentmindedly dunking a ginger biscuit in his tea. 'Could this tragedy be what Lily was referring to when she spoke about other people being hurt?'

'It might be.'

'Assuming your and Sylvia's suspicions are correct, do you think Lily might have decided to take a belated revenge on Flavia?'

'If you mean, do I think she killed her, I think it's unlikely. She might take a hatchet to someone in a fit of rage, but not poison – I wouldn't have thought that was her style. In any case, why wait all these years? It doesn't make sense, but of course we still don't know the full story.'

'All right, let's assume for the moment that Lily didn't kill Flavia. But if Flavia was murdered, that means there must be someone else from her past living at Framleigh House, maybe someone whose career was blighted by Bernie Arnold's decision not to back the show.'

'That seems a fair assumption – but who? How does one go about finding out? I can't very well ask Geraldine Wardle for details of everyone's history.'

'No, of course not, but if you could track down Bernie Arnold he might come up with something. It shouldn't be too difficult, assuming he's still alive.'

'Gawain seemed fairly sure that he is.'

'This is rather a long shot,' Joe said slowly, 'but have you noticed any other residents who look as if they might have a theatrical background?'

'I can't think of anyone off hand.' Melissa thought for a moment, flicking through mental images. 'There are two dapper old boys who always seem to be together, but I've no idea what they used to do before retiring. Mum says they're gay,' she added as an afterthought.

'Really?' Joe cocked an eyebrow in surprise. 'I'm surprised she's heard of the expression after leading such a sheltered life.'

'I think she's been on quite a steep learning curve since she met Lily.'

Joe reached for the teapot and refilled their mugs. 'Any idea how long ago all this happened?' he asked.

'I never thought to ask. How stupid of me.' Melissa did some rapid calculations. 'I believe Mum said Lily's been a widow for about ten years, so it was at least that length of time ago. But Flavia must have been pushing seventy, so if she really is Esther then we could be talking about thirty years ago, maybe even longer.'

'I think you said that Pudgie was quite a bit older than Lily?'

'That's what Mum told me.'

'So if Esther was much younger than Bernie and was the nympho that Gawain suggested, the two women might well have been in the same age group, which adds weight to the idea that somewhere along the line Esther became Flavia. When are you planning to visit your mother again?'

'I thought tomorrow. Why?'

'Suppose you were to try and catch a word with Lily and tell her about your chat with old Hardcastle? Mention how the subject of her late husband came up, how interesting it was to learn that he used to be a showbiz angel and see how she reacts? She might even know if Bernie's still alive and if so where you can contact him.'

Melissa hesitated, then shook her head. 'I'm not sure. Even if I were to catch Lily on her own it might get back to Mum and she'd pounce immediately, wanting to know what my interest was and why I hadn't said anything to her.'

'You could spin her the same yarn as you spun Hardcastle.'

'I suppose I could, but—' Melissa gnawed her lip as she mentally weighed up the pros and cons of Joe's suggestion. 'It's a good idea, but I think I'll leave it until Bruce has had time to check with his contact at the hospital. I'm still hoping that he'll be able to confirm the accuracy of the report in the *Gazette* so I can convince Mum that there are absolutely no grounds for her suspicions.'

'Perhaps you're right, but' – Joe gave her a searching look – 'will it convince you?'

She met his gaze with a rueful smile. 'Probably not.'

Soon after breakfast the following morning, Bruce telephoned to say that he had learned from what he described as 'a reliable source' that there was to be no post-mortem on Flavia Selwyn-Tuck and that the coroner had given permission for her body to be released for burial. There did, however, seem to be a problem in that so far it had not been possible to trace her next of kin, which meant that the body would remain in the hospital mortuary for the time being. He added the somewhat gloomy news that a further elderly victim of the outbreak of food poisoning had died during the previous night.

'Let's hope that will satisfy Mum,' Melissa remarked to Joe as she relayed the message. 'I'll go and see her later on. Oh, that'll be Gloria,' she added as the doorbell sounded. 'She'll be thrilled to bits to meet you. She "oohed" and "aahed" like anything when I told her about our engagement.'

Gloria's round cheeks were pink with excitement as Melissa made the introductions. 'Ooh, Mr Martin, I were that thrilled when Mrs Craig told me she were getting wed,' she exclaimed. 'Me and my Stanley wishes you both every happiness.' She beamed at them both with pure delight shining in her toffee-brown eyes. 'I've told him that many times, Mrs Craig's a lovely lady who deserves to find Mr Right,' she went on. 'We thinks you be a very lucky gentleman and—'

She paused for breath, and Joe took the opportunity of saying, 'Thank you very much. I think so too,' and taking the plump hand she held out to him in both his own.

Sensing that Gloria would if given half a chance embark on a lengthy eulogy to her own sterling qualities, Melissa quickly interposed, 'I have to go and see my mother this morning, but you know where everything is and there aren't any special jobs for today. Mr Martin will be here, working in my study.'

'Oh, right. I'll be sure and not disturb you,' Gloria assured Joe, treating him to another radiant smile. 'I always keeps quiet when Mrs Craig's at her writing.'

'You're welcome to disturb me at about eleven with a cup of coffee,' he said gallantly and was rewarded with a coy simper.

'Ooh, that'll be a pleasure, Mr Martin. I'll have to learn to call you Mrs Martin, won't I?' she went on, turning to Melissa.

'I'm sure you'll get used to it.'

'I won't be the only one. You'll find it a bit strange yourself. I remembers it were quite some time when someone called "Mrs Parkin" before I realised they was talking to me! You comes from London, that right, Mr Martin?'

'That's right. Mrs Craig's from London too, originally.'

'So she be. I'd quite forgotten. She do seem like one of us now.'

'I hope you'll soon say the same about me,' said Joe.

'Well, I'll leave you to it,' said Melissa. She sensed that Joe was in for a grilling despite the hint that he had work to do. 'Just bear in mind that whatever you tell her will be all over the village by teatime,' she whispered as they parted at the front door.

Sylvia Ross had spent the greater part of Tuesday trying to devise a strategy for approaching the two gentlemen whom everyone referred to as Seb and Chas. She had of course been introduced to them the day of her arrival, and she recalled with a twinge of mingled amusement and embarrassment how she had assumed, because of the way they had openly stared at Lily, that they had both been attracted by her. After Lily's explanation of why this was unlikely she had thought no more about it, but the previous night, just as she was dropping off to sleep, it occurred to her to wonder what other reason there might have been for their interest. She tried to recall the moment when she had observed them with their eyes fixed on Lily, who – like her – had only recently arrived at Framleigh House. They had exchanged glances and whispers; on reflection it struck her as being the way people might react if they thought they recognised someone but were unsure. Whatever conclusions they had come to, so far as Sylvia was aware they had not spoken to Lily. Being such an open, confiding sort of woman, Sylvia reasoned, she would surely have mentioned it if they had. The possibility she had mentioned to Angela Fuller – that Lily might be 'covering up for someone' – came back to her mind with a rush. Was it possible that Seb and Chas had known Flavia Selwyn-Tuck years ago? Perhaps they had been among those who, according to Lily, had had their lives blighted by something Flavia had done. For Sylvia did not share her daughter's doubts that it was Flavia who had been the subject of that conversation in the garden.

She awoke later than usual the following morning and was the last to reach the dining-room for breakfast. There were empty places at only two tables. At one, Laurence Dainton and Angela Fuller appeared to be deep in conversation; at the other, Seb and Chas were eating toast and marmalade while scanning what looked like a tabloid newspaper propped against the coffee pot in front of them. Neither pair had noticed Sylvia, who hesitated for a moment before deciding that the opportunity was too good to miss. She approached Seb and Chas and said shyly, 'Do you mind if I sit at your table? I won't interrupt if you want to read your paper.'

'It will be a pleasure to have your company,' said Chas, with a gesture of welcome towards the empty chair.

'Thank you so much. I'm usually one of the early birds, but I overslept this morning,' Sylvia explained as she sat down. Tracy appeared at her elbow with a pencil poised over her order pad. 'I'll have cornflakes and then scrambled eggs with wholemeal toast and coffee, please, and a glass of orange juice. If you want to go on reading, don't mind me,' she said to the two men as Tracy bustled off.

'We wouldn't dream of being so rude,' said Seb gallantly, with a nod at Chas, who returned the nod, beamed at Sylvia and put the paper aside.

Sylvia noticed that it was a copy of the *Stage,* which gave her an opening. 'You're interested in the theatre?' she asked.

'It's been our life,' Chas replied. It was Seb's turn to nod and smile.

'Oh?' Sylvia was intrigued. 'You mean, you're actors?' They smiled first at one another, then at her, and nodded yet again. They reminded her of Tweedledum and Tweedledee, not on account of any physical resemblance to the Tenniel illustrations but because of the manner of their responses to her questions, almost as if they had been rehearsed. The knowledge might not be of much use in her investigations, but it was exciting, and rather glamorous, to be talking to people who had spent their life on the stage, or 'treading the boards' as she had once heard the profession described.

Now she came to think about it, there was something

slightly theatrical about their appearance. Seb had luxu-
riant, silvery grey, beautifully cut hair, bright blue-green
eyes and a fresh, unblemished skin. He wore a cream linen
jacket over a black shirt with a medallion hanging from a
gold chain round his neck. Chas was partially bald and on
the rotund side; he was clad in a safari-style khaki shirt, open
at the neck to reveal a smooth, hairless chest. Despite the
wrinkles round their eyes and mouth and a tendency for
their chins to sag, both were remarkably well preserved
for men who, she guessed, must be at least in their early
seventies. She noticed that each sported a plain gold ring on
the third finger of the left hand.

Sylvia, whose knowledge of the world of the theatre was
limited, dredged her mind in search of something to say.
'Are you what they call "resting"?' she asked in a moment
of inspiration.

The two exchanged rueful smiles, which they then turned
on her. 'You could say that,' they said in unison.

'What kind of parts do you . . . used you to play? I'm
afraid' – Sylvia felt herself stumbling – 'I don't know very
much about the theatre. I mean, my late husband didn't like
it.' She forbore to mention that Frank Ross had considered
most forms of entertainment as intrinsically evil. He had
been prevailed upon to buy a television set only because she
and Lissie between them had managed to convince him that
many programmes had great educational value.

'Oh well, we've done most things in our time, haven't we,
Chas?' Seb smiled fondly at his partner, who agreed that
indeed there were few things they hadn't done at some point
in their careers and added that just lately it had mostly been
on TV.

'Only small parts these days,' Chas admitted with a sigh.

'Commercials, mostly. "A man's never too old to enjoy Bloggs's Lager," that sort of codswallop.'

'And have you lived at Framleigh House for a long time?'

'Oh, we don't live here,' said Chas.

'We just spend a month here every year while our house-keeper's on holiday,' Seb explained.

'Oh, I see. I'm only here for a short time as well – just until my daughter's had some alterations done to her house. Then I'm going to live with her.'

'How nice,' they said, almost in the same breath.

For a moment, Sylvia felt that the conversation had run into the sand. Then she had another flash of inspiration. 'Mrs Cherston – Lily – is only here for a few weeks as well, while she has some work done on her house.' Greatly daring, she added, 'You've met her, I expect?'

'Not since she arrived here,' said Chas.

'We think we recognised her from a while back, but we aren't sure,' Seb explained.

'We used to know a Pudgie Cherston,' Chas went on.

'That's what she calls her husband – Pudgie, I mean,' said Sylvia eagerly.

'Then it must be her,' said Seb.

'I told you so, didn't I?' said Chas.

'Well, it was a long time ago,' Seb reminded him. He rolled his eyes heavenwards and heaved a deep, dramatic sigh. 'Pudgie was an angel, God rest his soul.'

Sylvia was nonplussed. She had a feeling that to ascribe angelic qualities to Lily's late husband in tones of such reverence carried a hint that his widow was in some way open to criticism and she tried to think of something to say in defence of her friend.

At that moment Tracy appeared with her cornflakes and

orange juice. As if someone had pressed a button, Chas and Seb simultaneously folded their napkins, pushed back their chairs and stood up. 'We'll leave you to have your breakfast in peace,' said Seb politely.

'It's been so nice talking to you,' said Chas.

## 17

Sheila Barron, who acted as receptionist and secretary at Framleigh House, glanced up from her desk in the entrance hall as Melissa entered. Normally, they would exchange cheerful greetings and some inconsequential comments about the weather before Melissa went in search of her mother, but this morning, without any preamble or the usual smile of welcome, Sheila said, 'Oh, Mrs Craig, I wonder if you could spare a minute? Mrs Wardle would like a word with you.'

Melissa felt a stab of anxiety. 'Is there something wrong?' she asked. 'Is my mother . . . ?'

'Oh no, Mrs Ross is fine. I saw her not half an hour ago – I think she's attending to her flower arrangements. She does them so beautifully, doesn't she? This is one of hers.' Sheila indicated a cushion of small pink and white roses nestling among tender green foliage in a blue delft container on her desk. 'They make a real difference to the place; we shall miss her when she leaves.' While she was speaking, Sheila had picked up the phone on her desk and pressed a button. 'Mrs Craig is here,' she said into the instrument, waited a second and then said, 'Yes, of course.' She put the phone down and said to Melissa, 'If you wouldn't mind popping along to Mrs Wardle's office? She asked me to say she won't keep you long.'

It was clear to Melissa the moment she entered the office

that something was seriously amiss. At first sight, Geraldine Wardle presented her usual, well-groomed, discreetly understated appearance in her simple but beautifully styled dark blue dress, her pepper-and-salt hair neatly arranged and the dusting of make-up on her pale features expertly applied, but there was a troubled expression in her eyes as she invited Melissa to sit down and her hands moved restlessly over some sheets of paper spread out on the desk in front of her.

'It's good of you to spare the time to see me,' she began, and Melissa was struck by the change in her normally brisk, confident manner. 'Something very strange and disturbing has happened and I would appreciate your advice.'

'I'll be glad to give any help I can,' Melissa replied. 'What seems to be the problem?'

'It's these letters.' The manager gestured at the papers with a small, ringless hand. 'We found them in Mrs Selwyn-Tuck's room and I've been trying to decide what's the best thing to do with them. Normally I would consult the next of kin, but unfortunately the person whose particulars she gave us when she came here seems to have moved without leaving a forwarding address. That's why we were searching among her things,' she added, almost apologetically. 'We don't make a practice of—'

'Quite,' said Melissa, wishing she would come to the point. 'Don't the letters give you any help? Isn't there an address on them?'

'They're anonymous and . . .' Mrs Wardle hesitated for a moment before continuing, almost reluctantly, 'they appear to me to be threatening.'

Melissa's interest, already aroused by the prospect of learning more about Flavia's background, notched up another gear. 'Threatening?' she repeated. 'In what way?'

'Mrs Craig, I do want you to understand,' Mrs Wardle said earnestly, 'that in normal circumstances I would not dream of showing a resident's private effects to anyone but their next of kin, but as I believe you have some experience of this kind of thing – through your writing, I mean . . .'

'I can't claim to have any first-hand experience of threatening letters,' Melissa said with a smile, 'but if you'd like me to have a look at them, I'd naturally treat them as confidential.'

'And you would not let it be generally known that you had seen them? The other residents, you know, I would not wish them to think . . .' The managerial air of authority, so noticeable during their first meeting, had given way to an uncharacteristic indecision. Mrs Wardle gathered up the letters, patting them into a neat sheaf with nervous fingers but making no move to hand them over.

'I promise not to say anything to suggest that you have been guilty of a breach of confidence, if that's what's worrying you,' Melissa assured her.

'In that case . . .' Still with a hint of reluctance, Mrs Wardle surrendered the letters. She waited in silence with her hands folded on the desk while Melissa scanned the half dozen or so single sheets of cheap writing paper. Each bore a short message written in an untidy scrawl, the characters sloping first to the left and then to the right in what seemed an amateurish attempt at disguise. Crude insults like '*You oversexed tart*' were interspersed with others, slightly more menacing, such as '*You've got it coming, you heartless bitch!*', '*You think you've got away with it, but just you wait!*' and '*One of these days someone will get you for what you did.*'

'Well?' said Mrs Wardle as Melissa handed the letters back to her. 'Do you agree that they are threatening?' She took a deep breath and once more hesitated before adding,

'I know the doctors have put the cause of Mrs Selwyn-Tuck's death as food poisoning, but do you think it's possible—' She broke off, evidently unable to bring herself to put her worst fear into words.

'I'd say they're more abusive than threatening,' Melissa said thoughtfully. 'They aren't dated, of course, so we've no idea when they were written. I take it you didn't find any envelopes?'

'No, just the letters.'

'I wonder why she kept them?'

Mrs Wardle shook her head, evidently at a loss. 'Perhaps she thought of showing them to the police, but hesitated to do so because they might have asked embarrassing questions. They do appear to suggest she had been guilty of, how shall I put it, improper behaviour, don't they?'

Melissa's mind was racing through the information she had gleaned from Gawain Hardcastle, the scraps of conversation between Lily and Laurence that her mother had relayed to her, and Flavia's hint that someone at Framleigh might bear her a grudge. Her excitement was mounting like an incoming tide, but she did her best to stay outwardly cool and detached as she replied, 'They suggest *someone* has been guilty of improper behaviour, but apart from the fact that they were found in her room there's nothing to prove they were addressed to Mrs Selwyn-Tuck, is there?'

'I don't follow you. Why would she have them if they were sent to someone else?'

'I don't know, I'm just brainstorming at the moment. She could have written them herself to some other person, but for some reason decided not to send them.'

Mrs Wardle pursed her lips and frowned. 'That seems a little unlikely, don't you think?'

'Unlikely, I agree, but not impossible. Maybe she wrote

them in a fit of anger, to relieve her feelings. Do you know anything about her past life? This person you mentioned, the one whose address she gave you, did they come with her when she moved into Framleigh House?'

'No, she came on her own. All she told us was that she had been living in the north of England, had been recently widowed and decided to return to the Cotswolds because she lived in the area many years ago. Since coming here she has mentioned a few, shall we say, prominent people with whom she claimed to have an acquaintance . . .' For the first time since Melissa had entered the room, a smile flickered round Geraldine Wardle's thin lips.

'Yes, I gather she was rather good at name-dropping,' Melissa agreed.

'I suppose we might try to get in touch with one or two of them, to see if they have any knowledge of this other person's whereabouts. Personally, I have my doubts over some of the stories Mrs Selwyn-Tuck put about, but I feel I should make some effort to—'

Seizing her opportunity, Melissa said, 'Mrs Wardle, I have a friend, a detective sergeant in the local police. If you agree, I could show him the letters unofficially and ask him for his opinion.'

'I was hoping it would not be necessary to involve the police. That is why I have taken you into my confidence.' There was a faint note of reproach in the manager's voice, as if she felt that Melissa had failed her by not coming up with a magical solution that would absolve her from responsibility while ensuring that Framleigh House would remain untouched by any whiff of scandal or skulduggery.

'It would be entirely off the record,' Melissa repeated. 'The doctor has signed the death certificate, so there will be no call for an official police investigation.'

'I see.' The suggestion was clearly not what Geraldine Wardle had in mind, but after a few minutes' reflection, during which Melissa kept her fingers mentally crossed, she gave a deep sigh and said, 'Very well, Mrs Craig, I leave it to you.' She opened a drawer, took out an envelope, put the letters inside and handed it over. 'I cannot stress sufficiently that I am relying on your discretion. The good name of Framleigh House is very important to me, and to my staff.'

'I quite understand. Now, if you will excuse me, I'll go and find my mother.'

'Lissie, whatever's going on? Angela said you arrived a quarter of an hour ago.'

'Angela?'

'Angela Fuller. She said she heard Sheila telling you Mrs Wardle wanted to see you.'

'I don't remember seeing anyone while I was talking to Sheila.' It would, Melissa reflected, be unfortunate if the interest of some over-curious person had been aroused.

'I'm not surprised you didn't notice her.' Sylvia gave a slightly scornful laugh. 'She's such an insignificant little person, and not a bit enterprising. I tried to enlist her help with my enqu—' She broke off and looked sheepish.

Melissa pounced. 'You were going to say "enquiries", weren't you? About Flavia's death, would that be? I thought we agreed you'd let that drop.'

'Yes, well, she didn't want to know so that was that.' Sylvia made an impatient gesture as if to imply that the subject was closed. 'You haven't told me why Geraldine Wardle wanted to see you. Is there something wrong? With me, I mean?' She turned to look Melissa full in the face. There was acute anxiety in her gaze.

'No, Mum, of course not.' Melissa took her hand and gave it a squeeze. 'You're doing fine, everyone says so.'

'Truly? You wouldn't hide anything from me, would you?'

'Of course I wouldn't, and there's absolutely nothing to hide. You're making wonderful progress.'

'That's what I feel as well, but when I heard Geraldine . . .' Sylvia's expression changed from anxiety to curiosity. 'Then what did she want to see you about, if it wasn't me?'

'She just wanted to ask how the building work at Hawthorn Cottage is progressing,' said Melissa, desperately improvising while mentally cursing Angela Fuller for her well-meaning but inconvenient intervention. 'She wanted to know if it's going to be finished on schedule, but I explained it's too soon to tell.'

'What's that got to do with her?'

'She wanted to know when your room here is likely to be available for someone else.'

'It took fifteen minutes to ask you that?'

'No, of course it didn't. She was telling me how difficult running a place like this is nowadays, with all the new rules and regulations they keep bringing in.' Melissa's voice became more confident as the fiction took shape. It was, she thought, rather like plotting a novel, except that there was no opportunity to edit words once uttered and with her mother's mind growing sharper by the day the situation was becoming a little tricky. 'I had quite a job to get away,' she finished.

To her relief, Sylvia appeared to accept the explanation. She tucked her arm into Melissa's and said, 'Oh, that's all right then. Let's go and sit in the conservatory. It's almost time for coffee.'

They had the conservatory to themselves. They had just

settled into their chairs when Tracy popped her head round the glass door, beamed at them and said, 'Two in here for coffee then?' and served them from her trolley.

As soon as she was out of earshot, Sylvia turned to Melissa and said in a low voice, 'Have there been any new developments?'

'What sort of developments?' Melissa asked guardedly, knowing full well what her mother had in mind.

Sylvia tutted impatiently. 'You know, dear, about Flavia being poisoned.'

'Mother, she wasn't poisoned, at least, not in the way you seem to think.'

'What's that supposed to mean?'

'The cause of death was food poisoning, and another person has died as the result of the same outbreak. It'll be in this evening's *Gazette*.'

'How do you know that?'

'One of their reporters is a friend of mine.'

'He told you?'

'Yes.'

'Why should he have bothered to do that?' Sylvia's eyes narrowed slightly and she cocked her head at an angle in a way that took Melissa straight back to her childhood when she had been detected in some misdemeanour and was trying to talk her way out of it. 'Did you ask him to find out for you?' her mother persisted on not receiving an immediate answer.

'I did, as it happens,' Melissa admitted resignedly.

'So you have your doubts as well?' Sylvia retorted with an air of triumph.

'Not really.' For the second time within minutes Melissa found herself prevaricating. 'It was just . . . you seemed so determined to believe the worst, and it's bad for you to worry about things. I wanted to be able to reassure you. That's all, honestly. So I won't be hearing any more about your "enquiries", will I?' she added, a little sternly. 'Because there's nothing to enquire about now, is there?'

'If you say so, dear. Why don't we drink our coffee before it gets cold?'

Melissa, although far from convinced that her mother was satisfied, decided to leave it at that. The next step was to contact Matt Waters as soon as possible.

Sylvia had deliberately avoided telling Melissa about her breakfast-time chat with Seb and Chas. She had made such a thing about 'not overdoing it' and 'not upsetting people with a lot of questions' that she would almost certainly have started lecturing all over again.

Sylvia did not believe that her daughter was entirely satisfied with the official explanation of Flavia's death, nor did she accept the excuse she had given for asking a journalist friend to make a special check. On the contrary, she was convinced that she too had her doubts but was unwilling to admit as much to her mother. Why can't she trust me? Sylvia asked herself resentfully. It would have been great fun to join forces. It would have added a bit of spice to her present rather restricted existence. Spice was something that had been absent from her life for so many years. Looking back, it struck her that in some respects she had been like a prisoner of medieval legend, immured in a grim castle with little hope of rescue. She played with the notion for a minute or two, wondering how she would have reacted had some knight in shining armour suddenly arrived on the scene with the offer of freedom. Would she have had the courage to leave the husband she no longer loved? Probably not. She had submitted to his authority in all things for so long that to rebel during his lifetime would have been unthinkable – and in any case there had been no knight in shining armour. So the years had slipped remorselessly by, years spent secretly nursing the pain of separation from her only child and bitter resentment against the man who had turned from loving if somewhat puritanical companion into cold-hearted gaoler.

With Frank's death came the freedom she had craved for so long. It had also brought about a reconciliation with her daughter, but the trauma of finding his body and being suspected of his murder, followed almost immediately by the revelation that she needed brain surgery, had for a while knocked the stuffing out of her. Many women would have suffered permanent psychological damage or at least had a nervous breakdown. She told herself with justifiable pride that she was made of sterner material. She had bounced back. At the age of seventy she could hardly count on a lengthy future, but there was no reason why she should not make up for at least some of those wasted years. The enquiring mind and the spirit of adventure that had been subdued to the point of extinction had burst into new and vigorous life and were eager to find an outlet. Finding out who murdered Flavia Selwyn-Tuck was an exciting challenge. For Flavia had been murdered. Sylvia had no doubt whatsoever about that.

She decided that making a few notes would help her to sort out the jumble of odd thoughts and recollections teeming in her brain. She would start right away. 'No time like the present,' she said to herself. She was crossing reception on her way back to her room when she realised that she had no writing materials. In its attempts to create the atmosphere of a private hotel, Framleigh House stopped short of providing stationery in the residents' rooms. 'Bother!' she exclaimed.

Sheila looked up in surprise. 'Is something wrong, Mrs Ross?' she asked.

Not having realised that she had spoken aloud, Sylvia jumped and gave a self-conscious laugh. 'Not exactly wrong,' she replied. 'It's just that . . . I wanted to write something down . . .' To her astonishment, she found herself inventing an excuse. It tripped off her tongue so readily that when she thought about it afterwards she was almost shocked. Frank, with his unswerving insistence on the truth at all times, would have been horrified. 'I'll need lots of things when I move into my daughter's house,' she explained, 'so I thought I'd make a few lists, but I haven't anything to write on.'

'No problem.' Sheila rummaged in a drawer of her desk and produced half a dozen sheets of lined foolscap and a ballpoint pen. 'Will that do?'

'Oh, that's lovely, thank you so much,' said Sylvia. 'Lissie has promised to take me shopping for some new clothes and things.'

'I'm sure you'll enjoy that,' said Sheila with a smile.

'Yes, I'm so looking forward to it,' Sylvia replied brightly. As she turned away from the desk, Mrs Wardle appeared and she found herself quite unnecessarily repeating the explanation. 'I hope it's all right, I hope you don't mind me borrowing these,' she gabbled, feeling unaccountably confused. The manager merely smiled, said something reassuring and began speaking to Sheila about an administrative matter, but as she retreated Sylvia had a sudden irrational fear that she might not have believed her and would mention the episode to Lissie, hinting that her mother was behaving oddly. She would have to be more careful in the future.

Back in her room, she sat down and wrote *'Things I Need to Find Out'* at the top of her first sheet of paper. The questions came tumbling out in quick succession:

1. *I'm certain Lily recognised Flavia. Did Flavia recognise Lily? We don't know, but she didn't appear to.*
2. *Lily told Laurence about someone doing something dreadful a long time ago. Something that hurt other people. I'm sure it was Flavia, even though she didn't mention a name. What could it have been?*
3. *Lily wanted to expose Flavia, but Laurence advised her not to because that would hurt other people as well. What other people?*
4. *Flavia's dog was poisoned. Was Lissie right in thinking it was an accident or was it someone's way of punishing Flavia? If so, was that person Lily? Flavia definitely thought someone here had a grudge against her. Why?*
5. *Did Flavia die of the same poison as Gaston? If so, how was it administered, and by whom?*
6. *Lily definitely knows something she doesn't want to discuss. I know this because she wouldn't talk to me that evening after supper and then came to me next day with an excuse I don't believe. What was the real reason?*
7. *Seb and Chas thought they recognised Lily but she's never given any sign that she recognised them. They're actors, how would she know them? They knew her husband and thought a lot of him. Did he have something to do with the theatre? Now they seem sure who she is, will they go and speak to her?*

When she had reached this point in her deliberations, Sylvia put down her pen, reread her notes, put them in the drawer of her bedside cabinet alongside her purse and one or two pieces of jewellery and turned the key. She glanced at her watch. It was almost twelve thirty; the gong for the midday meal would sound any minute. Writing everything down, besides giving her the opportunity to tidy up the clutter in her mind and decide what her next step should be, had also given her an appetite. She went downstairs to the dining-room feeling hugely pleased with herself. How wonderful it would be, she thought with a sudden wave of excitement, if she could solve the mystery before anyone else did.

# 18

Impatient to put her plan into operation without delay, Sylvia had been hoping to find a table for two where she and Lily could have a private chat, but on reaching the dining-room she was disappointed to find all the tables occupied. Normally people tended to turn up for meals in ones and twos within a few minutes of the gong, but today most of them seemed to have arrived early *en masse* and some were already eating their first course. A glance round the room showed her that the only vacant seats were at a table for four, at which Angela Fuller and Laurence Dainton were at that moment being served with soup. As Laurence picked up his spoon she noticed him make some remark which she did not catch, but which Angela evidently considered amusing, for she tilted her head back and gave a coy, ladylike titter. What a silly creature she is, Sylvia thought crossly as, having no other option, she approached their table. Aloud, she said, 'Do you mind if I join you?'

With his usual courtesy, Laurence put down his spoon and stood up with a smile of welcome and said, 'Please do.' His seat was adjacent to one of the empty places and he held Sylvia's chair and slid it expertly into place as she sat down.

'Thank you so much,' she said, thinking how refreshing it was to meet a really polished, considerate gentleman.

Such a gesture would not have occurred to Frank. 'We're all very punctual today, aren't we?' she added brightly.

Laurence gave a polite nod and picked up his spoon again. 'I hope you'll excuse me if I get on with this?' he said.

'Of course. It gets cold so quickly, doesn't it?'

Sylvia's remarks and the smile that accompanied them were intended to include Angela, who, however, made no response to either. Evidently untroubled by the niceties of etiquette, she had continued to sip daintily at her soup and pop small pieces of bread roll into her mouth throughout the interruption. I do believe she's miffed because I broke up her tête-à-tête with Laurence, thought Sylvia with a hint of malicious glee.

Tracy paused on her way to the kitchen to offer Sylvia a choice of soup or avocado with a basil and tomato *coulis* for her first course and Laurence seized the opportunity of detaining her with a request to open a fresh bottle of wine from his private store in readiness for the evening meal. While he was reminding her of the correct way to carry out this important procedure, Sylvia leaned across the table to Angela and said in a low voice, 'I thought you'd like to know I'm making progress with my enquiries about . . . you know.'

Angela paused with her spoon halfway to her mouth and for the first time since Sylvia arrived at the table she showed a flicker of interest. After a furtive glance to make sure that Laurence's attention was still engaged, she whispered, 'What have you found out?'

'I can't tell you now. Can we have a chat later on?'

Angela hesitated for a moment before saying, 'I'm going out immediately after lunch. When I come back, perhaps.'

'Fine. I might have even more to report then.'

At that moment, Lily entered the dining-room, cast an eye round the tables and bore down on them to claim the one remaining place. 'Mind if I make it three to one?' she said breezily and sat down without waiting for a reply. The two women responded with conventional words of welcome. Laurence, who by this time had completed his negotiations with Tracy, merely nodded.

'Why's everyone so punctual today?' Lily demanded. 'Are they all going off to bingo this afternoon or what?'

Angela finished her soup, laid down her spoon and dabbed at her mouth with her napkin. 'A visit to the theatre in Cheltenham has been arranged for this afternoon,' she said. 'Sheila's ordered a coach for one forty-five.'

Lily looked aggrieved. 'I didn't know there was a trip to the theatre,' she said, a little petulantly. 'Why didn't someone tell me?'

'It was arranged some time ago.' Laurence appeared to address the piece of bread roll he had just broken off before placing it in his mouth. 'I imagine it sold out pretty quickly – these excursions usually do.' His tone made it clear that 'these excursions' were of little interest to him.

'What's the show?'

He shrugged. 'One of the Gilbert and Sullivan operettas, I believe. An amateur production.'

From the malicious gleam in her eye it was clear that Lily not only recognised the thinly veiled disdain in his tone, but found it highly amusing. 'I take it you're not honouring the company with your presence?' she taunted him.

'It isn't the kind of event that appeals to me,' he replied, still without making eye contact with her.

'Too plebeian for you, I dare say,' she retorted with a flash of her gleaming porcelain teeth.

'I'm told the local operatic society put on some very good shows,' said Angela. 'This one had an excellent review in the local paper.'

Laurence merely shrugged again, pushed away his empty soup bowl and leaned back in his seat, drumming his thin fingers on the table. It occurred to Sylvia that, while her own arrival had not been well received by Angela, his reaction to Lily's was even less enthusiastic.

'Well, it would have been nice to have the option,' Lily declared. 'I enjoy a bit of G and S meself. Still, I suppose there'll be other outings. How does one find out about them?'

'I asked Sheila and she told me she makes an announcement well in advance and sends round a list for people to sign if they want a ticket,' Angela explained. 'If there are spare places she puts a notice on the board in reception, but as Mr Dainton says, theatre trips are usually booked up pretty quickly.'

'Oh well, I'll have to keep me eyes open in future,' said Lily. 'I'll have some of that please,' she added as Tracy put a portion of avocado in front of Sylvia. 'Well,' she went on, evidently determined to keep a conversation going despite the slightly strained atmosphere, 'what have we all been doing this morning?'

The strategy enjoyed a limited success. Sylvia set the ball rolling with a mention of Melissa's visit and the news that the building of the extension to Hawthorn Cottage was under way and so far going according to plan. This prompted Lily to launch into a series of horror stories about the problems she was having with her builders. When that subject had been exhausted, Angela chimed in to sing the praises of a new biography of an eminent Victorian statesman that she had spent most of the morning reading; an unfortunate choice of topic as it happened, because it emerged that Laurence had reviewed the book for one of the literary journals and damned it with faint praise.

From then on they all concentrated on their meal with only the occasional request for butter or condiments to break the silence until dessert in the form of a bowl of fresh fruit was put on the table. Laurence helped himself to an apple, which he polished carefully on his napkin, declined coffee and left with the excuse that there was 'something on the radio' that he wished to listen to.

'Some boring highbrow discussion, I expect,' Lily remarked as soon as he was out of earshot.

'I find Mr Dainton a very intelligent, interesting gentleman,' said Angela with a hint of reproach in her soft, well-modulated voice.

Lily treated her to a condescending smile, but made no comment. Observing a general move to leave the other tables, she remarked, 'Looks like the theatre crowd's on the move. You going, Angie?'

'As a matter of fact . . .' Angela turned slightly pink, whether from irritation at hearing her name thus abbreviated or embarrassment at the admission in the light of Laurence's comments was not clear. She pushed back her chair and stood up. 'I . . . someone dropped out at the last minute and offered me their ticket. If you'll excuse me.'

'Sure. Enjoy the show and tell us about it at supper,' said Lily, adding with a hint of mockery, 'I'm sure *Mr Dainton* will be keen to hear about it. I do believe the silly little cow's taken a shine to him,' she whispered to Sylvia with her eyes on Angela's retreating back. She gave one of her sudden, ear-piercing laughs. 'She'd have kittens if she knew about him and me, wouldn't she? You never let on, did you, Sylv?'

'Of course I didn't. I promised, didn't I?'

'Course you did, love. You're a good sort.' Lily brushed Sylvia's hand with ruby-tipped fingers. 'Y'know,' she went on, stirring cream into her coffee, 'I've wondered several times what made me blurt out all that stuff about Lol and me. I suppose it was the shock of bumping into him again after all those years. I needed someone to confide in.'

'That's quite understandable,' Sylvia replied mechanically. Throughout the meal she had been trying to decide the best way to guide the conversation in the right direction and had still not come to a conclusion when the problem was solved for her. Among the handful of people remaining after the departure of the theatregoers were Seb and Chas, who were seated on the other side of the room. Out of the corner of her eye, she noticed them glance first at Lily and then at each other, after which they stood up and came over to their table. They were both smiling broadly and she was once more reminded of Tweedledum and Tweedledee.

'Mrs Cherston,' said Chas with a little bow. 'I don't suppose you remember us?'

Lily looked them up and down for a moment before shaking her immaculate blond head. 'Can't say as I do,' she said. 'Did we meet somewhere?'

'It was a long time ago,' said Seb.

'At an audition for a new musical called *The Merry Month of May*,' said Chas. 'You were there with your husband. Pudgie Cherston *was* your husband, I believe?' he added hastily as if anxious to reassure himself that he was not making a *faux pas*.

'Yeah, that's right,' said Lily. Sylvia, who was watching her closely, thought her tone sounded a little guarded. 'Now you mention it, the name of the show does ring a bell, but I don't recall any details.'

'It was a long time ago,' Chas repeated. 'Maybe you didn't notice us. We did rather well,' he continued with a touch of pride. The two exchanged slightly arch smiles. 'We both landed quite important parts.'

'We were so excited. It was going to be our first appearance in the West End, but nothing came of it after all.' Seb sighed deeply and spread his well-kept hands in a gesture of sorrowful resignation.

'The show was never put on,' explained Chas. He waited for a moment, as if hoping for some expression of regret. 'But I expect you heard about that.'

Lily shook her head. 'Can't say as I did.'

Her tone did not exactly invite further confidences, but Chas refused to be discouraged. 'We mustn't complain,' he went on. 'We've had our successes, I suppose, but somehow the big break never came again.'

'That's too bad,' said Lily. As if by way of an excuse for her apparent forgetfulness, she added, 'I'm afraid I've been out of touch since Pudgie died.' It was her turn to heave a sigh, which to Sylvia sounded a little forced.

'We do understand,' Chas assured her.

Seb nodded in agreement. 'Such a *dear* man,' he said with a warmth that was evidently sincere.

'He was very enthusiastic about *The Merry Month of May*,' said Chas. 'I recall him saying he was sure it was going to be a hit – the book and lyrics were *wonderful*.'

Sylvia, who until now had maintained a discreet silence, could not contain her curiosity any longer. 'What happened to it, then?' she asked. 'I mean, if it was so good, why was it dropped?'

'Money, my dear,' said Chas. 'Pudgie's business partner pulled out.' He spoke to Sylvia, but his eyes were on Lily. 'You remember Bernie Arnold, don't you, Mrs Cherston?'

'Vaguely,' she replied. 'I never really knew him.' She

picked up her handbag and pushed back her chair. 'If you'll excuse me.'

'Of course,' said Seb. 'I hope we haven't offended you? We just thought, once we were sure who you were, it might be nice to have a chat about old times. But perhaps you didn't care to be reminded about . . . I mean, it wasn't just us who suffered. There was that awful tragedy.' It was his turn to sound anxious.

'Like I said, I'm right out of touch,' said Lily.

'Yes, of course. We apologise for having disturbed you,' said Chas.

'No problem.'

The two bobbed their heads, smiled first at the two women and then at each other, and made their exit.

'Silly old buggers!' Lily remarked once they were out of earshot. 'That's the trouble with actors, they can't stop rabbiting about their past triumphs.' Her tone was light, but Sylvia had a feeling that she had been uncomfortable during the entire conversation and was relieved when it ended.

'I think they're rather charming,' said Sylvia. 'I sat with them at breakfast and we had such a nice chat. They spoke very highly of your late husband, by the way.'

'Oh? What did they say?'

'They said he was an angel.'

Lily gave an uncomprehending stare before letting out another raucous cackle. 'Oh, Sylv, you are priceless!' she chortled.

'I don't understand,' said Sylvia in bewilderment.

'Pudgie was a darling, but even if he'd been an out-and-out bastard he'd still have been an angel to them. He put up half the money for the show – that's what angel means in theatre-speak. He backed one or two very successful productions.'

'I see.' Sylvia thought for a moment. 'This other man – Bernie Arnold, did Chas call him? I suppose he was to put up the other half?'

'That's right.'

'Why did he change his mind?'

Lily shrugged. 'How would I know? These things happen.'

'It must have been very disappointing for a lot of people beside Seb and Chas.'

'I suppose so.'

Once again, Sylvia felt a twinge of excitement. I'm on to something, I know I am, she thought. She doesn't want to talk about it. Why? Aloud, she said casually, 'Seb said something about a tragedy. I wonder what he meant?'

'Haven't a clue.' Lily's temporary good humour had evaporated. 'It must have been getting on for thirty years ago. Just drop it, will you?' she added irritably as Sylvia opened her mouth to ask a further question. She stood up and shoved her chair under the table as if she had a personal grudge against it. 'I can feel another of my headaches coming on.'

'Oh, I'm so sorry,' said Sylvia politely. She waited for a moment or two before leaving the table and returning to her room, where she took out her notes, read them through several times and then added some more:

8. *I know now how Lily came to know theatre people. She looked uneasy when Seb and Chas were talking about the show that folded because the other 'angel' changed his mind about putting money into it. She said she didn't know the reason, but I don't think she was telling the truth. Why?*

9. *Was it the tragedy Seb mentioned that she and Laurence were talking about in the garden? Did Flavia have*

*something to do with it? Did she have some connection with Bernie Arnold?*

At this point, something clicked in Sylvia's brain and she added one more question to her list:

10. *Was it Flavia who persuaded Bernie Arnold to take his money out of* The Merry Month of May?

## 19

Melissa held open the door of Hawthorn Cottage and Detective Sergeant Matthew Waters of the Gloucestershire CID stepped inside. 'Matt, it's good of you to come at such short notice,' she said as she closed the door behind him.

'You made it sound so intriguing I couldn't stay away,' he replied as he followed her along the short passage leading to the sitting-room. 'I've heard of children taking up their parents' professions, but a mother following in her daughter's footsteps is something else. Especially when the footsteps are in pursuit of crime,' he added with a wry smile.

'We don't know yet whether there's a crime to pursue, that's why I need your advice,' she said. 'Anyway, first things first. I'd like you to meet my fiancé, Joe Martin.'

'Delighted!' A smile of mingled surprise and pleasure lit up Matt's clean-shaven features, still comparatively unlined despite his thatch of grey hair. 'Congratulations to you both!' He kissed Melissa on both cheeks and shook hands with Joe. 'Perhaps you'll be able to persuade her to keep her involvement with crime between the covers of her books from now on!'

'I doubt it,' said Joe with a smile. 'She seems to attract mysteries.'

'I'm doing my best by giving up writing them,' Melissa

reminded them. 'I'm into the so-called "literary" genre now. Matt, do sit down. Would you like some tea?'

'No, thank you. I haven't much time, actually; I'm on duty at four. You said you had some letters to show me – anonymous letters, is that right?'

'Yes, they're in here.' She handed him the envelope.

He took out the letters and skimmed through them. When he had read the last one he patted them into a neat sheaf and laid them beside the envelope on a small occasional table beside his chair. His expression was thoughtful, but he made no immediate comment.

'What do you think?' she asked after a moment. 'Would you say they were threatening?'

He locked the fingers of both hands together and rested his chin on them, frowning in concentration. 'They certainly contain an implied threat of some kind,' he said slowly, 'but there's nothing in them to suggest the writer had murder – or any other kind of violence – in mind. Where did you get them?'

'They were found among the possessions of one of the victims of the recent outbreak of salmonella poisoning. I dare say you've heard about it?'

'Not officially, but I read something in the local paper. You mentioned on the telephone that your mother has a fixation about one of the residents at Framleigh House having been deliberately poisoned. Would that be the person in whose room they were found?'

'Yes. A lady called Flavia Selwyn-Tuck.'

'Can you fill in a few details? You didn't explain what put the notion into your mother's head in the first place.'

'It all started when she overheard a conversation between two of the other residents that suggested one of them – the woman – not only recognised Flavia but had some sort of grudge against her. At least, Mum assumed the person they were talking about was Flavia, but she had to admit she never heard them mention a name.'

'And then Flavia died of this salmonella bug and Mother put two and two together and made five?'

Melissa gave a rueful laugh. 'That's exactly what I said to her. The trouble is,' she went on, growing serious again, 'I'm not convinced she accepts the doctor's diagnosis. I'm afraid that in the absence of an official police investigation she's determined to carry out one of her own.'

Matt pursed his lips and shook his head. 'Not a good idea,' he said thoughtfully.

'You mean, you think there may be grounds for her suspicions?'

'I didn't say that, but we can't at this stage be certain there aren't. This conversation she overheard – did she hear either of the parties refer to any possible violent action?'

'On the contrary. The woman seemed to want to expose whoever they were talking about for some past mis-demeanour that apparently caused a lot of grief. The man was trying to talk her out of it, to avoid reopening old wounds, he said, or words to that effect.'

'And you still don't know for certain who they were talking about?'

'No. That's what I keep pointing out to Mum, but I have a feeling I'm wasting my breath.'

'I take it you've done your best to persuade her to accept the medical evidence?'

'Of course I have. I've also reminded her that she should be taking life quietly after her operation for removal of a brain tumour, and I've warned her that she could easily antagonise people if she goes round asking a lot of leading questions, but her responses have been ambivalent, to say the least. When my father was alive she was afraid to say boo to a goose without his approval, but now . . .' Melissa spread her hands and lifted her shoulders in a gesture of exasperation. 'My common sense tells me there's nothing suspicious about Flavia's death, but I don't believe I've managed to convince Mum.'

Matt gave her a penetrating glance and said, 'I have a feeling you're not entirely convinced yourself.'

'I admit I'd be far happier if I knew it was proved beyond doubt that she died from salmonella poisoning,' she admitted.

'You're questioning the medical evidence?'

'I've been asking myself whether, because Flavia was one of several admitted to hospital at the same time and all suffering from the same symptoms, it never occurred to anyone that there might be a different reason for her illness? It wouldn't be the first time a slip-up has happened; hospital staff are pretty stretched these days.'

'It's not impossible,' Matt acknowledged. He sat with knitted brows for half a minute or so before saying, 'You mentioned your mother recently had brain surgery. Do you think that has anything to do with this fixation, as you call it?'

'We've been wondering about that, haven't we?' Melissa glanced at Joe for confirmation.

'The surgeon did warn us to keep an eye open for signs of paranoia,' he said, 'but we've talked it over and from what Mel has told me there haven't been any.'

'That's right,' Melissa agreed. 'She seems perfectly rational in other respects. It's more a bee in her bonnet than an obsession, really. If anything the operation seems to have sharpened her wits. Not that I'm complaining about that, of course, but—'

'Does she know about these letters?'

'Good heavens, no! She'd see them as irrefutable confirmation of her suspicions.'

'So who does know about them?'

'Apart from you – and Joe, of course – no one but the manager of Framleigh House and her secretary.'

'Let's go back to these two people your mother overheard. What do you know about them?'

'Quite a lot, as it happens. One is Laurence Dainton, a well-known and highly respected journalist and political commentator; you've probably heard of him. The other is Lily Cherston, his ex-wife. They had a rather bad-tempered divorce about forty years ago and hadn't seen one another since until Lily moved into Framleigh House. I have reason to believe that Lily knew Flavia years ago and had quite a lively spat with her, but again I can't be sure.' Melissa gave Matt a brief summary of the information she had gleaned from the bibulous Gawain Hardcastle.

He listened attentively, thought for a moment or two and then said, 'Do I gather you suspect Lily of writing these letters?'

'If Flavia really is – or rather was – Esther Arnold, that would seem a reasonable assumption, don't you think?'

Instead of replying to the question, Matt said, 'This chap Arnold – have you any idea where he is now?'

'No, but Gawain seems to think he's still alive. Do you think it might be worth trying to trace him?' Melissa decided not to mention that she had already asked Bruce to do just that.

Matt shrugged. 'Presumably he had some knowledge of the incident, but he might not care to talk about it if Gawain's version is accurate. It might be possible to find some other way of checking whether Esther and Flavia

What's-her-Name are one and the same person. It's a long shot, though; all this must have happened a hell of a long time ago and as the woman's dead . . .' Matt made a dismissive gesture. 'In any case,' he added, 'some people change out of all recognition as they grow older.'

'According to Mum, Lily sounded pretty confident of her facts, but of course—'

'There's no proof she was talking about Flavia,' Matt finished.

'We seem to be going round in circles,' said Melissa with a sigh. 'Do you think this might be a case of mistaken identity?'

'It might well be. On reflection, there's one thing that makes me inclined to think it is.'

'What's that?'

'Let's assume for the moment that it *was* Flavia Lily was claiming to have recognised; and I'm inclined to think that it was. But there's no suggestion that Flavia recognised Lily, which seems unlikely if she was the woman who had the run-in with her that Hardcastle described.'

'That's a point.' Melissa thought for a moment. 'Unless she did recognise her but had a particular reason to keep quiet about it.'

'Why would she do that?'

'Look at it this way. If Flavia was Esther, then at some time in the past she obviously changed her name. Perhaps she changed her identity as well.'

'Why her identity? She could have simply remarried.'

'Perhaps she married someone in a higher social class and didn't want it to be known that she was once one of the hoi polloi. By all accounts she was a terrible snob and claimed to know half the names in *Debrett*. She had a posh accent you could cut with a knife, but the first time I heard her open her mouth I was sure it was phoney.' Melissa felt her excitement rising as she developed this new possibility. 'That could explain the change in her first name,' she suggested. 'Maybe she thought Flavia sounded more classy than Esther. Perhaps she did recognise Lily, but didn't want to acknowledge her and have her cover blown.'

'Wouldn't that give Flavia more of a motive to kill Lily than vice versa?' said Matt dryly.

Melissa stared at him. 'You're not serious?'

'No, of course not, but you still haven't convinced me that anyone had a motive for topping Flavia.'

'Matt, I've already said that nothing Mum overheard suggested either Lily or Laurence was contemplating violence, but I do know that Flavia thought someone might have a grudge against her because she said so, after her dog was poisoned.'

Matt, who had been making a few notes in his pocket book, stopped writing and said sharply, 'Her dog was poisoned? You didn't say anything about that. When did that happen?'

'Just a few days before she died. Everyone thought he must have picked up something noxious while she was taking him for a walk, but she insisted it had been done deliberately to get at her. She even asked me to try and find the culprit, on the strength of my reputation as a crime writer!'

'Sounds a bit of a nutcase,' Matt commented.

'I wouldn't say that, but she certainly doted on Gaston and she was heartbroken when he died. I managed to figure out how he could have ingested oleander pollen by accident. Flavia jumped at it – when I told her she seemed really relieved.'

'So at this stage neither you nor your mother suspected foul play?'

'Not exactly, except that at one point it did cross Mum's mind that someone could have given Flavia a poisoned cake, knowing that she'd promptly feed it to the dog. She dropped that idea when I said that Flavia would probably have *shared* it with the dog, and eaten some of it herself. At that point no one seriously thought anyone intended to murder Flavia; except that, come to think of it, Gloria came up with the suggestion that the cake was intended for Flavia all along and she scuppered the attempt by feeding it to Gaston. Gloria thought that was hilarious!'

'It sounds as if Flavia wasn't exactly popular,' Matt commented wryly.

'I think she upset some of the staff over her obsessive devotion to the dog, and her rather autocratic manner, but I can't believe any of them would wish her any harm,' Melissa began, but even as she spoke her doubts returned and would not be ignored. 'Just the same, it does seem odd that Flavia should die of some kind of poisoning so soon after her dog died in similar circumstances.'

'Odd, yes, but it could be pure coincidence.' Matt put away his notebook, picked up the letters and returned them to the envelope. He sat for a moment deep in thought while Melissa and Joe waited to hear his conclusions. 'To be honest,' he said at last, 'I don't feel that these letters on their own are sufficient to warrant an official enquiry, provided all the proper tests were carried out at the hospital. If they were, and they confirm beyond doubt that Flavia's death was due to complications after a severe bout of salmonella poisoning, then I think my Super will agree that there are no grounds for action on our part. If they weren't, then the coroner will certainly have to be informed.'

'So what do I say to Mrs Wardle in the meantime? She's

desperate to protect the good name of Framleigh House, but equally anxious to do the right thing. If she'd been able to contact Flavia's next of kin, the responsibility would be out of her hands, but as it is . . .'

'Yes, I see her predicament, but I'm afraid that's the situation. You hold on to these for the time being' – Matt handed over the envelope containing the anonymous letters – 'but if it turns out that we have to launch an enquiry, we'll need them as evidence.' He glanced at his watch and stood up. 'I must be going. I'll keep you posted.'

'So what do we do now?' Melissa asked, a little despondently, after seeing Matt out.

'We wait,' said Joe. 'Let's have that cup of tea your friend turned down.' He went into the kitchen and filled the kettle.

Melissa followed him and flopped into a chair. 'I suppose I'd better put Geraldine Wardle in the picture,' she said. 'I promised to let her know what Matt said about the letters.'

'I wonder why Flavia kept them?'

'Geraldine suggested she might have thought of showing them to the police, but was too embarrassed.'

'That makes sense if she really was Esther Arnold. I take it you kept that part of the story to yourself?'

'Yes, of course.'

'Anyway, what are you going to tell Geraldine?'

'At this stage, simply that as the coroner hasn't called for any further tests and has released Flavia's body for burial, Matt doesn't think an enquiry is called for.'

'You aren't going to mention that he's proposing to ask the medics to confirm all the proper tests were carried out?'

'Is there any need at this stage? I don't want to cause her unnecessary worry.'

Joe shrugged. 'I suppose not.' He put the teapot on the Aga to warm and began setting out the tea things while waiting for the kettle to boil. Melissa picked up the phone and called Framleigh House.

As she anticipated, Geraldine Wardle was greatly relieved to hear the edited version of Melissa's conversation with DS Waters. 'I'm most grateful to you for your help,' she said. 'As I'm sure you realise, the death of Mrs Selwyn-Tuck has caused us a great deal of distress and if it should turn out that there was anything untoward . . . the publicity, you know.'

'I quite understand,' Melissa assured her. 'I'm sure all your residents and your staff will have been affected by it. My mother—'

'I can put your mind at rest as far as Mrs Ross is concerned,' Mrs Wardle broke in. 'She's in a very positive frame of mind and looking to the future.'

'Oh? Has she been talking to you about it?'

'Not exactly. I happened to come along as she was borrowing some writing materials from Sheila and she was telling me about her plans.'

Melissa felt a prickle of suspicion. 'What did she want writing materials for?'

'She said it was to make a list of things she's going to need when she moves into your house.'

'Did she say what sort of things?'

'She didn't go into details; oh, yes, she said something about shopping for some new clothes. She seemed quite excited. I'm sure it will be a very good therapy for her to start thinking of practical matters.'

'Therapy my foot,' said Melissa as she put down the phone after the usual polite signing-off remarks. In response to Joe's enquiring glance, she relayed the latter part of the conversation. 'She's up to something, I know she is.'

'Darling, aren't you getting a little paranoid?' he said

gently. 'You mentioned yourself that you've offered to take her shopping. Why should you get suspicious just because she's making a list of things she wants?'

Melissa sighed and combed her hair back from her face with her fingers. 'You're probably right,' she said, a little wearily. 'I just hope Matt comes back soon with positive confirmation that Flavia died of natural causes. That should put everyone's mind at rest, even Mum's. Thanks, love,' she added as Joe put a mug of tea in front of her and sat down. On a sudden impulse she reached across the table, took one of his hands between both her own and gave it a squeeze. 'And thanks for being such a rock,' she said softly.

'No problem,' he said as he returned the pressure.

A few hours later, Bruce telephoned. 'Hi, Mel,' he said. 'I thought you'd like to know right away that I've managed to track down Bernie Arnold.'

'Bruce, that's brilliant! However did you manage it so quickly?'

'Through my theatrical connections,' he replied airily.

'Where is he? Have you spoken to him?'

'He's in a nursing home in Gloucester.'

'But that's great. I'll go and see him and—'

'I'm afraid it's not that simple. The poor old chap is suffering from Alzheimer's and hardly knows what day it is. I spoke to the manager of the home and she says his memory's pretty well non-existent.'

'That's a blow,' sighed Melissa. 'Well, thanks anyway.'

'Ah, that's not all I found out.' From the slightly smug note that crept into Bruce's voice Melissa knew at once that there was better news to come. 'Bernie's got a son who pays his fees and keeps in regular touch with the home. He lives in London, but he visits his father every Thursday.'

'And it's Thursday tomorrow. What a bit of luck!' Melissa's spirits rose again. 'I'll have a word with the manager first thing in the morning. What exactly did you tell her, by the way?'

'Only that an old friend who'd lost touch with Bernie was enquiring after him.'

'Fine. What's the address and phone number?'

Bruce gave her the information and then said casually, 'Did you get any joy out of Matt Waters?'

'Who told you I'd spoken to Matt?' she asked in surprise.

'Oh, these things get around.'

'Through your police connections, I suppose.'

In reply, he merely chuckled and repeated the question. Knowing that through one contact or other he would find out anyway, she told him what he wanted to know.

# 20

'It's very good of you to spare the time to see me, Mr Arnold,' Melissa began.

'No problem. Have a seat.' Max Arnold pointed in the direction of a group of easy chairs in the small book-lined room that the manager of the Granville Nursing Home had put at their disposal. 'Shall I ask them to bring us some coffee?'

'No, thank you. I won't keep you long or your father will be wondering where you are.'

'I wish that was true,' he said with a faint, sad smile. 'Nine times out of ten when I come here, he doesn't even recognise me.'

'That must be very difficult for you.' She realised as she spoke that her words were inadequate, but could think of nothing more helpful to say.

'It isn't easy,' he agreed, with a movement of his hands and shoulders that struck her as not entirely English. His features, too, spoke of foreign, possibly Eastern European origins: high cheekbones, a prominent nose, slightly swarthy skin and dark eyes beneath strongly arched brows. His black hair was heavily streaked with grey but his skin was firm, clear and relatively unlined. Melissa judged him to be about fifty.

If his appearance and mannerisms held a hint of the exotic, his accent was unmistakably native to the Home

Counties. 'Mrs Richards introduced you as Melissa Craig,' he remarked. 'Would you by any chance be Mel Craig, the writer?'

'Well, yes, I am.' She was – as always – gratified at the recognition, but checked herself from asking if he had read any of her books. The question often had the effect of sparking off a flood of fulsome praises followed by embarrassingly detailed analyses of aspects of a plot that she herself had either overlooked or completely forgotten. 'My wife will be very interested to hear that I've met you,' Arnold went on. 'She buys all your books and recommends them to her friends.'

'That's very nice to know.'

'I've never got around to reading them myself – don't have much time for reading except for the City pages – but now I've met you . . .' He sat back in his chair, giving the impression that he would be quite happy for the conversation to continue on these lines.

Melissa, however, had no wish to be sidetracked, much as she normally enjoyed chatting to a fan – or, in this case, a relative of a fan – about her work. She was here to seek information about a possible connection between Esther Arnold and Flavia Selwyn-Tuck. She was about to put the first of her previously prepared questions to him when he too appeared to remember the reason she was here and said, 'I understand you knew my father some years ago?'

'Oh no, I've never met him personally.' Aware of Arnold's questioning gaze she added, 'But I recently met someone who used to know him very well and was wondering how he was.' It sounded lame even as she spoke and it was clear that Arnold thought so too.

'Who is this person?' he asked. The sub-text of the question was quite clearly, *If they were that interested, why couldn't they make their own enquiries?*

'It was the actor, Gawain Hardcastle,' she said. Arnold's brows lifted and she hurried on, 'Actually, we were talking about the theatre. He was helping me with research for my new book. It has a show business background and I was asking him how people who have an idea for a show go about raising the money. He told me about angels; that's what theatre folk call people who put money into a production, isn't it?'

'That's right.' This wasn't the way she had planned the conversation, but paradoxically, by appearing so naïve, she seemed to have aroused his sympathy. His indulgent smile was like a pat on the head.

'Anyway,' she went on, 'I asked him if he knew of any angels I could go and talk to. He mentioned your father.'

'Oh, yes.' Arnold's tone was wistful. 'Papa must have put thousands into various productions. Some of them turned out to be turkeys, but he backed a few winners as well. The theatre's been one of his lifelong passions.' Suddenly animated, he leaned forward and gripped his knees with strong, tapering fingers. 'D'you know, he used to tell me how when he first came to England he used to go to the Penge Empire every week. That's a rep theatre in south London where he used to live,' he explained, seeing Melissa's enquiring glance. 'He said it helped his English no end.'

'He wasn't born in this country, then?'

'No. My grandparents came here from Poland before the war when Papa was still a schoolboy. He'd learned English at school, but his mother and father could hardly speak a word of the language.'

'Well, they obviously prospered,' said Melissa. Arnold

acknowledged the remark with a sideways tilt of the head
and the characteristic movement of hands and shoulders.
'Tell me, how did your father become an angel?'

'Through a business contact who had a share in a West
End production that was on at the time.'

'Would that be a man called Pudgie Cherston?'

His face lit up on hearing the name. 'That's right. Nice
old boy, died about ten years ago.' He gave Melissa a keen
look. 'What did Gawain tell you about him?'

'Not a great deal, except that there were some problems
with a joint venture he and your father were involved in. It
was expected to be a big hit, but it never saw the light of day
because funds ran out when your father pulled out unexpectedly. Do you happen to know why?'

'He had his reasons.' There was an icy edge to Arnold's
voice that told Melissa she was approaching fruitful, but
possibly chancy territory. She would have to tread carefully;
the wrong remark could bring the shutters down with a
bang. She tried a different approach. 'I never knew Pudgie
Cherston, but I do know his widow, Lily.'

His smile returned, once more alight with affection.
'You're a friend of Lil's? How is she? I haven't had news of
her in years.'

'Her heart's a bit rocky, but she's quite a live wire for all
that. Actually, she's a friend of my mother's; they're both
staying in a residential home for a spell to recuperate.'

'I always thought Lil was a good sort. Do give her my
regards next time you see her.'

'I'll certainly do that.' Melissa had a sudden inspiration.
'I imagine your father knew her as well, if he and Pudgie
were so close. Perhaps if you were to mention her name to
him, it might jog his memory?'

Arnold shook his head, his expression dubious. 'I doubt

it,' he said. 'He's gone downhill steadily in the past few months. Speaks in Polish a lot of the time and talks to my mother as if she were still alive.'

'Ah yes, I believe that often happens in cases like his.' At last, Melissa had the opening she had been seeking. 'Gawain mentioned your mother, but he didn't seem to know whether she was still alive. I think he said her name was Esther.'

The look of rage that contorted Arnold's features was almost frightening. His jaws snapped together with an audible click. 'That bitch Esther was not my mother!' he snarled through gritted teeth. 'How dare you mention her name to me!'

'I'm sorry, I didn't mean to offend you,' she said hastily, but he was in no mood to be placated.

'What exactly is your game?' he demanded. 'And don't give me that bullshit about researching a book or looking up an old buddy of that doddering has-been Hardcastle,' he went on before she had a chance to speak. His eyes narrowed; his jaw set like granite. 'She's put you up to this, hasn't she? Sent you to find out how long my father's got to live so she can stake a claim. She's got a bloody nerve, but it's no more than I'd expect from a bloodsucking vampire like her.' He leaped out of his chair and stood in front of Melissa, towering over her, his gaze boring down into her eyes. 'I'll kill that sodding cow with my own hands rather than let her have a cent of Papa's money and you can tell her I said so!'

'Please, Mr Arnold, I assure you—'

'Just get out of here.' Beside himself with rage, he flung out a hand and pointed to the door. 'Do you hear me? OUT!'

Her heart was pounding, but she remained seated. 'Very

well,' she said calmly, 'I'll go if you'll answer one simple question.'

'Which is?'

'Does the name Flavia Selwyn-Tuck mean anything to you?'

The question appeared to take the wind out of his sails. He thought for a moment before saying guardedly, 'Why do you ask?'

'It's the name of one of the residents of the retirement home where my mother and Lily Cherston are staying. Mum overheard Lily talking to someone about her and got the impression that she not only recognised her, but that there had been bad feeling between them some years ago.'

Arnold sat down again. 'What else do you know about this Flavia woman?' he asked.

'Nothing – nothing for certain, that is – except that she died last Sunday.'

'Died?' A sardonic smile flickered across the saturnine features. 'Could it be her?' he muttered to himself.

'The name does mean something to you, then?'

'My stepmother's name was Tuck before my father married her,' he admitted. 'What became of her after she and Papa separated I've no idea. She could have married again, or changed her name for some other reason. She was capable of anything.' Clenched fists and white knuckles spoke of bitter anger still close to the surface. 'What did she die of, by the way?'

'According to the hospital it was food poisoning, but my mother believes the poison was administered deliberately.'

'You mean she was murdered?'

'Mum's convinced of it and to be honest, the more I think about it, the more I'm inclined to think she's right. That's what's worrying me.' Melissa quickly outlined the reason for her fears and the trail of somewhat nebulous clues that had led her to seek him out.

He listened in silence until she had finished. 'You're afraid that someone in the home is responsible and will try and silence your mother if she looks like stumbling on the truth?' he said thoughtfully.

'Exactly.'

'I have to admit everything you've told me suggests that this Flavia woman could well have been my former step-mother. If so, then she was directly responsible for the tragedy.'

'Gawain Hardcastle hinted at a tragedy, but he wouldn't go into details.'

Arnold did not appear to have heard her, but continued speaking in a faraway voice as if he was thinking aloud. 'Everyone connected with *The Merry Month of May* was pretty devastated when Papa pulled out of it. No one blamed him, of course – they knew that cow was behind it. He never could stand up to her. Ironically, she walked out on him six months later when someone else took her fancy. I pleaded with him to divorce her, but he wouldn't. I think he always hoped she'd get tired of the new man and come back to him.'

'This tragedy you were speaking of . . .' Melissa reminded him.

'Oh yes, that was very sad. Most of the cast took it more or less philosophically once they'd got over the initial dis-appointment. Acting's a pretty uncertain profession anyway and sooner or later they either got other parts or found alternative work. But for one poor chap it was one setback too many. A very talented actor called Ryan Roper. You probably don't remember him.'

Melissa shook her head. 'It doesn't ring a bell, I'm afraid.'

'That's hardly surprising. We're going back thirty years or so. He never made the big time, but he had small parts in a few successful productions in the provinces after leaving RADA and looked all set for a promising career. He actually landed a lead in a show that was due to transfer to the West End, but collapsed with peritonitis on the opening night.'

'That must have been a terrible blow. But if he got a part in a new West End show he must have recovered?'

'Oh yes; after a long period of recuperation he landed a leading role in *The Merry Month of May*.'

'And then the show folded before it even opened. That must have been hard to take, on top of everything else.'

'It seems it was just too much for him. He'd staked everything on it: traded in his old banger for a new car, put down a deposit on a flat, fixed the date of his wedding.' Arnold finished the sentence with the now familiar body language.

'So what happened?'

'He went on a bender, took a taxi home – the driver said he was pretty well paralytic and had a job opening his front door – and that was the last time he was seen alive. His fiancée found his body two days later. He'd OD'd on paracetamol.'

'How awful. She must have been devastated.'

'Must have been.'

'You didn't know her, then?'

'Not personally.'

'Do you know what became of her?'

'I've no idea, I'm afraid. I wasn't directly involved in Papa's showbiz games. I just heard about things second-hand.'

'I don't suppose you remember her name?'

He shook his head. 'Sorry, but . . . thinking back, if she

was about the same age as Ryan she might well be living in a retirement home by now.'

Melissa took a moment to digest the significance of this remark. Then she said, 'There are several single women and widows living at Framleigh House. I suppose any one of them could be in the right age group.'

'Well, there you are. See what you can find out about them.' He got to his feet. 'Now, if you'll excuse me, I really should go and see Papa.'

Melissa too stood up. 'Yes, of course,' she said. 'I do appreciate your help, and I'm sorry if I—'

He swept aside her attempt at an apology with a sweep of one hand. 'Forget it.' He went to the door, opened it and stood aside to let her pass. 'There is a slight chance I might be able to help.'

'Yes?'

'Now and again, Papa has a kind of window when he suddenly recalls something that happened long ago. I could try mentioning Ryan Roper's name; it's a long shot, but . . .'

'I'd be so grateful if you would.' Melissa took one of her business cards from her handbag and gave it to him. 'If he should come up with anything, please give me a call.'

He nodded. 'I'll certainly do that, but don't hold your breath.'

'Well, I think we can be pretty sure now that Flavia is the former Esther Arnold,' said Joe. 'Cheers!' he added as he handed her a glass of gin and tonic.

'So it would seem.' Melissa put down the knife she had been using to slice chicken breasts for a stir-fry to take the drink from him. 'Thanks, love, just what I needed.'

He perched on the edge of the kitchen table and sipped his drink. 'So where does it leave us?'

'I'm not sure. It certainly seems to confirm that at least one person had a motive for killing Flavia, but I can't help wondering why they waited all these years.'

'You're thinking of the dead actor's fiancée?'

'She'd seem to be the obvious suspect. Maybe she was the one who wrote the letters. But we know that Esther walked out on Bernie Arnold soon after the tragedy and she – the fiancée, I mean – was probably too grief-stricken to think of plotting a more serious form of revenge until much later, by which time—'

'Esther had disappeared from the scene,' Joe finished as Melissa broke off to take a mouthful of her drink. 'Okay, suppose it happened like this: out of the blue, she bumps into her again in of all places a retirement home. Like Lily, she recognises her despite the change of name and the passage of time. After years of sorrow and bereavement, she suddenly finds herself face to face with the woman who ruined her life.'

Melissa put down her glass, picked up her knife and went back to slicing chicken breasts. 'So we're looking for a single woman.'

'Probably. Who do we have?'

'Several. There's Angela Fuller and two old dears who hardly speak to anyone except each other. There may be others; I haven't met all the residents.'

'So what's your next move going to be?'

'I could ask Bruce to do a bit more research for me. He can use the theatrical connections he's so proud of to try and track down the fiancée.'

'You reckon she's the most likely suspect?'

Melissa shrugged. 'Who knows? She might have married someone else and be a perfectly contented matron living in Tunbridge Wells, but we have to start somewhere.'

'I take it you don't have much hope of Bernie Arnold remembering anything useful?'

Melissa shrugged and reached for the phone. 'Not really, but I'll put Bruce in the picture and see if he can come up with something; and for what it's worth I'll make a note of what I learned at today's meeting and pass it on to Matt Waters.'

Later that evening there was a call from Max Arnold. 'Papa did show signs of remembering when I mentioned Ryan Roper's name,' he said. 'He rambled on for several minutes about wasted talent. Then he got quite upset and lapsed into Polish. I've forgotten most of mine, but I did catch a reference to "poor little Frosty" being heartbroken by the tragedy. It occurs to me he might have been talking about Ryan's girlfriend.'

'You mean she might have been a Miss Frost?'

'It's a long shot, but if there's anyone of that name at Framleigh House . . .'

'I'll find out tomorrow. Thank you so much.'

'Hope it's some use. Tell your mother to mind how she goes.'

He rang off and Melissa relayed the information to Joe. 'I'll check with Mrs Wardle first thing in the morning,' she said excitedly.

He stared thoughtfully into his glass for a moment or two before saying, 'Don't get too carried away, love. We still don't know for certain that Flavia's death wasn't natural, do we?'

'No, but we do know that at least one person had a very strong motive for killing her – and now we've got a possible lead on who it might be.'

# 21

For Sylvia, eager to follow up what she considered to be significant questions arising from her notes, the remainder of Wednesday seemed interminable. She strolled in the grounds, chatted to the gardener and some of the other residents who were out enjoying the afternoon sunshine, returned to the house to attend to her flower arrangements and then, thinking a swim would be enjoyable, went along to the pool, only to find it closed as it was the physiotherapist's day off.

To add to her frustration, there was no sign of Lily taking her customary 'snifter' in the lounge before supper. The dining-room was half empty because, Tracy explained, the theatregoers were staying in town for shopping and a meal after the performance. She also mentioned in response to Sylvia's enquiry that Lily had asked for her supper to be served in her room. 'She must be feeling tired after her afternoon's shopping,' she remarked cheerfully. 'I saw her come home in a taxi about five o'clock, simply laden with carrier bags from some very expensive boutiques,' she added in a confidential whisper.

The following morning Lily turned up at breakfast, but although she sat at the same table as Sylvia and chatted amiably throughout the brief meal, she excused herself the minute she finished eating, saying that she had appointments with her hairdresser and beautician and would be

having lunch in town. Sylvia wandered somewhat discon-
solately into the lounge and picked up a newspaper, her
mind still mulling over the unanswered questions and asking
herself when, if ever, she would have the opportunity to put
them to Lily. She began to feel discouraged; perhaps, after
all, Lissie was right to urge her to drop her enquiries. Then
she told herself to stick to her guns; surely there would be a
chance to tackle Lily later on.

That evening she made a point of being in the lounge in
good time, but once again there was no sign of Lily and this
time it was Angela Fuller who provided the explanation.

'Mrs Cherston's gone out with her stepson,' Angela said
excitedly as she sat down beside Sylvia with her glass of
sherry. 'He arrived to collect her just as I came downstairs
and she introduced me. His name's Desmond; he seems
very nice, I can't think why she speaks so unkindly of him.'

'She thinks it's all an act,' said Sylvia. 'She told me that
what's really behind the care and concern is that he's afraid
she might alter her will and leave all the money she inherited
from his father to someone else.'

Angela's eyes rounded at what she evidently considered
a shocking suggestion. 'Oh, I'm *sure* it isn't that,' she said
earnestly. 'He really seemed most attentive, so polite and
considerate, holding the car door open for her and making
sure she had her seat belt fastened; he struck me as a real
gentleman.'

Sylvia let the eulogy pass without further comment. She
was feeling a little waspish towards Lily as she had by
now convinced herself that the convenient onset of a headache and her subsequent elusiveness had, as on a previous
occasion, been a ploy to avoid any further discussion of the
demise of *The Merry Month of May* and the mysterious
tragedy that had ensued. It occurred to her to ask Seb and

Chas – it was impossible to think of them as other than a duo – for enlightenment, but there was no sign of them either. A casual remark to Gary about their absence brought the information that they had given notice to Terry, the cook, that they had gone to a concert in Cheltenham Town Hall and would be having a late supper in town afterwards. So she was forced to sit and make polite responses to an enthusiastic account of the previous afternoon's performance of *The Mikado*.

'I do so love Gilbert and Sullivan, don't you?' Angela said earnestly. 'Of course, I know they're not *grand* opera, but they're so jolly and tuneful, don't you think?'

'My parents took me to see *The Gondoliers* once,' said Sylvia absently while half of her mind was elsewhere. 'I don't remember much about it, I'm afraid.'

'I believe *The Mikado* is on until Saturday. Perhaps your daughter would take you if it isn't sold out?'

'I could ask her, I suppose.' Sylvia made an effort to appear interested in the suggestion. 'I'll give her a call in the morning.'

At that moment Laurence Dainton entered the lounge. He went straight to the bar and ordered his habitual Scotch. 'He's late, he's usually one of the first down,' Angela commented.

Sylvia noticed her watching him as he carried the drink to his usual corner seat, hoping, no doubt, to catch his eye and try to lure him to join us, she thought, a little scornfully. There was no doubt the silly creature had taken a fancy to him. She longed to question him about Flavia Selwyn-Tuck, as she was quite sure he knew as much as Lily about the dead woman's past. Yet even had the opportunity arisen, she doubted whether she would have had the courage. There was something about the man that filled her with awe. Along with the friendly courtesy and the polished manners were a hint of arrogance and an air of intellectual superiority that made her hesitate to approach him on such a potentially explosive topic. In any case, she could hardly raise it without revealing what she had overheard and lay herself open to a charge of snooping. It was all very frustrating.

Angela took a few sips from her sherry, cleared her throat and said, 'You mentioned yesterday that you'd found out something interesting about . . .' She glanced round to make sure no one was within earshot before saying, 'Mrs Selwyn-Tuck's death.'

'Oh yes, I did, didn't I? It was something the two theatrical gentlemen said to Lily.'

'Do you mean the ones who call themselves Seb and Chas?'

'That's right.' In a low voice, with frequent furtive glances over her shoulder, Sylvia repeated the conversation between Lily and the two elderly actors, and their reference to a mysterious tragedy following the collapse of the production of *The Merry Month of May.* 'Lily pretended not to remember much about it, but I'm sure she wasn't telling the truth.'

'What makes you think that? You said it happened many years ago. Anyway, what has this got to do with Mrs Selwyn-Tuck's death?'

'Supposing she had something to do with Mr Arnold taking his money out of the show? Supposing that somehow led to the tragedy they spoke about? A lot of people must have suffered as a result.' Sylvia leaned forward and lowered her voice still further. 'Supposing one of them is living here, someone who recognised Flavia and murdered her out of revenge? And supposing Lily knows who it was? I said earlier she might be covering up for someone, didn't I?'

Angela, who had sat open-mouthed and apparently mesmerised while Sylvia was developing her hypothesis, gave a determined shake of her head. 'It's an intriguing notion,' she said firmly, 'but – please don't be offended, Sylvia – it sounds more like something out of one of your daughter's novels than real life. I don't believe for a moment that Mrs Selwyn-Tuck was murdered and if I were you I'd just forget all about it. Oh, there's the gong,' she added in evident relief.

It appeared that several people were out for the evening as numbers in the dining-room were considerably reduced. The bridge-playing foursome were at their usual table, as were the elderly spinsters who, it seemed, had staked a permanent claim to a corner table for two. Angela announced her intention of joining a couple of her fellow theatregoers and, in a complete change of attitude, suggested that Sylvia sit with them. 'When you hear how good the show was, I'm sure it will whet your appetite,' she said chirpily and, unable to decline without appearing rude, Sylvia agreed. She noticed that Laurence, again contrary to his usual habit, was one of the last to reach the dining-room. He took the only remaining seat at a table for four already occupied by three other single residents. At no time did he glance in her or Angela's direction; it crossed her mind that Lily might have said something that caused him to want to avoid them.

As usual, coffee was served in the lounge after the meal, but Angela, pleading a touch of indigestion, retired to her room. As soon as she could without causing offence, Sylvia followed suit. She sat for a long time at her window, looking out at the garden and watching the slowly gathering dusk while reflecting on recent events. First, there had been

Lissie's visit yesterday morning. With hindsight, she began to ask herself whether her daughter had been completely open about her conversation with Geraldine Wardle and why she was so adamant that there was nothing unnatural about Flavia's death, so insistent that her mother should refrain from ferreting around. One would have thought that, being a writer of crime novels, she would have shown a professional interest instead of being so discouraging. Once again, she found herself wishing she would agree for the two of them to join forces. It would make the hunt much more fun. Then another thought struck her; she got out her notes and added a further question: *Angela Fuller was very keen to know what I'd found out, but when I told her she poured cold water on my theory and as good as told me to lay off. Why?*

As she locked her notes away there was a tap at the door. When she opened it she was surprised to find Lily standing outside. Evidently she had just come in, as she was clutching an evening bag and wearing a short sequin-trimmed jacket over her calf-length black dress. Her face was flushed and she appeared slightly unsteady on her feet.

'Hi, Sylv,' she said. 'Mind if I come in?' Without waiting for a reply she lurched into the room, sat down heavily on the edge of the bed, threw the bag aside and kicked off her shoes.

'Have you had a nice evening?' Sylvia asked politely.

'Not bad. Des took me to a place near Oxford, down by the river. Very pretty, it was, watching the boats. We had dinner there.' Lily gave one of her characteristic, harsh cackles. 'Dinner, not supper like we have to call it here.'

'Oh well, what's in a name?' Sylvia said, a little uneasily. It was many years since she had encountered anyone the worse for drink. Frank had been a total abstainer and nothing stronger than non-alcoholic cider was allowed in the house while he was alive. During her nursing days, Saturday night drunks had been commonplace in the A and E department of the hospital where she worked, but they were strangers and had to be handled with professional detachment coupled with a certain amount of diplomacy. 'They can easily turn nasty if you say the wrong thing, so whatever you do don't get involved in any arguments,' Sister used to say.

Lily burped, put a hand to her mouth and gave a tipsy giggle. 'Oops, manners! Bit over the odds tonight, I'm afraid. Not s'posed to have more than a couple while I'm on these pills. Me doctor would slap me wrist if he knew. Won't do it again, Doc, promise!' She turned suddenly serious. 'Don't look so shocked, Sylv,' she said earnestly. 'I'm only the teeniest bit tight. Not going to puke or anything like that.'

'I'm not shocked,' Sylvia assured her. 'You took me by surprise, that's all. Would you like a cup of coffee?'

'Love one if it's not too much trouble.'

'No trouble at all, I was just going to have one myself.' It wasn't true and the caffeine would probably keep her awake, but it might help Lily to sober up. She went into the en suite shower room to fill the kettle.

When she returned she found Lily sitting full-length on the bed with her back against the headboard and her feet up. She was playing with the sweet left on the pillow by the maid who turned the beds down during the evening while the residents were at supper, holding it by the end of its shiny gold plastic wrapper and swinging it to and fro with a dreamy expression on her face, almost as if she was trying to hypnotise herself. 'Such a thoughtful touch,' she sighed. 'Reminds me of staying in hotels with Pudgie.' Suddenly her face crumpled. She dropped the sweet into her lap and covered her face with her hands. 'Oh, Pudgie, I do miss you,' she sobbed.

Sylvia plugged in the kettle, switched it on and went over to the bed. She put an arm round Lily's shoulders. 'It's all right, it's all right,' she said soothingly. 'We all feel like this at times.' She took a paper tissue from a box on the bedside cabinet and pushed it into Lily's hand. 'The kettle's coming to the boil; you'll feel better after a nice strong coffee.'

Lily dabbed her eyes and blew her nose. 'Don't you believe it,' she muttered brokenly. 'If you only knew . . .'

'Knew what?'

'I can stand Des pretending to be so concerned for me; it used to rile me at first because I know what his game is, but I've got used to it and he's not a bad sort really, I suppose.' She shifted her position and put her hands behind her head. 'Meeting up with Lol after all these years was a bit of a facer,' she went on, 'but I've got used to that too. It was recognising that bitch that got to me; brought everything back, turned it all sour. And now she's dead and we don't know—' She broke off and clutched Sylvia by the arm. 'I'm scared, Sylv. Suppose they find out?'

In her excitement at the realisation that Lily was about to reveal something of significance, Sylvia was on the point of saying, 'Find out what?' but checked herself just in time. Recalling Sister's lessons in diplomacy and sensing that such a direct question might be counter-productive, she said in a quiet, matter-of-fact voice, 'Well, what if they do?'

'Don't you see? If they find out that I knew her, they'll find out about that awful row I had with her, and the letters I wrote. I never signed them of course, but I'll bet she guessed who they were from and hung on to them in case she ever had a chance to use them against me. It's just the sort of thing she would do, the scheming, poisonous cow.

They show how I hated her because of what happened to Ryan. It nearly broke Pudgie's heart. He felt responsible, you see.' Her voice quavered again and she reached for another tissue. 'He never backed another production after that, couldn't bear the thought. Why did that evil bitch have to come here and bring it all back?' Suddenly Lily's mood changed and her face, by now smudged and blotchy, contorted with venom. 'If someone did kill her then jolly good luck to them, and I hope it was painful,' she said viciously.

'Are you talking about Flavia Selwyn-Tuck?' asked Sylvia cautiously.

'Flavia Selwyn-*fuck*!' Lily spat out. 'Giving herself a fancy name and poncing about as if she were royalty. Esther Arnold, that's who she was. Common as muck and nympho of the year . . . whenever it was. Led poor old Bernie a dog's life. Led any man a dog's life if he wouldn't have her. Not that many of them turned down the chance. Just the one. I often wonder if the poor sod ever realised what he'd done by giving her the elbow.'

By this time, Sylvia was becoming completely bewildered. She wished Lissie were there to help her make sense of it all. After her final outburst, Lily seemed to fall into a kind of reverie; she leaned back again and closed her eyes. Telling herself that she was unlikely to notice if she did not drink coffee herself, Sylvia made one cup, put it on the bedside cabinet and shook her uninvited guest gently by the shoulder.

Lily started, opened her eyes and mumbled, 'Whassamatter?'

'Nothing's the matter. I brought you some coffee.'

'Oh, ta very much.' Lily sat up and swung her legs over the side of the bed. The sweet that had fallen into her lap began sliding towards the floor. She grabbed it and with some difficulty unwrapped it and popped it into her mouth. 'I do love chocky creams, don't you? These are yummy. I wonder where they get them?' She chewed the sweet with little murmurs of enjoyment, swallowed it and reached for her coffee cup. She drank in silence for a few minutes while Sylvia sat down in her chair, reflecting on Lily's extraordinary, if confusing, revelations and trying to think of a strategy for getting her to enlarge on them.

Her thoughts were interrupted by a thud as Lily's half-empty cup fell to the floor. Her immediate reaction was one of irritation at the sight of the brown stain spreading over the rug and at her own inattention. She might have known that Lily's hands were unsteady; she should have kept an eye on her instead of going off into a daydream. But as she reached down to retrieve the cup, she caught sight of her friend's face. A few minutes ago she had been flushed with the effects of wine; now, she had a sickly pallor and there were beads of sweat on her forehead. Her eyes were staring and she was clutching her stomach. 'Oh, my God, I feel terrible, I'm going to puke,' she groaned. 'Where's the loo?'

'This way.' Taking her by the arm, Sylvia propelled her into the toilet, propped her over the washbasin and put a firm hand on her forehead. It was damp and clammy to the touch; mechanically, she reached for Lily's wrist and checked her pulse. She had no need of a watch to recognise its unnatural beat. Leaving her patient gasping and vomiting, she rushed back into the bedroom, picked up the phone, called the emergency services and informed the operator that an ambulance was urgently needed at Framleigh House to deal with a suspected case of acute poisoning.

## 22

The arrival of the ambulance sent shock waves through Framleigh House. It was only a little after ten o'clock and although some of the older residents had already retired, a number were still in the lounge, reading, chatting over a nightcap or – in the case of the bridge-playing quartet – playing their regular evening rubber. Others were in the television room or enjoying a furtive cigarette in the 'smoke hole'. At the shrieking crescendo of the siren all activities were momentarily suspended; the flashing light that sent strobe-like blue darts through gaps in the curtains as the vehicle approached caused heads to turn as if pulled by wires.

After a brief moment of anxious silence and an exchange of disturbed, questioning glances, one member of each little gathering stood up with the muttered comment 'Better see what's going on,' and went out, returning shortly with the news that Mrs Cherston was being taken to hospital for observation after complaining of what Mrs Wardle, who had emerged from her private quarters to take charge of the situation, described as 'feeling a little unwell'. On being pressed, she justified the need for an ambulance by explaining that Mrs Cherston's general health was 'a little delicate and one couldn't be too careful'.

This message had a somewhat mixed reception; some people found it reassuring while others, recalling that Lily had dined out that evening, thought the manager was deliberately playing things down and speculated about a possible new case of food poisoning. One of the bridge players, who happened to have paid a visit to the toilet during a break between games and had observed Lily's return on her way back, commented acidly that she had quite possibly fallen over and knocked herself out, which was, she added, 'hardly surprising considering the state she was in'. This uncharitable remark caused some mildly disapproving head-shaking and the expression of pious hopes that 'it wasn't anything too serious' before everyone returned to their previous occupations. As the sound of the retreating siren faded, Laurence Dainton closed the book he had been reading and quietly left the lounge without wishing the other occupants his customary courteous 'Goodnight', an omission which caused a few eyebrows to be raised.

He made his way to Mrs Wardle's sitting-room and tapped on the door. There was a pause before she opened it a fraction and the expression on her face made it clear that his appearance was far from welcome.

'What is it, Mr Dainton?' she said.

'May I have a word with you?'

'Can't it wait until the morning? I would remind you that these are my private quarters and—'

'I've lived here long enough to be well aware of that,' he interrupted brusquely. 'I'm concerned about Mrs Cherston! What exactly is the matter with her?'

'Really, Mr Dainton, I hardly think that's any business of yours.'

'If you'll allow me to step inside for a moment, I'll try to explain why I think it is.'

Reluctantly, she allowed him to enter, but somewhat

pointedly remained by the door without releasing the handle. 'Well?' she said impatiently.

Laurence was accustomed to being in command, but under Geraldine Wardle's cold eye he felt unexpectedly ill at ease and at the same time acutely embarrassed. The snobbish instincts that had proved so destructive of his marriage made him feel diffident about confiding in her, although he guessed that she had probably deduced from Lily's reaction on their first meeting that they had once been acquainted. As an experienced journalist who made a point of preparing his ground in advance of an interview, and being well aware of Geraldine Wardle's regard for protocol, he should have given himself more time to consider his approach, but anxiety about Lily had, to his own astonishment and consternation, swept all other considerations aside. He cleared his throat. 'It may not be generally known,' he began, 'but Mrs Cherston and I were once' – he hesitated, unable to bring himself to admit the complete truth – 'quite closely acquainted.'

'I had that impression the day she arrived here,' Mrs Wardle remarked.

There was a touch of irony in her voice that irritated him, but he did his best not to let it show. 'Although it's many years since we last met,' he went on, keeping his tone conciliatory, 'I still retain a certain . . . feeling for her, and I am naturally concerned—'

'Mr Dainton, if you are asking me to give you details of Mrs Cherston's condition, I'm afraid I must decline. The proper person to be informed is her next of kin and I have left a message for him, asking him to contact me as soon as possible. That is all I am prepared to tell you.'

'At least let me know where they've taken her.'

'To the general hospital, I imagine.'

'Did anyone go with her?'

'She was in the care of trained paramedics.'

He sensed a hint of defensiveness in her reply, which prompted him to say, 'I mean, anyone from here?'

There was a pause during which Mrs Wardle appeared to be deciding how to answer. It was, he thought afterwards, the need to show that there had been no negligence on the part of Framleigh House and its personnel, rather than a readiness to part with any further information, that drew the reluctant response, 'Her friend Mrs Ross was with her when she was . . . that is, it was she who called the ambulance. She followed in a taxi shortly after it left here.'

Taxis, it appeared, were in great demand that evening and it was some time before Laurence managed to track down a service with a driver free. By the time he reached the hospital almost an hour had elapsed, and there was a further delay in the Accident and Emergency department while a harassed-looking receptionist endeavoured to find a nurse to look after a man with a badly cut eye while trying to placate a distraught mother and her hysterically screaming child. Eventually he was directed along what seemed like half a mile of grey-painted corridors. In his agitation he realised he had forgotten the name of the ward he was seeking and was on the point of intercepting a passing porter who was pushing a patient in a wheelchair when he caught sight of Sylvia Ross. She was sitting beside a desk at which a nurse was immersed in some paperwork; her hands were folded in her lap, her head was bowed and her lips were moving as if she was praying. She was evidently unaware of his approach; when he touched her gently on the shoulder she started and stared up at him in alarm before she recognised him and exclaimed, 'Mr Dainton! What brings you here?'

He found a chair, pulled it alongside hers and sat down. 'How is she?' he asked.

'I don't know. No one's told me anything, but I heard a doctor say something about gastric lavage. That means—'

'Yes, yes, I know what it means. Mrs Wardle said you were with her when she was taken ill. What happened?'

'She suddenly clutched her stomach and began vomiting. She was pale and sweating and her pulse was racing, so I called the ambulance.'

'You checked her pulse? Are you a nurse?'

'I used to be; that is, I never finished my training, but I learned enough to be reasonably certain that it was something more than a bilious attack brought about by overeating and I felt sure she needed to see a doctor urgently. I think Mrs Wardle was a bit annoyed I hadn't consulted her first, but when she saw Lily she agreed I'd done the right thing.'

'Have you any idea what made her ill?'

'Not really, except that she'd been out to dinner with her stepson and I think . . . that is, she admitted she'd had a little too much to drink.'

'I see.'

There was an awkward silence, broken by the arrival of a thick-set, middle-aged man in a dinner jacket who marched up to the desk and said, 'My name's Desmond Cherston and I'm here to see Mrs Lily Cherston, who was admitted a short time ago.'

'Mrs Cherston is undergoing treatment,' said the nurse. 'I'm afraid you can't see her at the moment.'

'Treatment for what?' he demanded. 'How bad is she?'

'I'm afraid I can't answer that. I haven't actually—'

'Then find me someone who can.'

He glared at the woman through dark-framed spectacles and she hastily put down her pen, got to her feet and said,

'I'll see what I can do. Why don't you sit with that lady and gentleman? They're waiting for news of Mrs Cherston as well.'

'Oh, are they?' He swung round and cast an unfriendly eye on Sylvia Ross and Laurence Dainton. 'What's your interest in my stepmother?' he demanded.

'I was with her when she was taken ill,' Sylvia explained. 'There was no member of staff at Framleigh House available to accompany her to the hospital so we—'

'Well, I'm here now, so there's no reason for you to stay.' It was unmistakably a command rather than a polite suggestion.

'Er, no, I suppose not,' said Sylvia meekly. She got to her feet and Dainton somewhat unwillingly followed suit. 'When you see Lily will you give her our best wishes, and please let us know—'

'And you are?' Cherston interrupted.

'I'm her friend Sylvia Ross, and this gentleman is—'

Before she could complete the introduction, Cherston took a step forward and thrust his face towards Dainton. 'I know you, don't I?' he said. 'Seen your ugly mug in the papers; you're that bloody right-wing scribbler Lily was once married to. You've got a nerve, poking your nose in.'

Dainton started as if he had been stung. 'How dare you speak to me like that, you ill-mannered young oaf!' he snapped. 'I've as much right to show concern about Lily's health as you have.' He was a good head taller than Cherston and at the sight of the anger blazing in his greenish-blue eyes the younger man appeared taken aback.

'Please, gentlemen, not so loud.' The voice of the nurse, who had returned unobserved, caused the pair to swing round. 'It's late, the patients are trying to sleep.'

Cherston brushed aside the reproof and demanded

whether she had any further news of his stepmother. On learning that a doctor would be available to speak to him shortly, he sat down in one of the empty chairs, clasped his hands and glowered at the floor. Dainton went over to the nurse and spoke to her in a low voice. She wrote something on a slip of paper and handed it to him. He returned to Sylvia, took her by the arm and said, 'Come along, Mrs Ross. We'll keep in touch by telephone. I've got the number.' Deliberately raising his voice, as if to make sure that Cherston was able to hear, he added, 'Nurse has promised to give your message to Lily as soon as possible.'

They made their way back to the entrance without speaking. Dainton went to a public telephone to call for a taxi and they sat down to wait. After a moment he said, 'I suppose you already knew that Lily and I were once married?'

'Yes, she told me.'

'It didn't work out, but that doesn't mean I don't care what happens to her.'

'Oh, I'm sure it doesn't.'

'Can you tell me any more about what happened?'

'She came to my room after her stepson brought her back after their outing. She was a little . . . well, as I said, she admitted she'd had more to drink than she should have done because of the pills she has to take. She began talking about her late husband, and she cried a little, and then she suddenly started on about Mrs Selwyn-Tuck. She said she knew her many years ago.' At this point, Sylvia hesitated. 'I'm not sure I should be telling you all this. I mean, she was speaking in confidence.'

'It's all right, I know about that. What else did she say?'

'Nothing that made very much sense to me, I'm afraid. She was becoming rather excited and I thought that was bad for her. I offered to make her some coffee and she suddenly calmed down and stretched out on my bed while I was making it. She'd only drunk about half when she started to be violently sick.'

'Do you think it was the mixture of drink and her medication that caused it? Did she take any pills while she was with you?'

'Oh no, she didn't take anything, only the coffee, and she ate a chocolate cream. I think it's more likely to have been something she ate in the restaurant.'

'You're probably right,' Dainton agreed. 'Ah, I think our taxi's arrived.' They rode back to Framleigh House in an anxious silence. On arrival they exchanged expressions of hope that there would be better news in the morning before retiring.

Back in her room, Sylvia undressed, washed and got into bed. She felt physically weary and mentally confused by the events of the evening. She was cross with herself as well; it had been stupid not to take advantage of the opportunity to ask Laurence Dainton what he knew about the tragedy that first Seb and Chas, and now Lily, had so tantalisingly hinted at.

Despite having told Laurence Dainton that, in her opinion, Lily's illness had been caused by something she had eaten in the restaurant that evening, she had a strong suspicion that it was nothing of the kind. Someone had tried to kill Flavia Selwyn-Tuck. Lily thought so too, and now Lily had been poisoned. Could it have been by the same hand? If so, how was it administered? And in any case, why should Lily have been a victim? She had implied that her hatred for Flavia, when she was known as Esther Arnold, had something to do with somebody called Ryan, but who was Ryan and how did he fit into the puzzle? The questions poured into her mind in an endless stream.

Unable to sleep, she got out of bed, took a fresh sheet of paper from the drawer where she kept her notes and wrote down as much as she could remember of Lily's tipsy ranting. First thing tomorrow, she resolved, she would telephone Lissie and talk it over with her. Never mind that Lissie was being so discouraging. After this evening, she would have to take her mother's suspicions more seriously.

When she had finished writing she put away her notes and swallowed one of Doctor Freeman's pills with a glass of water. She got into bed, put out the light and settled down to wait for the drug to do its soothing work. She said a prayer for Lily, who was fighting for her life in a hospital bed. In the darkness, she felt her eyes grow misty at the recollection of her friend, a childlike smile on her face, playing with the chocolate cream before unwrapping it with slightly unruly fingers and popping it into her mouth.

It was as well for her peace of mind that sleep intervened before she pursued the thought any further.

# 23

Sylvia was roused the following morning by the sound of the telephone. She turned over and reached for it in some alarm. The last time she used it had been to summon the ambulance for Lily and in her half-waking state her immediate thought was that she was about to hear bad news. In a voice husky with sleep and unsteady with apprehension she croaked, 'Hello.'

A man's voice said, 'Mrs Ross?'

'Yes, who is that?'

'This is Laurence Dainton here. I thought you'd like to know there's encouraging news from the hospital.'

'Oh, thank God!' Now fully awake, Sylvia sat up. 'What did they say?'

'She's still in intensive care, but she's conscious and her condition is stable. I'll be going to see her presently. Would you like me to give her a message?'

'Oh yes, please! Give her my love and say I hope she'll soon be better.'

'I'll do that with pleasure.' There was a momentary silence before he said, 'I just want to congratulate you on your prompt action. It may well have saved her life.'

'I'm thankful I was with her when it happened. Did they say what it was that made her so ill?'

'They don't know yet. They're carrying out some tests,

but the nurse made it clear that in any case they wouldn't be giving me that sort of information. I'm not one of the family, you see.' A rasping note crept into Dainton's voice. 'That young upstart Cherston is claiming the privilege.'

'Forgive me,' said Sylvia hesitantly, 'but surely Lily's . . . I mean, your sons are—' She broke off, fearful that she had overstepped the mark. There was another, longer pause, which seemed to confirm her fears. 'I meant no offence,' she added hastily.

'None taken,' he replied gruffly. 'You're absolutely right, of course. Thank you.' There was a click as he replaced the receiver.

The time by Sylvia's bedside clock was a little after eight. She felt rested, refreshed and almost overcome by relief and thankfulness. She put on her dressing-gown, went to the window and pushed it open. The air was soft and cool on her face, chasing away the remaining vestiges of sleep. The garden lay washed in golden light and white puffballs of cloud hung motionless in a speedwell-blue sky, promising another fine summer's day. Yesterday there had been talk on the radio of rain at the weekend putting an end to the current spell of fine weather, but for the moment the sun continued to hold sway.

Glancing down, she saw a fledgling blackbird sitting in the grass beside a flowerbed while a parent flew to and fro with food for its gaping beak. Suddenly aware that she too was hungry, she had a hasty wash and got dressed. As she folded her nightdress and put it on the bed, her eye fell on the coffee stain on the rug and it crossed her mind that the cleaning charge would probably be put on her bill. She would mention it to Lissie when she phoned to tell her about what had happened last night. Lissie had been looking after that side of things for her since her operation. Then she reproached herself for bothering with such a trivial matter. There were far more important things to talk about, but for the moment the priority was breakfast.

There was the usual lively buzz of conversation in the dining-room, but as she entered everyone fell silent and turned towards her. Someone said, 'Ah, here's Mrs Ross, perhaps she can tell us a bit more.' Evidently word had got round of her involvement in the drama of the previous evening. Even the two reserved and inseparable ladies looked up from their eggs and bacon as she passed their table and one of them put out a tentative hand to intercept her. 'Do you know how Mrs Cherston is this morning?' she whispered anxiously. 'My sister and I were so distressed at the news.'

Before Sylvia had a chance to reply, Geraldine Wardle entered the room and everyone fell silent. 'I have one or two announcements to make about today's arrangements,' she began, 'but first of all, I'm sure you will all be relieved to know that I have spoken to the hospital this morning and they tell me that Mrs Cherston's condition has much improved. She will, however, be kept in for a few days for observation. If anyone would like to send flowers or messages they can leave them with Sheila, who will arrange for them to be delivered later today.'

'What about visitors?' someone asked. 'What ward is she in?'

Mrs Wardle shook her head. 'I understand she will not be well enough for visitors today,' she said firmly. 'Now, I'd like to draw your attention to one or two things that may be of interest to some of you.' She reeled off a brief catalogue of local events and then withdrew.

The minute she had gone, some half a dozen residents seeking more detailed information approached the table where Sylvia, in response to a gesture from Angela Fuller, had just sat down.

'I really don't know any more than you do,' she protested in reply to the barrage of questions. She had no intention at this stage of revealing her suspicions about the cause of Lily's illness.

'But you were with her when it happened and it was you who called the ambulance.' The speaker was a recent arrival at Framleigh House, a white-haired man with a military bearing who, Sylvia vaguely remembered, was called Major someone. 'What exactly is wrong with the lady?' he demanded. 'Has she had a stroke, or what?'

'Oh no, nothing like that. She was vomiting and complaining of very severe stomach pains.'

'You called an ambulance because she had a bellyache?' The man's tone carried a mixture of scorn and indignation that the emergency services should have been summoned for such a minor complaint.

'In the ordinary way I might not have done,' said Sylvia defensively, 'but I happened to know, because she told me, that she has a heart condition, so I felt it was wise to get medical help immediately.'

There was a muted chorus of 'Quite right too', 'Can't be too careful' and 'Better safe than sorry', although the military gentleman gave as his opinion that too many people made panic demands on the health service and it was no wonder so many seriously ill patients had to wait weeks for treatment.

At this point Angela Fuller remarked with a hint of reproach in her gentle voice that 'Perhaps we shouldn't bother Mrs Ross with too many questions just now. It must have been quite a stressful experience for her,' and to Sylvia's relief everyone nodded in agreement and either drifted back to their own tables or, having finished their breakfast, left the room. 'Don't worry about Major Filton,' Angela whispered to Sylvia. 'I'm sure you did exactly the right thing. Have you any idea what made Mrs Cherston so ill?'

'None at all.' Sylvia lowered her voice and added, 'She did admit to having had rather a lot to drink, though, and she is on some kind of medication.'

'Where did all this happen, by the way?'

'In my room. She dropped in for a chat when she came back from her evening out with her stepson. She seemed a little . . . unsteady, so I gave her some coffee, but I can't believe that had anything to do with it.'

'Hardly.' Angela appeared to be on the verge of asking another question, but at that moment Tracy approached the table, pad in hand.

'Good morning, Mrs Ross,' she said brightly. 'What can I get for you this morning?'

'Some scrambled eggs please, with toast and coffee.'

'Right. I hear Mrs Cherston gave you a bit of a scare last night.'

'It was a little alarming, but thank goodness she's recovering.'

'That's good news.'

'Isn't it amazing how things get around?' Sylvia whispered to Angela as Tracy returned to the kitchen.

'Yes, isn't it? I noticed that even the "secretive sisterhood" went out of their way to ask you what had happened.'

'Do you mean the two ladies who always sit by themselves?' asked Sylvia in surprise. 'What made you call them that?'

'Oh, it wasn't me, it was Major Filton. I heard him talking to Mr Dainton and he said, "I know their sort, keep themselves to themselves but make sure they know everything that's going on." They do sort of creep about, don't they?'

'He doesn't seem to miss much himself, although no one could accuse him of creeping about,' Sylvia observed.

'That's true.' Angela gave one of her tinkling, ladylike giggles. Becoming serious again, she added, 'You must be very relieved to know Mrs Cherston isn't seriously ill. I don't suppose you' – at this point she lowered her voice to a dramatic whisper – 'that is, do you think there's any connection with what happened to Mrs Selwyn-Tuck?'

'It's funny you should say that,' Sylvia said slowly. 'I've been asking myself the same question.'

'You did suggest Mrs Cherston might know something about her past, and that she might be "covering up for someone", I think you said.'

'That's right, I did, and last night . . .' Sylvia experienced a chill in the pit of her stomach as extracts from Lily's confused ramblings began to emerge from her memory. 'She said something about a row with Flavia; at least I assumed that's who she was talking about although she never mentioned her name. And she mentioned having written letters, and being afraid someone might find out.'

Angela's eyes became round with excitement. 'If it's true, and someone did poison them both,' she said breathlessly, 'I wonder how they did it?'

'I've been thinking about that,' said Sylvia guardedly, 'but I don't want to talk about it here.'

'Oh, all right then. You have your breakfast and we can have a chat later.'

'Yes, all right.' Sylvia looked down at the plate that Tracy had just put in front of her and decided that ordering scrambled eggs had not been a good idea. The euphoria that the news of Lily's improvement had brought about began to dissolve, to be replaced by a vague feeling of nausea. 'I don't think I'm very hungry after all,' she muttered, half to herself. She put down her knife and fork and helped herself to coffee.

'Oh dear,' said Angela nervously. 'I do hope you aren't going to be taken ill as well.'

Sylvia paused with her cup halfway to her mouth 'Whatever put that idea into your head?' she asked sharply.

Angela coloured. 'Oh, nothing at all. I mean, shock sometimes has delayed effects and you were quite ill not long ago, weren't you?' Seemingly overcome with embarrassment, she pushed back her chair and stood up. 'I'll leave you in peace. I didn't mean to . . . that is, do try and eat a little something.' She hurried from the room and Sylvia, after swallowing one cup of coffee and pouring out another, abandoned the eggs and nibbled half-heartedly on a slice of buttered toast before hurrying back to her room. She must get in touch with Lissie as soon as possible, but first she must bring her notes up to date.

Melissa was working in her study after an early breakfast when the telephone rang. The second she picked up the receiver and heard her mother say, 'Lissie, are you very busy?' in an urgent whisper, an alarm bell sounded in her brain. 'I need to talk to you,' Sylvia went on without waiting for a reply. 'It's very important.'

'Is something wrong?'

'No; at least, it's all right now, but—'

'Mum, you sound upset. What's happened?'

'I don't want to say anything over the phone.'

Doing her best not to show exasperation at this almost pathological insistence on secrecy, Melissa said quietly, 'Do you want me to come over?'

'Oh yes, please.'

'All right, I'll join you for coffee. No, on second thoughts, why don't I bring you here and we can spend the day together? Joe's just off to London for a couple of days and Iris has gone to an exhibition in Oxford and is spending the night with a friend there, so it will be nice to have your company.'

'I'd like that, but what about the workmen? This is terribly confidential.'

'Mum, they're all working outside,' Melissa pointed out patiently, 'and I haven't noticed any of them with their ears pressed to the windows.'

The joke was evidently lost on Sylvia. 'Oh, that's all right, then,' she said earnestly. 'What time shall I expect you?'

'Shall we say about eleven o'clock?'

'That'll be lovely.'

'What bee has she got in her bonnet now?' asked Joe, who had popped his head round the door in time to catch the last part of the conversation.

'I've no idea. All she would say was that something has happened, but it's all right now.'

'It doesn't sound too horrendous, then. I'm off now, love. I'll let you know when to expect me back.'

They went downstairs together. Joe put his overnight bag in the car, gave Melissa a farewell kiss and drove away. She watched him go with slightly mixed feelings. Despite his apparently limitless patience with her mother's moods and eccentricities, it might not be such a bad thing that he was going to be spared a long-winded account of some happening that her mother's over-heated imagination had persuaded her had sinister implications. At the same time, her own niggling doubts about recent events made her feel that if anything of serious moment had happened she would prefer to have Joe close at hand instead of at the end of a telephone.

When she reached Framleigh House she found her mother waiting for her in reception. Her anxiety increased at the sight of her troubled expression and pale face, which lit up with relief at the sight of her daughter. During the drive home Sylvia parried every question with repeated assurances that she was 'quite all right, really', and would explain everything once they were indoors.

On arrival at Hawthorn Cottage Melissa led the way into the kitchen and made coffee while Sylvia stood at the window watching the builders. She appeared tense and nervous, making little or no response to Melissa's comments on the progress of the work, and when the coffee was ready and Melissa suggested taking it into the sitting room on the grounds that it would be quieter in there, she jumped at the suggestion.

'It's not that I don't trust them, but it's better to be completely private, don't you think?' she said as she sat down in one of the comfortable armchairs and glanced round with an attempt at a smile. 'Besides, this is such a cosy room and I love the view.'

'Yes, so do I. I never get tired of looking at it. Now, drink that and tell me what's bothering you.' Melissa put a cup of coffee and a plate of biscuits on a small table and drew up her own chair alongside. She noticed with concern that although the room was comfortably warm her mother was shivering and when she picked up the cup her hand shook so violently that the coffee slopped into the saucer. Then, to her alarm, Sylvia put down the cup, covered her face with her hands and burst into tears. She hurried to her side and put an arm round her shoulders.

'Mum, whatever is it? What's happened to upset you like this?'

'Oh, Lissie, I'm so frightened,' Sylvia sobbed. 'All these terrible things that keep happening: first Gaston, then Flavia – and now Lily.'

'What about Lily?'

With an effort, Sylvia controlled her sobs and mopped her eyes with a handkerchief. 'She nearly died last night,' she gulped. 'If I hadn't been with her, I'm sure she would have done.'

'What happened? Was it a heart attack? I know you said—'

'No, it wasn't that.'

'What then?'

'She was poisoned, I'm sure of it. And I can't be certain, but I think I know who did it.'

# 24

Apart from the occasional prompt or word of encouragement, Melissa heard her mother's story without interruption, despite the many stumbles and frequent backtracking which made it difficult at times to follow the sequence of events. She was intensely curious to know who her mother suspected of being responsible for Lily's sudden illness but, feeling that it was better not to add to her confusion by too much probing at this stage, added it to the list of questions she had been mentally lining up while listening to the faltering and at times garbled account.

When she had finished Sylvia drew an envelope out of her handbag. 'I've made some notes and I'd like you to read them,' she said hesitantly. 'I'd have given anything to talk them over with you before, but you kept saying there was no reason to be suspicious and I was letting my imagination run away with me and I knew you'd tell me off for being silly.'

'I'm sorry, Mum. I was only thinking of your health. I didn't want you to get over-stressed when you're supposed to be convalescing.'

'Yes, dear, I understand that, but surely after what's happened to Lily you agree I was right to be so concerned?'

'Yes, Mum, I do, and after I've read your notes I'll tell you one or two things I've learned in the past day or two.'

Sylvia, who had leaned back in her chair with closed eyes

as if exhausted by the need to relive the traumatic events of the previous evening, sat upright again with a jerk. 'You've been making some enquiries of your own!' she exclaimed accusingly. 'Why did you do that if you were so sure there was nothing to investigate?'

'Because I was curious, I suppose,' said Melissa. Anxious not to excite her mother by revealing her own doubts and suspicions, she began improvising. 'I gave up writing mysteries some time ago, but I suppose the instinct is still there.'

'You might have told me. We could have worked together.'

'After I'd advised you to stop poking around? That wouldn't have made much sense, would it?'

Sylvia looked wounded. 'You don't think I'm clever enough, do you?' she said reproachfully.

'Oh, Mum, it isn't that, I promise. Now, if you'll bear with me for a few minutes while I read these?' Melissa held up the envelope.

'Yes, dear, of course. I'll have some more coffee if I may.'

'Help yourself.'

Melissa took from the envelope the half-dozen sheets of paper covered with her mother's neat handwriting and began to read. Her mind had been working on two levels during Sylvia's narrative. At the mention of Lily's admission to having crossed swords with Flavia Selwyn-Tuck in the past, followed by the reference to Ryan – presumably the Ryan Roper whom Max Arnold had told her about – plus the revelation that she had written anonymous letters to Flavia, things began clicking into place at bewildering speed. At the same time, the vague fears she had harboured earlier concerning her mother's safety assumed new and more ominous proportions. Might Framleigh House have become a dangerous place for an amateur sleuth who made no secret of what she was about? First a dog and then its owner had died, both as the result of suspected poisoning. Next, a woman who had nursed a corrosive hatred of the human victim over a long period had very nearly met the same fate, while the aforesaid sleuth was not only asking a lot of leading questions, but openly boasting that she was 'making progress'. Melissa's concern was increasing by the minute.

By contrast, Sylvia's appeared to diminish, as if sharing her thoughts and suspicions had reduced them to manageable proportions. She refilled her cup from the cafetière and began tucking into the biscuits. 'I'm afraid I'm being a bit piggy,' she apologised as Melissa, having finished reading the notes, refilled her own coffee cup. 'I didn't have much breakfast, you see. I couldn't face it,' she added with a grimace.

'No problem, help yourself,' Melissa replied absently. She laid the notes aside and sipped her coffee, frowning. There were so many gaps in the story and her mother almost certainly had knowledge – probably without being aware of it – that would help to fill at least some of them, yet she was reluctant to put too many questions at this stage for fear of causing additional stress.

Meanwhile Sylvia, having finished her second cup of coffee and polished off two pieces of shortbread and a chocolate finger, said eagerly, 'Well, what do you think?'

Melissa decided that the line she had taken with Geraldine Wardle over the anonymous letters would probably be the most useful one to fall back on now. 'I have a friend who is a detective,' she said. 'I think the best thing would be to tell him everything you've told me and ask his advice.'

Sylvia clapped her hands in delight. 'There, I said all

along the police should treat Flavia's death as murder!' she
said triumphantly. 'If they had, poor Lily might not have
been attacked.'

'Just hold your horses, Mum. What I have in mind is
simply to tell Matt everything you've told me—'

'And everything you've found out,' Sylvia broke in. 'You
haven't told me yet.'

'No, that's right, I haven't.' Melissa was already regret-
ting her careless admission. 'It's something Mrs Wardle told
me in confidence and I'm not sure on second thoughts that
I ought to tell you.'

'Oh, Lissie, you can trust me. I won't say a word to
anyone.'

'All right. You mentioned that Lily said something about
having written anonymous letters to Flavia.'

'Yes. What of it?'

'It seems that Flavia kept them. They were found in her
room after she died.'

'Well I never!' Sylvia's eyes saucered. 'Did Mrs Wardle
show them to you? What did they say? Where are they now?
Can I see them?' The questions tumbled out with barely a
pause for breath.

'Hang on, Mum, one thing at a time. Yes, she showed
them to me.'

'Did they contain death threats?'

'No, nothing like that. They were abusive rather than
threatening.' Sylvia's face fell; evidently she had been
expecting something more dramatic. 'But they did indicate
that whoever wrote them held a grudge against Flavia,'
Melissa went on, 'so I suggested to Mrs Wardle what I just
said to you about showing them to Detective Sergeant
Waters, and she agreed.'

'And what did he say?'

'I'm afraid you're going to be disappointed by this. Because Flavia's death was caused by food poisoning, he doesn't think there's any reason to start an investigation, but' – Melissa raised a hand as Sylvia was about to protest – 'he's promised to have a word with a senior officer.'

Sylvia gave a contemptuous sniff. 'I hope the senior officer has the sense to take the matter more seriously. No one would listen to me when I said Flavia was poisoned. Perhaps they'll listen now, after what's happened to Lily.'

Melissa decided that this was the moment to refer to her mother's earlier assertion. 'You said something on the phone about her having been poisoned and you thought you knew who did it,' she said. 'Who have you got in mind?'

'Well, isn't it obvious? It must be that stepson of hers.'

Melissa gaped in disbelief. 'What on earth put that idea into your head?'

'We know her money will go to him if anything happens to her. Maybe he's in debt or something and needs it urgently, so he took her out to dinner and somehow managed to—'

'Mum, just stop it, will you? We don't even know yet what it was that made Lily ill, do we? You said yourself that she has to take pills and she'd had too much to drink.'

'She was poisoned, I know she was,' Sylvia said obstinately. 'I was there and I saw what happened. I used to be a nurse, remember?'

'Yes, Mum, and you did brilliantly in getting her into hospital so quickly, but we can't know anything for sure until the pathologist finds out exactly what caused her illness. Now listen,' Melissa went on, forestalling the protest that Sylvia was about to utter, 'I've had an idea. Why don't you spend a few days here with me? I've got a spare room. It'll make a change for you and' – seeing her mother's dubious expression, she cast around for some further inducement – 'if I get any feedback from Matt I'll be able to tell you straight away.'

The ruse worked. 'Oh yes, and we can put our heads together and see if we can think of any other ideas,' Sylvia enthused. Then she hesitated. 'But what about Joe? Where will he sleep when he comes back?'

'Ah, that's a point.' When making her suggestion, Melissa had overlooked the fact that her mother entertained some-what old-fashioned ideas about relationships between engaged couples. Once more, she found herself thinking on her feet.

'There's no problem tonight as he's in London,' she said. 'I'm not sure when he's planning to come back, but perhaps Iris can help out. I'll speak to her tomorrow, when she gets back from Oxford.'

'All right.'

'So that's settled then. Now, would you like to go for a little walk before lunch?'

'That's a lovely idea.'

The weather had lived up to its early promise and the peaceful valley was bathed in sunshine. They climbed the stile and descended the grassy slope to the footpath that followed the course of the swiftly flowing stream, picking their way round clumps of brambles whose pale flowers promised a rich autumn harvest of blackberries. Sylvia was entranced by everything she saw, from the lambs frisking and chasing one another like children in a school play-ground to the springs that gushed out of the earth and tumbled, gurgling and foaming, down the hillside. Listening to her exclamations of pleasure, Melissa found herself reliving her early days at Hawthorn Cottage and her own delight in the novelty of country sights and sounds after so many years as a town dweller. Impulsively, she took her mother's hand.

'Do you think you'll be happy living here, Mum?' she asked.

'Oh, yes!' Sylvia breathed contentedly. 'Everything's so beautiful and the air smells so sweet and the trees are so green and fresh.'

'It isn't always like this, you know. It can be a bit bleak in winter.'

'Then I can stay indoors and read lots of books. Books I can choose for myself,' she added, half to herself, and Melissa, recalling the subterfuges she had resorted to in order to keep up with the books her friends at school were reading without having them confiscated by her father, gave the hand she was holding a squeeze in tacit understanding.

They returned to the cottage and Sylvia pottered happily in the kitchen, helping with preparations for lunch. When they had finished eating she said, 'Lissie, would you mind if I took a nap? I'm feeling quite sleepy; it must be all that lovely fresh air.'

'That's fine. I'll make up your bed and make one or two phone calls, and then we'll go back to Framleigh House and pick up the things you'll need while you're here.'

As soon as Sylvia was comfortably installed in an armchair with her feet on a stool, Melissa hurried upstairs to her study and punched out Matt Waters' mobile number. When he answered she said, 'Matt, it's Melissa. Are you free to talk?'

'Sure. I was going to call you anyway. I checked with the

hospital and you were right, no special tests were carried out on Flavia Selwyn-Tuck. I spoke to my DI and he agreed we should ask for them as a matter of urgency. Meanwhile, the coroner has withdrawn permission to bury the body for the time being. I'll let you know the outcome.'

'Thanks, Matt, but there's something else you should know. You remember those anonymous letters?'

'Of course.'

'I've found out who wrote them.'

'Well done, Miss Marple. Tell me more.'

'It was Lily Cherston, the woman Mum overheard having that conversation in the garden with her ex. It seems she went out to dinner yesterday evening with her stepson, got a bit sloshed, dropped in to see Mum and started on about how she'd had a run-in with the woman who'd died, and how she was scared it might become known if it turned out that someone had topped the old bat; and then she admitted she'd written the anonymous letters.'

Matt whistled. *'Did* she! That's interesting, isn't it? Well, thanks for the lead, Mel. If it turns out there's something dodgy about those tests, I'll make a point of having a word with Lily Cherston.'

'There's one other thing you should know,' said Melissa.

'What's that?'

'Lily was rushed into hospital last night. Mum was with her when she was taken ill and she's convinced that she'd been poisoned. She also thinks her stepson did the foul deed, although I think she's a bit off message there.'

'Hmm.' Matt was silent for a moment. Then he said, 'I imagine in this case the path lab will carry out some routine tests.'

'Sure to. One theory is that Lily had too much booze on top of her medication, but we have to wait for the results.'

'Well, as the saying goes, we'd better watch this space. Cheers, Mel.'

The telephone rang a few moments after Melissa put it down. Bruce was on the line. 'We've struck oil!' he announced. 'I checked on Ryan Roper and his girlfriend. And guess what her name was!'

'I don't know. Amaze me.'

'Jane Iceley.'

'Iceley?' It took a couple of seconds before Melissa made the connection. 'Of course! "Poor little Frosty" – that must have been Ryan's pet name for her. Well done, Bruce. Anything else?'

'Oh yes. This is the best bit. It seems Frosty didn't exactly live up to her nickname; there was a child, a daughter, born six months after Ryan's death.'

'Have you any idea what became of them?'

'Sorry, that's where the trail goes cold.'

'I see. Well, thanks anyway, Bruce.'

'No problem. Anything new your end?'

Melissa hesitated, uncertain for the moment whether she had mentioned the anonymous letters to Bruce. By the time she realised that she had not – having given her word to Geraldine Wardle to keep their existence confidential – he had pounced.

'You're keeping something back,' he accused her.

'Not really.' At least, she thought, there's no harm in telling him about Lily's illness. Aloud, she said, 'I'm not sure if it's relevant.'

'Tell me anyway.'

'Lily Cherston was rushed to hospital last night after developing severe stomach pains. They don't know the cause yet, but Mum's convinced her stepson tried to poison her when he took her out to dinner last night.'

'I see.' There was a pause; evidently Bruce was assessing the significance of this development. 'D'you reckon there's anything in your mum's theory?'

'I don't know what to think. She's insisting he did it to get his hands on her money.'

'Well, rich widows have been murdered before, so I guess it's feasible. How is Mrs Cherston anyway?'

'Recovering, I understand.'

'That's good. Well, keep me posted and I'll let you know if I turn up anything else. *Ciao!*'

While she was making up the bed in the spare room for her mother, sorting out clean towels and placing a few of Joe's clothes strategically in the wardrobe, Melissa considered the new information Bruce had uncovered and tried to assess its relevance, if any, to the situation at Framleigh House. No immediate explanation occurred to her; the only practical step she could think of was to enquire whether any of the residents was called Iceley rather than Frost as she had originally intended. It might, she feared, be a little tricky; she would have to be discreet in order to avoid rousing her mother's suspicions.

That small problem, however, was resolved by Sylvia herself. When Melissa woke her with a cup of tea and reminded her that they had to go back to Framleigh House to pick up her toilet things and a change of clothes, she said anxiously, 'I do hope Mrs Wardle won't be cross. Will you speak to her for me, Lissie?'

'Of course, Mum.'

Sylvia's fears were groundless; apart from pointing out that there could be no reduction in her fee for the duration of her absence, Mrs Wardle raised no objection. In reply to Melissa's enquiry, she shook her head and informed her that there was no resident at Framleigh House by the name of Iceley. As Melissa was about to leave, she said, 'By the way, perhaps you'd kindly tell Mrs Ross that Mrs Cherston will be discharged from hospital tomorrow morning,' adding, in a tone that carried more than a hint of surprise, 'It was Mr Dainton who gave me the news. He has been in constant touch with the hospital ever since she was taken ill and I understand he has undertaken to collect her.'

'That's very kind of him. Mum will be delighted.'

'I'm sure it will be a great relief to us all.'

When Melissa returned to her mother's room she found her chatting to one of the domestic staff, who was apologising for not having serviced the room earlier.

'We're short-handed today,' the girl explained as she gathered up her cleaning materials. 'I've finished now so I'll get out of your way.'

As she disappeared down the corridor wheeling her trolley, Melissa passed on the message about Lily. Sylvia clapped her hands in delight.

'How absolutely wonderful!' she exclaimed. 'I've been hoping all along that she and Laurence would be reconciled.'

'I wouldn't set too much store by it,' Melissa warned.

'But surely it proves he still cares about her?'

'Up to a point, yes, I suppose so.' As she spoke, Melissa stooped to retrieve something she had spotted lying half concealed under the bed. 'Your chambermaid didn't do a very good job of tidying up,' she remarked, holding up the discarded sweet wrapper before dropping it into the waste bin.

'It's from yesterday's chocolate cream,' said Sylvia. 'They put one on the pillow every evening when they turn the beds down.' She gave a sudden giggle. 'Lily ate mine last night while I was making her coffee. She'd been playing with it like a little girl. Oh, I'm so relieved she's going to be all right. I just hope she'll be more careful from now on.'

It was as well, Melissa thought afterwards, that her mother was concentrating on folding clothes and putting them into her suitcase rather than looking in her direction while they were speaking. Had she done so, she would have seen the expression of horror on her daughter's face, and wanted to know why she had retrieved the sweet wrapper from the waste bin and slipped it into the pocket of her dress.

## 25

During the drive from Framleigh House Sylvia chattered excitedly about her hopes for a renewal of the relationship between Lily and her ex-husband. Melissa made only monosyllabic replies and on being chided for her lack of interest gave the excuse that the unusually heavy traffic made it essential to give all her attention to the road. The truth was that she was still trying to come to terms with the awful possibility that the chance discovery of a discarded sweet wrapper had opened. Could it be the case that Lily's sudden illness had nothing to do with a mixture of medication and alcohol and everything to do with the chocolate cream she had absent-mindedly picked up and eaten while sprawled in an alcoholic haze on Sylvia's bed? If the sweet had indeed been poisoned it was plain that the intended victim was not Lily but Sylvia, which led inescapably to the conclusion that Flavia's death was no accident and that the killer was determined to silence the woman who was not only doing her best to prove it, but looked like getting dangerously near the truth.

When they reached Hawthorn Cottage it was almost six o'clock. Melissa led her mother upstairs, showed her where she was to sleep, gave her clean towels and pointed out the bathroom.

'Just sing out if there's anything else you want,' she said, but Sylvia was too busy exclaiming in delight over the outlook along the valley to respond. 'Right then, I'll leave you to unpack. I'm going down to start preparing our dinner.'

Almost reluctantly, Sylvia turned away from the window and opened her suitcase. 'Thank you, dear. I'll just sort my things out and then I'll come down and give you a hand.'

'No rush, take your time.'

The moment Melissa reached the kitchen she snatched up the telephone and punched out Matt Waters' number. She ground her teeth in frustration on receiving a recorded request to leave a message.

'Matt, it's Melissa,' she said. Fear gave a harsh edge to her voice, making it sound strange in her own ears. 'Something's happened and I think my mother could be in danger. Please call me as soon as you can, but be discreet as she's here with me for the weekend and I don't want to alarm her.'

She put down the telephone and began, almost mechanically, to assemble the ingredients for their meal. As she prepared fillets of salmon for the microwave and chopped vegetables for a stir-fry she tried to piece together everything she could recall of their various conversations on the subject of Flavia's death. Sylvia's conviction that it was murder rather than a simple case of food poisoning probably stemmed from her earlier triumphant claim to have solved the death of Gaston. Tests had proved that the dog had ingested what the report described as a 'cardiac stimulator' which, according to a book on poisons that formed part of Melissa's research library, was a known ingredient of the oleander plant. If the tests currently being carried out on samples from Flavia and Lily showed a similar result there could be little doubt that the substance had been administered deliberately to both women, whereas the dog could have picked it up by accident. There was absolutely nothing to suggest that either Flavia or Lily could have done so, although in Lily's case a simple question would be enough to settle the matter once she was well enough to be interviewed.

Meanwhile, nothing could be confirmed one way or the other until the test results became known. Melissa found herself clinging, a little desperately, to the hope that Flavia's death and Lily's illness were due to similar but unrelated causes, but her underlying fears had all along refused to be dismissed and had now, after the business of the chocolate cream, been reinforced to a frightening degree. It was, she felt, rather like having to spend a night in a house reputed to be haunted. Common sense might insist that belief in the supernatural had no place in this scientific age, but common sense could not entirely banish the uneasy premonition that at any moment some ghostly manifestation would appear.

Overhead, she could hear Sylvia moving to and fro, humming to herself as she opened and closed drawers and cupboards, serenely unaware of the turmoil in her daughter's mind. At least, Melissa told herself, by removing her from Framleigh House she had placed her in a safe en-vironment, and she uttered a silent prayer of thankfulness for the inspiration that had led her to make the suggestion. Her next concern was to protect her, if humanly possible, from a different kind of danger: if she were to suspect that she was under serious threat, what effect would that have on her mental condition?

The question was answered almost immediately. The humming suddenly ceased and was followed by a silence lasting several minutes. Absorbed in her own thoughts, Melissa paid no attention until Sylvia came very quietly into the kitchen and stood beside her at the sink where she was scrubbing some of her newly dug potatoes.

'Hi, Mum,' she said, making a determined effort to appear relaxed and cheerful. 'You're going to have a treat this evening: home-grown earlies from your daughter's Cotswold garden. I just managed to lift them before the builders began wrecking my vegetable patch.'

'Lovely,' said Sylvia. Her voice had a flat, toneless quality and she clutched the edge of the sink as if in need of support.

Melissa looked at her in alarm. 'Is something wrong?' she asked. 'You're looking a bit pale – don't you feel well?'

'I'm all right. I mean, I'm not ill, but I've just had a very frightening thought.'

Melissa's heart sank. She hastily dried her hands and steered Sylvia to a chair. 'What is it, Mum?' she said quietly, although she had little doubt that she already knew the answer.

When Matt called back later that evening his first words were, 'Is it all right to talk?'

'No problem,' said Melissa. 'I'm in the study and she's downstairs watching the telly. In any case, she knows already.'

'Knows what?'

'That someone tried to poison her. That is,' she went on hurriedly, 'it looks very much as if whatever nearly killed Lily was meant for Mum.' She gave a brief account of the discovery of the sweet wrapper that Lily had carelessly dropped after consuming the contents. 'It occurred to me straight away what it might mean, but I naturally didn't say anything to Mum because I didn't want to frighten her. As it happened, her first thought when Lily was taken ill was that her stepson was trying to top her in order to inherit her money. And ever since Lily's ex showed up at the hospital full of concern she's been cherishing hopes of a romantic reconciliation. It wasn't until after I left the message for you that all of a sudden something clicked and she realised that she could have been the target of a murder attempt.'

'That must have been a shock for the poor lady. How is she?'

'She was pretty shaken at first, but she bounced back after a glass or two of wine, since when she's hardly stopped telling me that it just goes to prove that she was right all along.'

'I can see where you get your single-mindedness,' said Matt with a wry chuckle. 'You've bent my ear on more than one occasion when you thought I'd missed some vital clue.'

'I have been known to be right,' she pointed out.

'Indeed you have,' he conceded. 'Can I take it your mother will be up to answering a few questions should the need arise?'

'She'll be outraged if you don't question her. She sees herself as a key witness.'

'She may well turn out to be just that. Do you have the sweet wrapper, by the way?'

'Yes, I managed to smuggle it out without Mum noticing. Thought I was being so clever, didn't I?' she added with a rueful laugh. 'I put it in a plastic bag when I got home, but I'm afraid I handled it first. I didn't realise the possible significance until after I'd picked it up and chucked it in the bin.'

'That's a pity. It could be crucial evidence if the test results on Lily and Flavia lead us to believe we have a murder enquiry on our hands.'

'Have you any idea when you'll have the results?'

'They're promised for tomorrow. If they're positive I'll call round for a chat with you and your mother. I can pick up the letters and the wrapper at the same time. How's Mrs Cherston, by the way?'

'Much better. She's being discharged from hospital tomorrow.'

'Do you suppose she'll be well enough to be interviewed?'

'I imagine you'll have to check with her doctor.'

'Okay, Mel, I'll be in touch.'

Melissa put down the telephone and went back to the sitting-room, where her mother was watching a wildlife programme. 'That was Matt on the phone,' she said. 'I've told him everything that happened last night and he says that if the tests prove positive he'll call round some time to pick up the sweet wrapper.' She was about to add 'and the letters' but remembered just in time her promise to Geraldine Wardle of complete confidentiality. It was better for her mother not to know that they were actually in the house, since she would undoubtedly demand to see them.

'Of course they'll prove positive,' said Sylvia impatiently. 'How much longer do we have to wait?'

'He's hoping to get them some time tomorrow. If they show traces of poison he may want to ask you a few questions.'

'There'll be no "if" about it, and it will almost certainly be oleander.' Sylvia pointed the remote control at the screen, plunging a school of dolphins into blackness. 'I've been giving it a lot of thought while you've been on the phone. Preparing the poison would be fairly easy. All it would need is putting pieces of the plant in to soak for a few days and leaving it to evaporate or boiling it up to make a really concentrated solution. The problem would be getting it into the sweet. How do you think that was done?'

Melissa shook her head. 'I've no idea.' Then, noticing her mother's slightly superior smile, she said, 'I have a feeling you've got it all worked out. Smeared it on the outside, perhaps?'

'Too risky, it'd be certain to show. I'd have been sure to notice it because I always look at anything before I put it in my mouth.'

'Yes, but you didn't eat it, Lily did.'

'The killer couldn't have known that was going to happen. In any case, what you've suggested would have meant unwrapping the sweet and then wrapping it up again. That would show as well.'

'All right, Madame Sherlock, tell me how you think it was done.'

'With a hypodermic needle, of course. And who would be likely to have one?'

Melissa thought for a moment. 'A nurse?' she said doubtfully. 'There are actually two at Framleigh House – Geraldine Wardle and her deputy – but they don't give injections to any of the residents, do they?'

Sylvia shook her head impatiently. 'I wasn't thinking of them.'

'Who, then?'

'I think,' said Sylvia, speaking slowly as if for dramatic effect, 'that our murderer is a diabetic who has to inject herself every day.'

'Are there any diabetics at Framleigh House?'

'It's more than likely, don't you think?'

'You could be right,' Melissa admitted. Then a thought

struck her. 'You said "inject *herself*". You reckon it's a woman?'

'I think so. Poison's more of a woman's weapon than a man's, isn't it?'

'So they say. I have to hand it to you, Mum. If you were a bit younger they'd have you in the CID in no time.'

Sylvia beamed. 'Why don't we have a look at that wrapper and see if we can find the hole where the needle went in?' she suggested eagerly.

'Certainly not,' Melissa said firmly. 'That's a job for the experts.'

'But there wouldn't be any harm in our having a look first, would there?'

'Mum, there are such things as fingerprints. It's been handled enough already, but forensics might pick up something useful.'

Sylvia pulled a face. 'Oh, all right,' she said sulkily.

By way of compensation for the disappointment, Melissa said, 'I'm sure Matt Waters will want to question you very closely about anyone at Framleigh House who might have picked up on all the questions you've been asking. Have you given any thought to that?'

'Oh yes.' Sylvia's slightly downcast expression brightened. 'And I think I can give him one or two helpful suggestions.' She gave a smug, slightly mysterious smile.

'Meaning?'

'I'm not saying. I'll wait until I see Mr Waters tomorrow.' And despite Melissa's coaxing, she refused to say another word.

As the forecasters had predicted, Saturday dawned damp and cloudy. When Melissa brought Sylvia an early cup of tea, she found her standing at the open window in her dressing-gown, inhaling deeply and with obvious enjoyment.

'Doesn't the air smell lovely!' she exclaimed. 'So fresh and clean.' She picked up the mug of tea and sipped it appreciatively. 'Thank you, dear. What time shall I come down for breakfast?'

'Whenever you like; there's no rush.'

'We want to be ready when Sergeant Waters gets here.'

'He has to wait for the test results and he won't come unless they're positive.'

'How many times do I have to tell you? They'll be positive all right.'

Knowing that there was no point in arguing, Melissa said, 'If it clears up I thought perhaps you'd like to come to the shop with me to collect the paper.'

'But supposing he calls while we're out?'

'He'll phone beforehand. If he doesn't get a reply he'll leave a message.'

Eventually, Sylvia allowed herself to be persuaded and as the sun was shining when they set off she even agreed to a short walk round the village on condition that Melissa took her mobile phone with her. By the time they returned the builders had arrived and begun work; watching their progress, studying the plans for her new quarters and trying to decide how to arrange her furniture kept Sylvia entertained until lunch, but after the men packed up and disappeared for the weekend she became fidgety, checked the time every few minutes and wondered aloud what was going on. She suggested calling Framleigh House to find out whether Lily had returned and if she could speak to her, but Melissa, fearing that she would say something indiscreet, managed to talk her out of it by saying that DS Waters would not approve.

At about four o'clock they were in the kitchen making tea when the phone rang. Sylvia grabbed it before Melissa could reach it, said an eager 'Hello!' and then handed it over. 'It's Joe for you,' she said. 'I'll let you talk in private.' She went out of the room, making no attempt to conceal her disappointment.

'I get the impression she was expecting someone else,' Joe remarked as Melissa came on the line. 'Is something going on? I was expecting to hear from you about your mother's call yesterday and when I didn't I assumed there was nothing important.'

'I didn't call because I didn't want to worry you.'

'Worry me?' His voice was full of concern. 'Is everything all right? I should have called you last night but I went to a concert with Paul and didn't get back to the flat until late.'

'Things have been a bit hairy,' she admitted. As concisely as she could, she outlined the previous day's events.

'That's appalling!' he exclaimed when she had finished. 'Do you want me to come down? Paul and I were going to play golf, but I can easily—'

'No, there's no need to cancel,' Melissa interposed, knowing how much Joe enjoyed his all too rare opportunities to spend time with his son. 'We're quite all right and Matt's coming round presently. He'll advise us what action we need to take, if any.'

'How has Sylvia taken it? It must have been a terrible shock for her.'

'It was when she first realised, but you'd never think so to see her now. She's been on pins ever since she got up this morning, waiting for Matt to call so that she can tell him her story. We're expecting to hear from him any time.'

'Then I'd better clear the line. I'll call you again later. Take care, love.'

'You too.'

Almost another hour passed before they heard from Matt. When he called, the message was brief and simple. 'It looks like murder and attempted murder,' he said. 'I'd like to come round straight away if that's all right.'

# 26

'Mum, this is an old friend of mine, Detective Sergeant Waters,' said Melissa. 'He thinks you may be able to help him with his enquiries into the two cases of poisoning at Framleigh House.'

'I'll do my best,' Sylvia said in a small, slightly tremulous voice.

'I'm sure you will, Mrs Ross, and it's very good of you to agree to talk to us,' said Matt warmly. 'Your daughter tells me you have suspected all along that Mrs Selwyn-Tuck was murdered, despite her best efforts to persuade you other-wise.' There was a twinkle in his eye as he glanced in Melissa's direction.

'It seems that Mum knew best after all,' she agreed with studied meekness.

'Just so,' he replied. 'We now have evidence that appears to confirm her suspicions.'

'I gathered that from your phone call, but you didn't give me any details.'

'No, and I'm afraid I'm not able to disclose any evidence at this stage.'

'I quite understand.' Thank goodness, Melissa thought, he's taken to heart my warning that Mum hasn't a clue about what I've been up to.

Matt turned back to Sylvia. 'This is Detective Constable

Ruby Stokes,' he went on, indicating the pale, sharp-featured woman clad in a black suit and shiny leather boots who stood beside him. 'She'll make a few notes while we're having our talk. Are you happy with that?'

'Yes. That is, I'd like my daughter to stay with me while you're asking your questions, if that's all right?'

'Of course she can stay. You never know, she may have something useful to add. Shall we sit down?'

Matt's voice and manner positively oozed reassurance, reminding Melissa of warm treacle. It was an aspect of his questioning technique she had not previously encountered and she was curious to see how he would proceed. She was surprised, and a little concerned, that despite her mother's eagerness to be involved in the official enquiry she had long predicted would be necessary, her enthusiasm had visibly waned now that she was faced with the reality of telling her story to not one but two detectives. As they moved towards the table in the little dining-room of Hawthorn Cottage Sylvia cast an uneasy glance at DC Stokes, who, after acknowledging the introduction with a brief, unsmiling nod, took a notebook and several pencils from her shoulder-bag before hooking it over the back of a chair. At Matt's suggestion, Melissa brought a jug of water and four glasses and they all sat down. DC Stokes opened her notebook and waited with a pencil poised over a blank sheet.

'Now, Mrs Ross, if you're ready, let's start with the death of the little dog,' Matt suggested. 'Do you know what he died of?'

'He was poisoned.'

'How do you know?'

'The owner – Mrs Selwyn-Tuck – paid for some tests to be carried out. She thought it had been done deliberately.'

'So I gathered from your daughter, but she tells me she

was able to explain how it might have been an accident.'

'That's right.' Sylvia brightened visibly in response to the note of encouragement in Matt's voice and she continued without further prompting. 'It was always sniffing around in the garden, the way a dog does – before it lifts its leg, you know.' She gave a brief, slightly embarrassed laugh. 'When I told Lissie how the gardener had complained about the leaves of his oleanders going brown because of Gaston's attentions, she guessed at once that he'd been sniffing round the flowers, got pollen on his nose and then licked it off. She knows about poisons, you see.' There was pride in the smile Sylvia directed at her daughter.

'Maybe you didn't know, Ruby, that Mrs Craig writes detective stories,' said Matt, turning to his young colleague.

DC Stokes raised her eyes briefly from her notebook and gave a thin smile. 'That's very interesting, Sarge,' she said in a voice devoid of expression.

'So tell me, what did the dog's owner – Mrs Selwyn-Tuck – say when Melissa told her about her theory?'

'She seemed quite relieved.'

'Relieved?'

'Yes.'

'Have you any idea why she should have been relieved?'

'I think she'd been afraid that someone with a grudge against her had poisoned her dog out of spite.'

'I see.' Matt nodded, his expression thoughtful. 'You appear to have a very good memory, Mrs Ross. Can you possibly recall exactly what she said?'

Sylvia put a hand to her brow and closed her eyes for a second or two. 'She'd been complaining that Mrs Wardle wouldn't allow her to employ a private detective,' she said slowly. 'That's why she asked Lissie to find the person – I think the word she used was "the wretch" who . . . let me

think, yes, I've got it, the wretch who took out their resentment of her by poisoning Gaston.'

'Well done! You're an excellent witness, Mrs Ross.' Matt
turned to DC Stokes. 'Have you got all that, Ruby?'

'Yes, Sarge.'

He turned back to Sylvia. 'So Melissa told Mrs Selwyn-
Tuck how Gaston could have been poisoned by accident
and she seemed quite relieved?'

'Yes, that's right.'

'Good. Now, let's move on to the night this lady – the
dog's owner, I mean – was taken ill. Just take your time and
tell me everything you can remember.'

Melissa listened and watched with increasing admiration,
touched with a hint of amusement, as Matt's subtle blend of
flattery and guile overcame her mother's initial nervousness
until she was telling her story with increasing assurance and
surprising accuracy. When she came to describe the events
of the evening when Lily was taken ill, she positively glowed
under Matt's praise for the promptness of her actions.

Having heard it all before, Melissa found her own concentration interrupted once or twice as she made a mental
note of some point Sylvia had overlooked, but she was
brought back with a jolt when Matt asked point-blank if
there was anyone she particularly suspected of poisoning
Flavia. 'It would appear,' he said, 'that because of the
apparent attempt on your life, the killer believes you are on
his – or her – track.'

Sylvia hesitated and her newly regained confidence
appeared to falter at the reminder of her own recent brush
with death. 'Maybe I shouldn't say anything without being
sure,' she said. 'I wouldn't want you to arrest the wrong
person because of something I've said.'

'I assure you that we don't arrest people without evidence,' said Matt gravely, while Melissa detected a fleeting smirk on the impassive countenance of DC Stokes. 'Just the same,' Matt continued, 'it's very useful to know the opinions of people who have been as observant as yourself.'

'Oh well, in that case . . .' Sylvia cast an anxious glance at Melissa, who gave an encouraging nod. 'At first I thought it might be Lily and Laurence plotting it together, but then I said to myself, if Lily did it and was afraid I suspected her, she'd hardly come and tell me all those things about the letters and so on, so it must be someone else. That makes sense, doesn't it?'

'Certainly,' Matt agreed. 'So, having eliminated those two from your enquiries, who do you actually have in mind?'

'Can't you guess?'

'I'd rather you gave me your opinion,' Matt said patiently.

'Well, it's obvious, isn't it? The most likely suspect is the person I invited to share in my investigation, the one who did her best to talk me out of it.'

'I can't believe you mean your own daughter,' said Matt without a trace of a smile.

Sylvia gave a little squeal of laughter. 'Oh, Sergeant Waters, you are a goose!' she exclaimed. 'No, of course not. I'm talking about Angela Fuller.'

DC Stokes continued to scribble, her face inscrutable. If Matt was taken by surprise, he gave no indication. 'You suggested earlier that the killer might be a diabetic who self-injects,' he said. 'Does that apply to Ms Fuller?'

'Not that I know of, but it's not something she'd be likely to go round telling everyone, is it?' said Sylvia. 'Even if she isn't, there's probably at least one in Framleigh House so she could have stolen a needle from them. Or she might get one from a pharmacy. Perhaps you can buy them over the counter.' She was beginning to look uncomfortable again; plainly she had not developed her theory this far.

'Well, that's something we can look into,' said Matt. With a nod at his colleague he stood up and she followed suit after closing her book and stowing it, with her pencils, in her capacious shoulder-bag. 'Thank you, Mrs Ross, you've been a great help,' he said gallantly. He turned to Melissa. 'If you could just let me have the sweet wrapper and the letters?'

'Yes, of course, they're all in here.' She took an envelope from a sideboard drawer and handed it to him, aware as she did so that her mother's eyes were on her, their expression accusing. She would have some explaining to do once the two officers had gone.

'Thanks,' he said as he took the envelope.

Sylvia began loading the water jug and glasses on to a tray. Sensing that Matt wanted a private word with her, Melissa said, 'Mum, while you're in the kitchen, would you mind doing some spuds for our dinner while I see the officers out?'

'Oh, all right.' There was no mistaking the hint of resentment in her mother's tone.

At the front door, while DC Stokes was unlocking the car, Matt turned to Melissa and said in a low voice, 'What do you think about her suspect?'

'She could be right, I suppose, but she doesn't seem to know anything about the woman's background so I've no idea whether there's any connection with show business. It's possible she knew Ryan Roper. She might even be Frosty, which would give her a very strong motive for going after Flavia.'

'Frosty?'

'I've found out a bit more since we last spoke, but I haven't said anything to Mum. I've made some notes – they're in that envelope.'

'Right. I'll have a word with the two actors as well. On the face of it they don't seem very likely suspects, but as they were involved in the show that never was they should be able to fill in a few details. Thanks, Ruby,' he added as DC Stokes opened the passenger door of the car and he got in. As she started the engine, he wound down the window and said, 'I'll speak to Mrs Cherston about the letters as soon as she feels well enough. What about the other two old dears?'

'You mean the so-called "secretive sisterhood"? I don't know anything about them. They're about the right age, I suppose.'

'We'd better check on them as well.'

'You'll keep me posted, won't you?'

'Sure.'

Melissa watched them drive away and then went back indoors. Her mother was in the kitchen, polishing glasses with a tea towel.

'You never told me you had Lily's letters,' she said reproachfully. 'Don't you trust me?'

'Of course I trust you, Mum. It's just that Mrs Wardle showed them to me in the strictest confidence. She's very protective of the good name of Framleigh House and—'

'Yes, I can understand that,' Sylvia interrupted impatiently. 'I just thought . . . I mean, I hoped you and I could put our heads together to solve the mystery, but you kept saying there wasn't a mystery, even after you knew about the letters.'

'I know that's what I told you, but I was never a hundred per cent sure and I was concerned about your safety.' Melissa gently took the tea towel from her mother's hands and put an arm round her shoulders. 'As it's turned out, I was right to be concerned, wasn't I?'

'Yes, dear, I suppose so. But we can share our ideas now, can't we?'

'I think we'd better leave everything to the police from now on,' Melissa said firmly. 'Now, let's get on with preparing our dinner. Tomorrow's Sunday – shall we invite Iris to lunch? It will have to be vegetarian, of course.'

'Yes, that would be lovely. I really like Iris.'

'That was absolutely delicious,' said Sylvia as she laid down her knife and fork after her second helping of vegetable moussaka. 'My late husband – Lissie's father, of course – was very fond of meat so I'd never eaten vegetarian food before meeting you, Iris. I'm afraid I'd always thought it must be very boring.'

'Mel used to think so too,' said Iris. There was a mischievous twinkle in her sharp grey eyes as she added, 'First time I invited her to a meal and told her it would be veggie, her face nearly hit the floor. With luck you and I between us can wean her off meat altogether.'

'We could give it a try, couldn't we, Lissie?' said Sylvia. 'You read so much about the awful things that can happen to you if you eat meat.'

'I'm not sure Joe would be too happy about it,' said Melissa as she gathered up the empty plates and prepared to serve the dessert.

'Give him time,' said Iris. 'Jack was a carnivore till I married him and taught him the error of his ways.'

'If the truth be told, it was a choice between giving up meat and giving up Iris,' Melissa informed her mother in an exaggerated stage whisper. 'He was so besotted, it was no contest.'

'Not true, I told him he could eat meat if he did his own cooking where I couldn't smell it,' Iris declared. 'Soon changed his tune,' she added smugly.

'Do you serve vegetarian food at your arts centre in France?' asked Sylvia.

'What else? Won't have meat near the place. Neighbours think we're barmy.'

'Oh well, they're foreign, aren't they?' said Sylvia without the ghost of a smile.

After lunch, Melissa proposed a walk, but Sylvia declined. Instead, she settled in an armchair in the sitting-room and within minutes was fast asleep. Melissa and Iris retreated to the kitchen, brewed coffee and settled down for a gossip. They chuckled over Melissa's description of her encounter with Gawain Hardcastle and Iris entertained her friend with pithy descriptions of some of the eccentrics who attended the Hammonds' art courses.

'Heard when Joe's coming down again?' Iris asked during a lull in the conversation.

'He phoned last night and he's talking about being here some time tomorrow,' said Melissa. 'It could be a bit embarrassing. Mum thinks she's sleeping in his room.'

'Doesn't know you're co-habiting, eh?' Iris cackled. 'Old-fashioned ideas and all that?'

'Exactly.'

'No problem. She can have my spare room.'

'Iris, you're a pal.'

'Of course,' Iris added with a wicked twinkle, 'Joe could have my spare room if you think that's a better arrangement.'

'I'll stick with your first offer, thank you very much,' Melissa retorted cheerfully. 'I think,' she added, growing more serious, 'Mum had better stay until they catch the killer, if that's all right with you. I wouldn't have a moment's peace if she went back to Framleigh House.'

# 27

After breakfast on Monday, Lily went into the lounge, collected her copy of the *Daily Mail* and settled in an armchair, but instead of reading the paper she left it lying idly in her lap. She felt restless, partly because she missed having Sylvia to talk to. She had been told that had it not been for Sylvia's prompt action she might not have survived whatever had caused the violent stomach upset that had landed her in hospital, but when she got back to Framleigh House after her discharge she was told that Sylvia had gone to stay with her daughter and no one seemed to know when she would be coming back. Lol – no, she mustn't keep thinking of him by that name, knowing his dislike of it – *Laurence* had been surprisingly kind and supportive after her illness, but she still didn't feel entirely at ease with him and in any case it wasn't the same as having another woman to chat with.

'Sod it!' she muttered to herself as a wave of self-pity, brought on partly by weakness, caused her eyes to fill. She dabbed them with her handkerchief, reflecting wryly that it was a good job she'd been skimpy with the make-up this morning or there'd be mascara smudged all over her face. She'd paid less attention than usual to her appearance since her illness; she must pull herself together, not let herself go.

'Lily, what's the matter? Aren't you feeling well?'

She looked up, startled, to find Laurence standing beside

her chair. There was a look of concern on his face, an altogether new look she had noticed several times since Saturday morning when, to her astonishment, he turned up at the hospital to fetch her. He'd even had the forethought to get one of the staff at Framleigh House to look out some more suitable clothes than the ones she'd been wearing the night she'd been taken ill.

He drew up a chair next to hers and sat down. 'What's the matter?' he repeated.

'Just feeling sorry for meself, I suppose.' She sniffed, put away the handkerchief and patted ineffectively at her hair. 'I'll have to do something about me face – I must look a fright.'

'If you want my opinion,' he said gravely, 'I think you look better with less make-up.'

'No kidding?' She gaped at him in astonishment, not only at his words, but also because he had actually noticed what she looked like.

'No kidding. Now, tell me how you're feeling in yourself.'

'Oh, all right, I suppose. A bit wobbly on me pins and I've been told to be careful what I eat for the next few days, but otherwise I'm okay. Nice of you to ask.'

'I've just had a word with Geraldine Wardle,' he said. 'Or rather, she had a word with me.'

'Oh yes? What about?'

'About you.'

'What about me?' Panic sent a shiver down her spine. 'Is there something wrong with me that no one's told me about?'

'No, nothing like that. In fact, you've made a remarkable recovery.'

'What then?'

Laurence leaned forward and lowered his voice. 'It's about something that was found in Flavia Selwyn-Tuck's room after she died. It appears that the police are enquiring into the cause of her death and—'

The shiver congealed and became a chill that wrapped itself round her like an icy garment. What she had feared had come to pass after all. 'Those bloody letters,' she whispered. 'I should have known the bitch would hang on to them.'

'You mean Flavia? You wrote to her?' Lily nodded. 'You never told me that.' There was no anger in his tone, only surprise and a hint of reproach.

'What was the point? We agreed we'd keep quiet in the hope that it would turn out she'd died of natural causes. We thought it was all settled.'

'What made you do it?'

Lily shrugged. 'I wanted to put the fear of God into her, that's all. I was so furious with her when she scuppered *The Merry Month of May* and put all those young hopefuls out of work. And when young Ryan topped himself, I just saw red.'

'Well, it appears she did keep your letters and I'm afraid questions are going to be asked. The point is, do you feel well enough yet to answer them?'

The icy feeling gave way to a sense of weary resignation. 'Why not? Might as well get it over with. Will you stay with me, Lol?'

In her agitation, she had forgotten his dislike of the name, but he did not even wince. 'Of course I will,' he said gently.

'I know I wrote a load of rubbish about wanting to kill her, but I swear I didn't,' she said with sudden urgency. 'God knows, I'd cheerfully have throttled her at the time, but I truly didn't kill her. Lol . . . I mean, Laurence, you must believe me!'

'I do believe you,' he said quietly. 'I'll go and tell Mrs Wardle.'

The interview, when it took place later that morning, was brief. 'Yes,' Lily admitted, after answering DS Waters' questions about the circumstances surrounding the collapse of *The Merry Month of May,* 'I did write a few nasty letters to Esther. After what she did, I probably wasn't the only one – but these aren't the ones I wrote.'

'Are you absolutely certain?' Waters gave her a keen look, but she met his gaze without flinching.

'Absolutely. I've never seen these letters before. If you don't believe me, I'm quite willing to take a handwriting test,' she added defiantly.

The detective showed no reaction as he returned the letters to their envelope. 'Well, Mrs Cherston, that's all for the time being. Thank you for your co-operation,' he said politely, and the interview was at an end.

Melissa was in the kitchen of Hawthorn Cottage preparing lunch when Matt telephoned.

'I thought you'd be interested to know that according to Mrs Cherston the letters found in Mrs Selwyn-Tuck's room are not the ones she wrote all those years ago,' he informed her.

'Really?' The possibility had not occurred to Melissa and it took her a moment to digest its significance. 'That widens the field, doesn't it? If you believe her, that is.'

'I'm inclined to. For one thing, according to forensics the paper they were written on was made much more recently than the date she admits to having written to Esther Arnold, and secondly, she volunteered to take a handwriting test.'

'That sounds pretty conclusive. In any case, I don't know about you, but neither Mum nor I seriously thought Lily killed Flavia.'

'Neither did I, so in a way it's been helpful. It seems likely now that the killer wrote the letters. For what it's worth I've sent them for the usual tests, although I'm not very hopeful. By all accounts they've been handled by several people. One thing is reasonably certain, though: your mother was probably right about the way the poison was introduced into the chocolate cream. Forensics found a tiny hole in the wrapper that could have been made by a hypodermic needle.'

'She'll be chuffed to know she's been right about something. She really fancies herself as a detective, bless her heart, but some of her reasoning is a bit suspect.'

'She won't be so chuffed to learn that there are no diabetics at Framleigh House – at least, none who self-inject. The manager assured me that they insist on knowing the medical history of every resident.'

'That's a blow. So where does that leave you?'

'Forensics are carrying out more tests in the hope of finding identifiable traces of the poison, but that will take a little more time. Meanwhile, I strongly advise you not to allow your mother to return to Framleigh House for the time being.'

'That's all taken care of.'

'Good. Thank her once again for her help.'

'Will do.'

Sylvia expressed satisfaction at having been proved right on one count, accepted the setbacks philosophically and greeted with a mixture of pleasure and concern the news that her stay in Upper Benbury was to be extended.

'It's very kind of Iris,' she said doubtfully when told of the arrangements, 'but didn't you say she was going back to France soon? I'm not sure I'll be happy sleeping in her cottage on my own. Couldn't I share your room? You've got a nice big bed.'

'Ah, well . . .' Not for the first time, Melissa found herself thinking on her feet. 'She has business to attend to that'll keep her here for a few more days. Let's hope Matt can clear up the case quickly.'

'I hope so too. I'm sorry to be such a nuisance.'

'Mum, you're not a nuisance. We're concerned for your safety, aren't we, Joe?' she added as, lured by the sounds of food preparation, he entered the kitchen.

'Of course we are,' he said warmly, 'and I promise you won't have to sleep in Iris's cottage on your own, Sylvia.' Having been well briefed by Melissa, he added, 'I have to go back to London in a day or two to attend to some business.'

'Oh, that's all right then,' said Sylvia. 'I'll need some more clothes, though. I only brought enough for a couple of nights.'

'That's no problem. Make a list of what you want and I'll fetch them for you after lunch and explain the situation to Mrs Wardle at the same time.'

'Why can't I come with you?'

'Mum,' Melissa said gently, 'I'm not trying to frighten you, but someone at Framleigh House tried to kill you. We don't want to give them another chance, do we?'

Sylvia put a hand to her mouth. 'Oh my goodness!' she gasped. 'I was forgetting that.' She looked round in a sudden panic, as if half expecting an avenging Fury to spring out of thin air. 'Suppose they come here while you're out?'

'Don't worry, they can't possibly know where you are. In any case, Joe's here to look after you.'

Everything about Framleigh House appeared almost defiantly normal and peaceful as it basked in the warmth of the afternoon sun. The gardener looked up from his task of hoeing weeds from the gravelled drive and gave

Melissa a cheerful wave as she drove slowly past and turned into the car park. The driver of a delivery van from a nearby off-licence carolled a few lines from 'Summertime' as he unloaded cases of wine and cartons of beer and soft drinks. The time for afternoon tea was approaching and several residents who had evidently been strolling in the gardens were converging on the front door on their way to the lounge. One or two of them, recognising Melissa, nodded and passed the time of day as she locked her car and headed in the same direction. Unfazed by the human presence, a small contingent of jackdaws marched about the lawns with a proprietorial swagger, pecking busily at the grass.

Inside the house, the customary atmosphere of calm orderliness prevailed. The air smelled of flowers and wax polish; a cleaner in an immaculate blue overall was dusting the Impressionist reproductions hanging in the entrance hall. As Melissa entered, Tracy was making her way to the payphone just inside the front door. She smiled and said, 'Good afternoon,' as she passed.

Sheila Barron was sorting papers at her desk. She greeted Melissa with her usual friendly smile before saying, 'Mrs Wardle would like a word with you before you leave, Mrs Craig, but she's got Mr Cherston with her at the moment.'

'And we know what that means,' said Melissa with a sympathetic grin.

'Don't we just!' Sheila grimaced and rolled her eyes towards the ceiling. 'Perhaps you'd like to go to Mrs Ross's room first and collect the things she wants.'

'Yes, I'll do that.'

As Melissa waited for the lift she could hear Tracy enquiring over the telephone about the non-delivery of a parcel. 'It was promised for last Friday and it still hasn't come,' she complained, 'and if it hasn't arrived within twenty-four hours you can cancel the order.' Not an uncommon problem these days, Melissa thought idly as she stepped into the lift. As the doors slid to behind her, she heard Tracy say, 'No, it's R-O-P-E-R. That's P for Peter, not . . . yes, that's right.' Moments later, as she turned the key in the door of her mother's room, Tracy's last few words flashed into her head. *'It's R-O-P-E-R. That's P for Peter, not . . .'* Tracy's surname was *Roper.*

What had Bruce Ingram said? Ryan Roper's lover, whose name was Iceley and to whom he had given the pet name of Frosty, had borne a child, *a daughter,* after his death. Ryan and Frosty had built a dream future together, a dream that had crumbled when he lost the lead in the ill-fated production of *The Merry Month of May* and ended altogether with Ryan's suicide. What had happened to mother and baby after his death? Did they know the part Esther Arnold had played in the tragedy? Had the daughter grown up nursing a corrosive hatred for the woman who had destroyed her mother's dream of happiness? Had a desire for revenge driven the pair of them to seek Esther out, somehow keep track of her even after the metamorphosis into Flavia Selwyn-Tuck and eventually run her to earth at Framleigh House?

The questions chased one another through Melissa's brain in a bewildering stream. From what she knew, it was probable that the child – assuming it had survived – would be about Tracy's age. Her first impulse was to speak to her as soon as she had finished packing Sylvia's things and try by diplomatic probing to establish whether she was indeed the daughter of the actor Ryan Roper, but on second thoughts she decided that the proper course was to contact

Matt Waters as soon as possible with this potential new lead.

Mechanically, she set about assembling the items on the list her mother had given her. She had just made her final check and was putting them in the suitcase she had brought with her when there was a tap at the door. She opened it and found herself face to face with Tracy. Taken aback, all she could think of to say was 'Oh, hello,' and then, when there was no immediate reply, 'Did you want something?'

It was, she realised later, the first time she had given Tracy more than a cursory glance while thanking her for small services such as serving tea or coffee as she sat with her mother in the lounge or conservatory. Had she been asked to give a description she would have been hard put to recall more details than neatly cut blond hair, a fresh complexion dusted with freckles, a slim figure of average height in a spotlessly clean overall and a quiet, courteous manner. Now, with barely a couple of feet separating them, she was struck by what she later described as 'a haunted look' in the woman's eyes.

Those eyes, of a pale bluish green, had dark smudges beneath them, suggesting a recent lack of sleep. They slid past Melissa's shoulder and focused on the half-filled suit-case lying on the bed. 'I was just wondering . . . is Mrs Ross leaving Framleigh House for good?' Tracy's voice wavered a little – with anxiety, perhaps, lest her intended victim was moving beyond her reach?

'No, just for a few days,' Melissa replied briskly. 'She's been very upset by Mrs Cherston's illness.'

'Yes, I know. I was so sorry about that.' This time, the tone sounded almost apologetic.

Was this due to a guilty conscience at having almost killed off the wrong person? Melissa wondered. Forgetting in the excitement of the moment her resolve to keep silent until she had spoken to Matt, she found herself saying casually, 'I heard you say on the phone that your name's Roper.'

'That's right. What of it?' This time the tone was guarded, almost defensive.

'I just wondered . . . it's a fairly unusual name,' Melissa began, aware as she spoke that it was nothing of the kind; she had noticed at least half a dozen when, in what she realised at the time was a pointless exercise, she had checked in the local telephone directory. 'I seem to remember an actor called Ryan Roper,' she went on.

Without warning, Tracy grabbed her by the wrist, pushed her back into the room and kicked the door to behind her. 'What do you know about Ryan Roper?' she said in a harsh whisper.

'I once saw him in a play, a long time ago,' said Melissa, making a supreme effort to keep her voice calm and steady. 'Do you mind letting go of my wrist, you're hurting me.' She was quaking inwardly; the hand encircling her wrist was like a band of steel that did not relax in response to her request and she realised that should it come to a struggle the younger woman almost certainly had the advantage. At least, she thought a little desperately, there was nothing immediately to hand that could serve as a weapon. Not that anyone in their right mind would in the circumstances suppose that they could commit an unpremeditated murder and get away with it, but from the wild look in Tracy Roper's eyes it was clear, at this crucial moment, that she was far from being in her right mind.

'What else do you know about him?' the woman demanded.

'Not a great deal.' Melissa's powers of invention, stirred into action by an increasing sense of danger, sprang into action. 'I rather fell for him at the time,' she said with an attempt at a smile. 'I hoped to see him in other plays, but I never—'

The grip on her wrist tightened. 'You're lying!' Tracy hissed. 'You've been checking up on me, you and your nosey interfering mother!' Without warning, her free hand shot out and closed round Melissa's throat, forcing her head against the wall. 'What else do you know?' she demanded.

'Nothing, honestly,' Melissa croaked, barely able to get the words out for lack of air. 'Please, let me go,' she begged, but the pressure on her windpipe did not slacken. She tugged frantically at the restricting hand, but the woman's strength was phenomenal and slowly, remorselessly, it increased. Lights flashed before her eyes and she heard a rasping sound that she realised only later was caused by her own efforts to draw lifesaving oxygen into her tortured lungs. In a final despairing attempt to free herself before losing consciousness, she put one foot against the wall and, using it as a lever, managed to thrust her upper body forward. The top of her head caught Tracy squarely in the face and she staggered backwards, her grip momentarily loosened. With a supreme effort, Melissa freed her pinioned wrist and with both hands prised the constricting fingers from her throat. Using all the strength she could muster she pushed her attacker away from her; there was a thin, high-pitched scream as Tracy, clawing frantically at the air, lost her balance and landed on her back on the floor, striking her head on the corner of the wardrobe as she fell. Without waiting to find out whether she had sustained any injury, Melissa fled from the room, raced downstairs and burst into the office just as Desmond Cherston was leaving.

'Mrs Wardle, please come to Room 28 at once!' she gasped, ignoring Cherston's indignant 'What the hell . . . ?' and the manager's expression of outrage at being so

unceremoniously interrupted. 'At once, please!' she repeated as both Mrs Wardle and Cherston appeared to
hesitate. 'It's an emergency – and it might be a good idea if
Mr Cherston came too in case there's further trouble.'

The word 'trouble' spurred Geraldine Wardle into
action; she all but ran from the room and without waiting
for the lift sped up the stairs and along the corridor with
Melissa and Cherston at her heels. They found Tracy sitting
on the floor with her back against the wardrobe, blood
running from her nose, her mouth hanging loosely open and
slow tears trickling down her cheeks from eyes that stared
vacantly at the opposite wall.

# 28

'Did your mum twig that she nearly got you killed?' said Iris.

'Thank heavens, no!' said Melissa fervently. 'I managed to play down the attack on me when telling her about Tracy's confession and she was so shattered when she found out what had turned "that nice girl" into a killer that she even forgot to tick me off for not taking her into my confidence earlier. This chap' – she cast an affectionate glance at Joe, seated beside her on the couch in Iris's sitting-room – 'wasn't quite so easily fobbed off.'

Joe gave the hand he held in his a gentle slap. 'I'll be afraid to let you out of my sight from now on,' he said. 'I think I'll have a word with the rector about a modification to the marriage service: make you promise to love, honour and keep out of murder and mayhem.'

'Fat chance!' cackled Iris from the floor where, as was her habit, she was seated cross-legged, her back as straight as a ramrod and her voluminous skirt draped over her knees.

'I don't do it on purpose,' Melissa protested, 'and anyway, it was Mum who set the ball rolling this time. I was only trying to protect her.'

Joe groaned in mock despair. 'Tell me about it! Now I've got two of you to keep out of trouble!'

'She went all gooey-eyed when I told her about my meeting with Gawain Hardcastle,' said Melissa. 'She only wants me to arrange an introduction, if you please – says he was one of her teenage idols. I warned her it would cost an arm and a leg, but she says she'll be happy to pay for the drinks just for the privilege of meeting him!'

'No accounting for taste,' Iris remarked. 'How are things at Framleigh House, by the way?'

'Mum couldn't wait to get back so that she could "enquire about the background to the case", as she put it, but we haven't had a report yet.'

'We're keeping our fingers crossed she doesn't upset the manager,' Joe remarked.

'I impressed on her that she has to leave the enquiries to the police from now on,' said Melissa. 'Not that she'll take any notice,' she added resignedly.

'Can't do much harm, can she?' said Iris.

'I suppose not – provided she doesn't go making statements to the press and bringing unwelcome publicity to Framleigh House. Geraldine Wardle's quite capable of asking her to leave if that happened.'

Iris gave another of her characteristic cackles. 'Then she'd have to come back to Hawthorn Cottage. That'd put a stop to your fun, you two! You can only use this place till the end of the month, by the way; it's let from July till October.' Her grey eyes sparkled with merriment as she rose to her feet in the single, lithe movement that Melissa had tried – unsuccessfully so far despite many yoga sessions under her friend's tuition – to achieve. 'More bubbly?'

'Thanks.' They held out their glasses while she refilled them with the pale, frothy brew for which she was justly renowned among her friends.

It was Wednesday evening. A little over forty-eight hours had passed since the arrest of a traumatised Tracy Roper. Joe and Melissa had been enjoying a farewell dinner with

Iris – spicy bean stew followed by peach crumble with yoghurt – before her departure for her home in the south of France the following day. She had apologised for the fact that the vegetables were not home-grown: 'Couldn't lug them all the way from the Midi, but they are organic,' she assured them as she doled out generous portions.

By tacit consent they had avoided the subject of the arrest during the meal, but after Iris picked up that evening's edition of the *Gazette* from the floor in the hall and found the latest report on the case on the front page under the black headline 'Further Charges Against Care Home Killer', they found they could speak of little else.

'Geraldine Wardle will have a fit when she reads that,' said Melissa, frowning.

'Not much in the way of detail,' Iris commented after scanning the story. 'It just says something about a second murder attempt that went wrong. Where do you suppose they got that from?'

'There's no byline, but I think I can detect Bruce Ingram's fingerprints on it,' said Melissa wryly. 'At least he's kept Mum's name out of it.'

'How much did he know before the arrest?' asked Iris.

'About the background, quite a lot. And I told him about Lily's illness, although I pointed out that there was nothing at the time to connect it with Flavia's death. Knowing Bruce, he's been busy ferreting around since the arrest. He's got plenty of contacts, as he keeps reminding me.'

'If it's contacts you're after, Gloria's your woman,' said Iris. 'Didn't see her car this morning, by the way. Thought Wednesday was her day to come to you, Mel.'

'She couldn't make it today; one of her aunties had a fall and she's looking after her. She'll be furious at missing all the excitement.'

'She'll know about it on the grapevine,' predicted Joe.

'What did Tracy say when you and the others went back to Sylvia's room?' asked Iris.

'Hardly anything. All the rage seemed to have gone out of her and she was in a kind of trance. We managed to get her downstairs and into the office without being spotted by any of the other residents. I contacted Matt Waters and he and a policewoman – in plain clothes at Mrs Wardle's urgent request – turned up in an unmarked car and took her away. All she did while we were waiting for them to arrive was rock to and fro and wail, "I did it for you, Mummy," over and over again, with Mrs Wardle hissing at her in a stage whisper to keep her voice down.'

'Never mind the odd arrest for murder as long as it doesn't get around,' said Iris with a disdainful sniff. 'Or the odd personal tragedy,' she added thoughtfully.

'She is a bit obsessive about the reputation of Framleigh House,' Melissa agreed. 'I promised I'd use what influence I have to get the *Gazette* to play it down, but Bruce didn't think there was much he could do, especially when the nationals get hold of it.'

'Imagine nursing a grudge like that year on year,' Iris reflected, absent-mindedly fiddling with one of the tortoise-shell slides that secured her bobbed, mouse-brown hair. 'Must have a pretty destructive effect on the soul.'

'I guess so.'

'I wonder where Tracy got the idea of using oleander?'

'It could be she overheard me expounding my theory about the death of Flavia's dog. Or she may have read about it somewhere and tried it out on the dog first to see if it worked.'

'It'll have a devastating effect on her mother,' said Joe.

On that sobering thought, they allowed the matter to

drop. After their offer to help with the washing up was declined, Joe and Melissa got up to leave. They wished Iris a safe journey and sent affectionate messages to Jack. Hugs were exchanged all round as they said goodbye.

'Thought about your honeymoon yet?' asked Iris.

'Not yet – too busy solving murders,' said Joe.

'How about Les Genêts?' Jack and Iris had named their house in the Midi after the swathes of golden genistas that lined their drive. 'We've been having an old barn renovated for extra accommodation,' she explained. 'Should be ready in six weeks or so. It's yours if you want it.'

Joe and Melissa exchanged delighted glances. 'That would be wonderful!' they exclaimed and hugged her again.

'See you in August, then.'

Back at Hawthorn Cottage, Melissa checked her answering service and found a message from Bruce.

'Thought you'd be interested to know I've been having a chat with the Ropers' neighbours,' he said. 'They tell me Tracy's mother suffered from chronic diabetes with various complications. She was hospitalised for several weeks before her death six months ago.'

'So that's where Tracy got the hypodermic needles from,' said Joe after Melissa relayed the message to him.

'She must have known her mother was terminally ill and waited till her death before taking revenge on the woman who'd cast a blight on both their lives.' Her voice broke on the final words; the nervous strain of the past few days caught up with her and, overcome by an unexpected surge of pity for the victims of the thirty-year-old tragedy, she buried her face in his shoulder.

He stroked her head gently for a few moments until she was calmer. 'At least, the poor lady will never know her daughter was a murderess,' he said.

'I suppose that's some comfort,' Melissa admitted. 'Still,' she added after a moment's reflection, 'she must have brought her daughter up to share an obsessive hatred of Esther Arnold. I wonder if we'll ever get the full story of how they managed to keep track of her?'

'I doubt it.'

On Thursday morning Laurence Dainton waylaid his ex-wife after breakfast and said in a low voice, 'Lily, I have something of importance to say to you.'

A little taken aback, she hesitated for a moment before saying, 'Oh, right. Shall we go to the lounge?'

'This' – he lowered his voice still further although there was no one close by – 'is a very confidential matter. I should prefer a place where there is no risk of our being overheard. Suppose we go for a drive, and perhaps have a quiet drink in a pub?'

'Sounds nice, but . . .' It was on the tip of her tongue to ask what he could possibly want to discuss with her that demanded such a degree of privacy, but something in his expression and a rare hint of uncertainty in his manner made her check the question and say instead, 'I'd like that. It'd be good to get away from here for an hour or so.'

'Excellent. Shall we say about eleven o'clock?'

'Sure. I'll be ready.'

It felt strange, sitting in the front passenger seat of Laurence's car for the first time in over forty years. There was something strange, too, about Laurence himself. He had lost nothing of his urbane demeanour, nor the hint of arrogance that had always lain beneath the polished, courteous façade he presented to the world. Yet in some way he seemed more approachable, although he hardly spoke as he steered the Jaguar along the winding lane that led to the ring road round Gloucester.

After a while, finding the silence oppressive, she remarked, 'Lovely car. A bit different from the clapped-out job you had when we were first married.' As she spoke, she wondered if that had been the most tactful remark and she cast an anxious glance at him. His gaze was fixed on the road ahead, but to her relief his normally stern, aquiline profile softened into a hint of a smile.

'A little,' he agreed.

Encouraged, she confided, 'I've got an Audi – an automatic. It's at home in the garage. Me . . . *my* doctor advised me not to drive for a while, and I don't really need it at Framleigh House.'

'How long are you planning to stay?'

'At Framleigh? Till the conversion's finished, I suppose. Another three months, the builders say, so I reckon at least four.'

This time there was no doubt about the smile, and it was wholly sympathetic. 'Not the most reliable people, are they?' he said.

'You can say that again.'

The silence that followed as the big car bowled smoothly along the A38 was no longer strained, and Lily was content to relax and watch the countryside slip past. When Laurence slowed to turn off towards Berkeley she frowned and said, 'We're not going to that old castle, are we? You know how I hate—'

'Culture?' he interrupted slyly and she shot him a suspicious glance, but there had been no malice in the remark, only a gentle mockery that was so unfamiliar it made her uneasy.

'You know what I mean.'

'I know. Just relax.'

'So where are we going?'

'You'll see.'

He refused to be drawn until, rounding a bend, they saw ahead a stretch of smooth water where a barge puttered gently along with another in tow. 'That's the Sharpness Canal,' he informed her, 'and this is our watering-hole.' He turned into the car park of an inn surrounded by a garden that ran down to the water's edge. He helped her out of the car and escorted her to a seat at one of a number of tables set out on a brilliant green lawn. 'Now, what can I get you to drink? A white wine spritzer, perhaps?'

'My, you remembered!'

He gave a self-conscious laugh. 'Not really. I've heard you order them from Gary. But now you come to mention it—' He broke off and turned away, heading towards a door marked 'Saloon' in black gothic lettering. Lily sat back in her chair and watched the wake of the barges fanning out towards the banks, sending a pair of mallards rocking up and down on the rippling water. The air was soft and the sun warm on her skin; she relaxed, closed her eyes and speculated idly on the nature of the 'very confidential matter' he wanted to discuss with her. She decided that, since he was going out of his way to be pleasant, it was unlikely to be anything confrontational.

'Here we are.' He put the drinks on the table and sat down. 'Cheers!'

'Bung-ho!' She gestured at his tumbler of orange juice. 'You on the wagon?'

'I never drink alcohol during the day,' he said, 'especially when I'm driving.'

'Since when?' He shrugged, but did not answer. 'So,

what's this "something of importance" you want to talk about?'

He took a further swallow from his drink and sat staring into his glass for several seconds before saying slowly, and without meeting her gaze, 'Lily, I want to make it clear at the outset that I am not trying to . . . that is to say, I have no ulterior . . . I mean, improper motive in asking for this meeting.'

Lily put a hand over her mouth to stifle the shriek of mirth that threatened to escape from it. 'Are you telling me you aren't trying to score with me?' she spluttered.

'I suppose that's one way of putting it,' he said a little stiffly. 'I merely wanted to avoid giving a false impression.'

'Okay, we know where we stand,' she said cheerfully, resisting the temptation to add, 'You'd have been wasting your time anyway.'

'All right. To be frank, I feel that in some ways I have been less than fair to you.'

The laughter died within her. 'Only in some ways?'

'Please, don't make it any more difficult for me. We can't undo the past, but at least let us try not to let it poison the rest of our lives.'

'I seem to remember saying something like that to you a week or so ago and getting the brush-off.'

'Yes, I know, and I apologise for that.'

'That's a word I don't recall hearing from you before.'

'Well, you've heard it now.'

'So where's this taking us?'

'These last few days I've seen a side of you that I never saw before. Your courage, for a start, and your humanity. You're not in the best of health and the other night you nearly died, but you showed great sympathy for the woman who tried to kill your friend and almost killed you. And your sense of justice has made me think a great deal as well. Lily, if it's not too late, how would it be if . . . I mean, would you like to have more contact with your . . . that is, our sons than you've had in the past, and their children too, of course?'

Lily put down her half-empty glass. The wine had suddenly become bitter; the air had grown cooler as wisps of cloud drifted across the sun. After a while, she said, 'Have you asked them how they feel about this?'

'Naturally.'

'And what did they say?'

'The boys are willing.'

'Willing!' She made no effort to keep the scorn from her voice. 'Willing to meet their own mother? No thanks; they've made it quite clear over the years that they've no time for me.'

'They bring Dave and Billy to see you sometimes.'

'Once in a blue moon, when the kids ask them to!'

'The youngsters have always had a soft spot for you.'

'It's mutual. I'd love to see them more often. They're good kids – always write and thank me for their birthday prezzies.'

'They're studying hard for their A-levels. I've promised to take them out for lunch tomorrow to give them a break. Will you join us?'

'Just the four of us?'

'Just the four of us.'

She drew a deep breath and finished her drink. It tasted less bitter this time. 'All right,' she said. 'I'd like that.'

# 29

Melissa awoke on Friday with a sense of anticlimax. Her book was finished, Iris was back in the south of France and Joe was busy preparing for a visit to business associates in several European countries. With no mystery to investigate and the plot for her next novel little more than an idea at the back of her mind, she cast about for something practical to do. She did a few of the jobs that Gloria normally did on her Wednesday visits, discussed progress on the extension with the foreman and made a half-hearted effort to tidy the kitchen cupboards. By teatime, having run out of ideas, she confided her frustrations to Joe.

'Why don't you take your mother shopping?' he suggested. 'You've promised her several times.'

'I suppose I could,' she replied without enthusiasm.

When Sylvia came to the phone in response to her call, she exclaimed, 'Oh, Lissie, I was going to ring you!'

At the note of breathless urgency in her mother's voice, Melissa felt a pang of apprehension. 'Is something wrong?' she asked.

'No!' Sylvia almost shouted the word. 'Something wonderful's happened!'

'Tell me.'

'Not now, I'd rather wait till I see you. When can you come?'

'I was going to suggest a shopping trip tomorrow. I've promised you several times.'

'That would be lovely.'

'Where would you like to go? Bath, Cheltenham, Oxford?'

'I don't know – you decide.'

'Cheltenham's the nearest.'

'Then let's go to Cheltenham. What time will you call for me?'

'Say half past nine?'

'I'll be ready.'

When Melissa drove up to the entrance of Framleigh House the following morning she found her mother waiting in the front porch. She almost ran down the steps and scrambled into the car before Melissa had time to get out and open the door.

'Such wonderful news!' she said breathlessly. 'I've been dying to tell you since Thursday afternoon only I thought I'd better wait till Lily told me it was going to be all right and then you phoned me before I had the chance to—'

'All right, Mum, just take it easy. Have you fastened your seat belt?'

'Yes, dear.'

'Right.' Melissa put the car in gear and drove slowly back to the gate. 'So, what is this "something wonderful" you hinted at? I assume it has something to do with Lily.'

'And Laurence. He's been quite different since she was ill, really kind. I'm so thrilled for her.'

Melissa almost stalled the engine as she waited to pull out into the road. 'Don't tell me he's asked her to marry him again!' she exclaimed.

Sylvia burst out laughing. 'No, of course not – how could you imagine such a thing?'

'What then?'

'He took her out to lunch yesterday with her two grand-sons, and it was such a happy time for her. They all got on so well, and she's going to be seeing them more often.'

'That's great news. What about her sons – is she going to see them more often as well?'

Sylvia's smile faded. 'That's the sad part. She says she can't be bothered with them because of the way they've shunned her in the past.'

'Maybe she'll change her mind in time.'

'Oh, I do hope so.' Sylvia brightened again as she went on, 'The funniest part is, you know how beautifully Laurence speaks, and Lily's . . . well, just a little on the common side?'

'Yes, you could say that.'

'Well, she says the boys used to "talk posh" as she calls it, like their parents and grandfather, but since they've been going to a different school to do their A-levels they've started speaking more like she does, only worse! She says Laurence was *most* disapproving! I think even she was a bit shocked – she says they made *her* sound posh!'

'So Lily and Laurence have mended their fences,' Melissa remarked when they had finished chuckling over the picture Sylvia's news had conjured up. 'Anyway,' she went on as she joined the queue for one of Cheltenham's multi-storey car parks, 'it looks as if the field's still open for Angela Fuller if she's so inclined.'

'Oh, poor Angela. We had a long talk and she told me quite a lot about herself. She's had such a sad life. Her fiancé was killed in a plane crash and then she met someone else and he died too, a month before the wedding, so she ended up as companion to a crabby old uncle. At least he left her all his money, but she hasn't got any friends or other relations, so perhaps after all she and Laurence—'

'I take it you don't have designs on him yourself?' Melissa interrupted wickedly. 'I couldn't bear to have him as a step-father!'

'Oh, Lissie, what a goose you are!'

As they inched forward in the queue, Melissa said, 'I suppose everyone at Framleigh is talking about Tracy's arrest?'

'Naturally. They keep asking me lots of questions, but I pretend I don't know anything.'

'That must be difficult for you.'

'Well, you did impress on me that I had to be discreet,' Sylvia said earnestly. She appeared not to have noticed the hint of irony in her daughter's voice, nor the mischievous twinkle in her eyes. 'I did tell Angela a bit about Tracy, but I made her promise to keep it to herself. I felt in a way I had to because I'd tried to get her to, well—'

'Assist you with your enquiries?' prompted Melissa as her mother broke off in some confusion.

'Well, yes.' Sylvia gave a self-conscious giggle and then grew serious again. 'We both feel so sorry for Tracy. Do you think she wrote the anonymous letters?'

'I imagine so. It will all come out in court – if she's found fit to plead, that is. I understand she's been remanded for psychiatric tests.'

'Poor girl.'

They had reached the front of the queue. Melissa took a ticket from the machine and drove up the ramp in search of a parking space.

**DATE DUE**